**Here's wh[at] [reviewers are saying about]
Cath[y Pickens's mysteries:]**

Readers are sure to enjoy this playful tale...this book is bound to please anyone that is looking for an easy, satisfying read on the beach.
—*InD'tale Magazine*

"If you like your cozy mysteries complete with a cast of zany characters this is one for you. And guess what? Recipes are included which makes me really wish I could bake."
—*Night Owl Reviews*

"TASTES LIKE MURDER is an intriguing start to the *Cookies and Chance Mystery* series. I want to visit more with all of the quirky characters just to see what crazy and outrageous things they will do next!"
—*Fresh Fiction*

"Twistier than expected cozy read--great for beach or by the fire"
—*The Kindle Book Review*

# BOOKS BY CATHERINE BRUNS

*Cookies & Chance Mysteries*:
Tastes Like Murder
"A Spot of Murder"
(short story in the Killer Beach Reads collection)
Baked to Death
Burned to a Crisp
Frosted with Revenge
Silenced by Sugar
"Drizzle Before Dying"
(short story in the Pushing Up Daisies collection)
Crumbled to Pieces
Sprinkled in Malice

*Cindy York Mysteries:*
Killer Transaction
Priced to Kill
For Sale by Killer

*Aloha Lagoon Mysteries:*
Death of the Big Kahuna
Death of the Kona Man

# Sprinkled in Malice
## A Cookies & Chance Mystery

### USA TODAY BESTSELLING AUTHOR
# CATHERINE BRUNS

Sprinkled in Malice
Copyright © 2019 by Catherine Bruns
Cover design by Janet Holmes

Published by Gemma Halliday Publishing
All Rights Reserved. Except for use in any review, the reproduction or utilization of this work in whole or in part in any form by any electronic, mechanical, or other means, now known or hereafter invented, including xerography, photocopying and recording, or in any information storage and retrieval system is forbidden without the written permission of the publisher, Gemma Halliday.

This is a work of fiction. Names, characters, places, and incidents are either the product of the author's imagination or are used fictitiously, and any resemblance to actual persons, living or dead, business establishments, or events or locales is entirely coincidental.

*Acknowledgements*

Thank you to my usual suspects that includes retired Troy Police Captain Terrance Buchanan and Judy Melinek MD, Forensic Pathologist, for lending their areas of expertise to this book. Much love to beta readers Constance Atwater and Kathy Kennedy for providing valuable feedback, and as always, special gratitude goes out to Gemma Halliday and GHP Publishing. And a huge "thank you" to Kim Davis for creating the delicious sprinkle cookie recipe for me!

Readers, many thanks for continuing along on Sally's journey. I am grateful to all of you.

# CHAPTER ONE

Josie eyed me sharply as she filled the pastry bag with fudge frosting. "Okay, Mrs. Donovan, let's hear it. What have you got up your sleeve?"

I shrugged into my coat and gave her a little teasing smile. "And what's that supposed to mean?"

"It means I *know* you." She squirted frosting onto a tray of vanilla cookies with an effortless and accomplished movement, making perfect flower designs in the process. Josie Sullivan never burned cookies or botched frosting. That was my department. We'd been best friends since the age of eight, and without her talent, my cookie shop, Sally's Samples, would cease to exist. "Sure, you bake—sometimes—but that's all. What's the idea of having a big family dinner tonight at your house? Is your grandmother secretly cooking, but you're going to pretend you made the meal instead?"

I looked out the window and watched large, fat snowflakes descending from the gray sky above. It was another Buffalo winter, but this one had been worse than usual. Spring had officially arrived a couple of days ago, along with a blizzard that deposited three feet of snow on us. Having lived in Western New York for most of my life, I was used to this weather—to a certain degree. But it was nearing the end of March, and the snow and cold showed no signs of letting up.

Nothing could dampen my mood tonight, though. "It's Mike's thirty-first birthday, and I wanted to do something special, so I'm preparing a lasagna dinner. What's wrong with that?"

Josie's blue eyes widened in surprise. "Nothing, except you don't cook and you're inviting the entire family. I figured you'd rather spend an intimate night alone with your man."

I leaned against the wood block table where she was working, tempted to snatch one of the cookies off the tray but forced myself not to. During the winter, I tended to overeat. My comfort foods ran the gamut, from my grandmother's ricotta cheesecake to Stouffer's macaroni and cheese. With a sigh, I moved away from the tray. "Well, that was the initial plan, but my mother called yesterday and hinted that she hadn't seen us for a while, and we never invite them over, and they have a birthday present for Mike, so…"

The freckles on Josie's cheeks stood out as she grinned. "So you caved. Admit it."

My shoulders slumped forward. "Yeah. Something like that."

Josie whisked another tray of cookies into the oven. We usually didn't bake so late in the day, except for our trademark homemade fortune cookies that were made at all different times. A customer was coming by first thing in the morning to pick up their order for an office breakfast party, so Josie had to prepare them tonight. "Let's hear the menu," she said.

I tossed my curly, dark hair over my shoulder and fastened the hood to my winter coat around my face. "Lasagna, tossed salad, and fortune cookies. I'm also planning on making frosted sprinkle cookies. A recipe I've been working on."

Josie studied me, obviously catching the note of pride in my voice. "I didn't know you'd created your own recipe. That's great, Sal."

"With Funfetti cake mix, but I still think it's pretty good. You can sample some tonight, and then maybe we can start featuring them in the bakery. You're welcome to come for dinner as well, but I know Rob's working and there's no one to stay with the kids. My grandmother is making Mike a birthday cake. Bring the boys over about eight o'clock for a slice and some cookies." It would be crowded in my little ranch house, but I loved having kids around. Josie had four boys, whose ages ranged from three to twelve years old.

Josie looked at me like I had two heads. "Okay, let's return from La-La Land for a second. I have no desire to drag four kids out of the house by myself when they have school tomorrow. Plus, more snow is predicted for tonight. What's going on? Did you buy Mike a new snowmobile or something?"

I laughed. "Nothing's going on. I want you to be there to celebrate with us, that's all."

"Your grandmother really isn't cooking any of it?" Josie refilled the pastry bag. She and my grandmother were experts in the kitchen, while I was just plain adequate. I liked to think my strength lay in the financial side of the business, but sales had been down as of late.

I folded my arms over my chest. "Will you give me some credit, please? I've been married for almost two years and have managed to make a few meals, you know."

She snickered and tossed the mixing bowl into the sink. "Come on. This is me you're talking to, Sal. I know the schedule that you and Mike keep. Two nights a week it's off to the parents' house where your grandmother cooks, three evenings there's takeout, one night it's sandwiches, and the other evening consists of scrounging around in the freezer for your grandmother's leftovers. You've got it down to a science."

Damn, she was good. "Okay, there's some truth to that, but I did make fried chicken a couple of weeks ago."

Josie rolled her eyes. "The kind in the freezer at the supermarket doesn't count. Hey, don't be upset. If anything, I'm jealous. I love to cook, but after a whole day of baking here, I'm too wiped out to want to make the effort some days. Of course, I have no choice."

Josie and I had always led very different lives. After we graduated from high school, she'd gone off to the culinary academy. She could create and bake any cookie you asked for and think up a new recipe at the spur of the moment. Real life had intervened before Josie could complete school, though. She and her husband, Rob, had married when she was only nineteen, and their first child had been born shortly afterward.

My first marriage had ended in disaster when I caught my ex-husband, Colin Brown, cheating on me with my high school nemesis. Mike and I had dated in high school but broke up after a misunderstanding on our prom night. Fast forward ten years, after I was newly divorced, and we finally found our way back to each other and admitted we were still in love. We dated briefly and became engaged four months later. Unlike Josie, we had no children yet. It was the one thing that would make my world complete.

Josie nodded toward a plastic box on the wall shelf that was filled with fortune cookies she'd made earlier. Every customer received a free one with purchase, and they were very popular with our clientele. "Why don't you take some of those and save yourself the trouble?"

"Because I want to do personal messages for everyone. It will be fun."

Josie placed her hands on her hips. "It wasn't too long ago that the messages in these cookies scared you half to death." She opened the container, took out a cookie, cracked it open, and then handed it to me. "Okay, read."

"Why?"

"Because I want to see for myself that you're really over this phobia."

Good grief. I took the cookie and strip from her outstretched hand. "*Today is a day you will always remember.*" I laughed out loud and slipped it into my pocket. "See? A positive one. Nothing to it."

She gestured toward the back door that led to the alley where my car was parked. "You'd better get going. It's almost four. What time does my favorite crazy family arrive?"

"Not until seven. Mike won't be home till shortly before then either."

Josie offered me a sugar cookie, still warm from the oven. She must have noticed my eyes growing in size as I stared at them, but I refused. "I thought he finished that renovation project," she commented. "Are they *ever* going to start work on the expansion in *here*?"

My husband owned a small construction company. He'd been the only employee until recently, although sometimes he'd hire helpers if the job required more hands. Last summer he'd hired Trevor Parks. After a month of steady work, he'd felt comfortable enough to offer the man a full-time job.

Mike himself had been tied up for the last couple of months restoring a 19th century mansion. The new owners had bought it cheap and hired him last December to do a complete overhaul. The downside was that they only wanted Mike doing the work. There had been one problem after the next, but he'd finally completed the job a couple of weeks ago, and the owners were thrilled with the outcome. In the meantime, Trevor had taken on the other, smaller jobs Mike had been forced to overlook. Mike told me several times this winter that he didn't know what he would have done without him.

I shrugged. "You know how it is. When you remodel homes for a living, yours is always the last to get done." I'd been wanting to put in a lunch menu and expand the bakery for quite some time now. Mike had been all set to start work when the mansion had come along, and there was no way he could refuse such a significant job. "Someday it will happen."

"All right, I'll try to stop by," Josie said, "but no promises. Rob's mother is supposed to come over with some new shirts for the boys. If she shows up, I'll sneak out for a few minutes. But I'd better get a good fortune cookie message."

I winked and reached for the doorknob. "That I can personally guarantee."

A slow grin spread across her face. "And what's Mike getting from his lovely wife? Maybe a private striptease after dinner?"

My cheeks burned with embarrassment. Josie was anything but subtle. "Did anyone ever tell you that you're way too nosy?"

"You've known me for over twenty years and just figured that out?"

"See you later." I shivered as I hurried to my car and started the engine, willing the heat to emerge from the vents. Fortunately, the snow had just started, and I didn't have to worry about driving in crappy road conditions for once. Hopefully this would be the last storm of the season.

When I arrived home, I got the mail and parked my vehicle in the garage. Our house was a small yellow ranch that had been willed to Mike after his mother, Tonya, had died a few years ago. We'd been planning an addition here too, but as with the bakery, Mike hadn't found the time yet.

Once inside the kitchen, I followed my Grandma Rosa's recipe with precision and care. It took me close to an hour, but I was putting the last layer of noodles in the pan along with the sauce and cheese when my phone buzzed. I grabbed a dish towel to wipe my hands. "Hello?"

"Hey, baby girl," my father's deep voice greeted me. "Can we do the book signing at the bakery next Saturday? I think it will draw more people that day instead of doing it on Sunday like we originally planned."

*Head smack.* When my father announced that he was writing a book, it had become something of a joke between my younger sister, Gianna, and me. We'd attempted to humor him at first, hoping it was only another one of his crazy ideas. I loved my parents dearly, but some days they had a few loose screws—or nails, as my grandmother said. She had a charming habit of frequently getting her sayings mixed up.

Domenic Muccio was in his late sixties with a balding head and protruding stomach that seemed to grow larger in girth every year. He had retired from the railroad a few years back and had managed to turn his fascination with death into a profitable hobby of sorts. Dad had gone from planning his own funeral to driving a hearse for a local funeral home to running his own blog, where he referred to himself as Father Death. Morticians and casket suppliers were obsessed with it and paid money to advertise there—something I would never understand.

My father had been preoccupied the last year with writing a novel. It was called—of all things—*How to Plan and Enjoy Your Funeral.* The title alone gave me the creeps. It consisted of several posts from his blog, plus rambling ideas on how to enrich that special, final time in your life. He'd offered me the chance to read it, but I'd politely declined. I'd told him I'd wait for the movie.

"Uh, sure, Dad. That should be okay." Cripes. I hadn't mentioned this to Josie yet, and she would not be pleased. She thought my father's hobby was insane and wanted no part of his "crazy shenanigans" as she called them.

"You know those fudgy delight cookies that Josie makes?" He chuckled. "Well, you make them too, of course, but not as good."

"Gee, thanks, Dad," I said dryly. "What about them?"

"I was hoping Josie could turn the cookie part into the

shape of a coffin," he said. "They'd be a real killer at the signing. Ha-ha. Get it? I'll pay her for her time, of course."

Jeez Louise. "Ah, I'll have to check with her. How many were you looking for?"

"Not a lot," he admitted. "Only a couple hundred. She could put fudge frosting on the lid and then decorate it with vanilla—you know, a white cross design on top."

The idea was disturbing. "You're expecting 200 people? Dad, I'm lucky if I can fit thirty people in my bakery at once. Why don't you hire a hall?"

"But it's so much more personal this way," he protested. "And you've got the empty apartment upstairs that we can use. We can stagger people. Not everyone will come at the same time. My only other concern is the media."

Okay, this was worse than I'd imagined. "What media? Is someone coming from the local newspaper?" Please, God, no.

He snorted on the other end of the line. "Newspaper? Hah. I'm talking big-time, baby girl. One of my funeral director friends has a son who's a cameraman on Channel 11. They've promised to hook me up with star anchorman Jerry Maroon. But there will be newspaper reporters there too. Betsy Simmons from the *Colwestern Journal* and Regina Dillinger from—"

I'd heard enough. "Okay, I get it, Dad. If Josie can't do the cookies, I'll make them." Panic instantly set in. How was I going to make cookies in the shape of coffins? Did Josie even have such a mold in her possession? I honestly didn't know because no one had ever asked for them before.

"Aw, come on," he protested. "You do okay, baby girl, but yours don't come close to Josie's."

It was a good thing I had thick skin. "This must be Insult Sally Day," I said cheerfully.

"Don't be like that," Dad pleaded. "You know I love my baby girl. Everyone's good at something different, that's all. For your grandmother, it's cooking. With Josie, it's baking. For Gianna, it's winning an argument in court."

Gianna had always thrived on winning arguments, even when we were kids. It came as no surprise to me when she'd decided at a young age that she wanted to be an attorney. "What am I good at, then?" I asked with interest.

There was a long silence. "Uh, your mother's calling me. See you at seven, right?"

"Sure." Defeated, I sighed and clicked off. No matter. I wasn't going to let trivial things bother me today. I was in my own little happy place and, to my surprise, enjoying preparing the dinner.

I made a dozen fortune cookies and baked thirty sprinkle cookies. There were sprinkles in the mix, but too late, I realized I had none for the frosting. I'd wanted to use some on the fortune cookies too. Shoot. Now what would I do? The bakery had them of course, but I didn't want to drive over there now.

I popped the lasagna into the oven and reached for my phone. Five thirty. I could always frost the cookies and then add the sprinkles at the last second. Same with the fortune cookies. I pressed the button with Mike's name, and he answered on the second ring. "Is this my sexy birthday boy?" I teased.

"Who wants to know?" he shot back. "My gorgeous wife who's been working hard on my dinner all day?"

"Not all day, but close enough. Hey, could you do me a favor and pick up a bottle of sprinkles on your way home?"

He paused for a moment before answering. "We're having sprinkles on lasagna?"

"No, wise guy. I need them for the cookies I'm making for dessert. And for the fortune cookies too. What time do you think you'll get here?"

"Let's see, it's what—five thirty?" he asked. "I've got to gather up my tools and stuff, and with a quick stop at the market, you should see me by 6:15."

"That's perfect. The fortune cookies have personal messages for everyone. It's going to be fun watching everyone open theirs after dinner."

"Oh, really?" His voice became low and sexy. "What does mine say?"

I went into our combination living and dining room to set the table. "Hey, I never kiss and tell."

"Ooh, I love when you play hard to get. Hey, would it be okay if I invite Trevor for dinner?"

"Of course. There's plenty. But won't his girlfriend be expecting him?" I didn't know Trevor Parks well, although I'd met him on several occasions. He was always pleasant and polite and was a few years older than Mike. Trevor had recently gone through a bitter divorce but seemed happy with his current girlfriend, a woman named Tina whom I'd yet to meet.

"Guess she has plans tonight. His truck still isn't running right, so I'm giving him a lift home. As long as mine holds out, that is."

"Did you finally get a chance to bring it into the auto shop today?" I placed my rose-patterned china plates around the table. My grandmother had given the set to us as a wedding present.

Mike sighed. "Yeah, unfortunately. The struts are shot, and I need new brakes. It's going to cost close to two grand."

Ouch. Whenever we started to get a little ahead, something always happened to help put us behind. "Jeez, it's only a couple of years old."

"What can I tell you? I always seem to find the clunkers, and the warranty doesn't cover this type of repair. Anyhow, Trevor has seemed kind of down lately. I thought an evening with your parents might cheer him up."

"That's one way to put it." My parents were an embarrassment, but they could always manage to distract you from other problems in life.

"And of course, who would pass up a chance to sample my beautiful wife's cuisine?"

His words made me smile. "Flattery will get you everywhere, Mr. Donovan." My father's words from earlier came back to me. "What am I good at?"

Mike's voice sounded puzzled. "Excuse me?"

"My father was telling me that everyone is good at something. Josie's terrific at baking, Grandma Rosa at cooking, and you, of course, at building things. But what am I good at?"

"Oh, princess," he growled sexily into the phone. "You don't *ever* need to ask *me* that question. But I'll give you my answer—later tonight."

# CHAPTER TWO

---

I made the salad and put a loaf of garlic bread into the oven. It was the frozen kind, but I didn't think anyone would care. I hadn't yet mastered the art of bread making like my grandmother. Preparing the lasagna and sprinkle cookies had proven to be more work than I'd thought. Still, I'd enjoyed it and vowed to do this more often.

I wrote out the fortune cookie messages. Everyone in my family was getting one, and I'd made a few extra in case Josie changed her mind and brought the kids with her. The adult messages were specifically tailored for each person. I drew out the message from the cookie Josie had given me and smiled when I read it again.

*Today is a day you will always remember.*

Such a lovely, positive thought. Mike had been right. He had told me back on our honeymoon that I was taking these messages too seriously. There had been a time when I'd been convinced the messages were evil because they always seemed to come true in some shape or form. I'd almost stopped making them for the shop, and that wouldn't have been a smart move. Our customers loved them, and even though we gave most away for free, they boosted sales. Customers even ordered trays of them for parties.

I glanced at the clock. It was 6:15, and except for the sprinkle cookies, everything was ready to go. I gave Spike, our fourteen-year-old, black-and-white Shih-tzu, fresh water and food and then brought butter and drink glasses to the table, followed by the covered salad bowl. If the bread became cold, I could always microwave it at the last minute. I checked the time again—6:30. Mike was late.

I went to the bay window in our living room and glanced out into the darkness, illuminated only by the lamppost on our lawn and a couple of street lights. The snow was coming down heavier, but my parents had an all-wheel drive vehicle and didn't live far away. Gianna and her fiancé, Johnny Gavelli, were coming in a separate car. Gianna was eight and a half months pregnant and not her usual graceful self these days, but Johnny would take good care of her.

After another look at the clock, I drew out my phone and pushed the button for Mike's name. His phone rang three times and then went to voice mail. I didn't bother to leave a message. He'd see my number. He was probably driving and hadn't bothered to hook up his Bluetooth. A little niggle of doubt crept into my brain. No, I was being silly. Mike and Trevor were both fine. Still, I wished that Mike had gotten his truck fixed today. I didn't like to think of him maneuvering it with brake issues in this weather.

Okay, I had to stop with the incessant worrying. It was an annoying habit of mine. I went back into the kitchen to check on the lasagna, keeping warm in the oven, when the sound of our scanner startled me.

My parents had bought Mike the scanner for Christmas. He liked hearing emergency calls come in—when he was around to hear them, that is. We usually turned off the scanner when we went to bed, and he worked such long hours that I didn't know what the point was of having it, but hey, to each his own.

"Panic alarm at Colwestern Mini-Mart has been activated," a man's deep voice announced suddenly. "We have no record of this alarm going off before."

Within seconds, another male voice answered. "Officers have responded, but there seems to be some confusion over the location. Is this the Colwestern or Colgate Mini-Mart?"

"Colwestern," the previous male voice said. "Location is at 40 Birchwood Street."

An icicle formed between my shoulder blades. I stood there and continued to listen to the voices while a cold, sick feeling of dread built in the bottom of my stomach. *No.* It must be a mistake.

A few seconds passed and then another voice—or

perhaps it was the previous one—spoke again. "Shots have been fired at Colwestern Mini-Mart. *All* available units, please respond."

With trembling fingers, I reached for my phone and pressed the button for Mike's name again. *Please pick up, please pick up.* The phone rang once and went to voice mail.

"Damn it!" My hands shook violently, and I paused to try to calm myself. Maybe Mike and Trevor had been detained at a job. Maybe the truck had given them trouble. Or they might have stopped at a different grocery store, even though the mini-mart was the most convenient location on the way to our house.

*Think, think.* I scrolled through my contacts and pressed the button for Brian Jenkins' number. Brian was a Colwestern Police officer and a good friend. We'd first met when I had returned to Colwestern after my divorce, approximately two and a half years ago. His phone also went to voice mail. He might be one of the cops responding to the call. Even if he wasn't on duty, Brian was the type who would show up anyway.

"Brian, it's Sally. Please call me as soon as you have a chance. It's about the robbery at the mini-mart. I'm afraid that Mike—"

A woman's pre-recorded voice came on the line. "Your mailbox is full" rang out cheerfully in my ears. In frustration, I clicked off. Waves of panic rose from inside me, and I took several deep breaths to try to calm myself. The slow-moving hands on the wall clock were an agonizing torture for me. 6:40. My family would be here in twenty minutes. The market was only five minutes away—ten with the bad weather. Without thinking further, I picked up my car keys and ran into the garage, not even stopping to grab my coat. I'd simply run to the market and make sure Mike's truck wasn't there. I'd be back before my family even arrived. Besides, they had a house key and could let themselves inside if necessary. But I couldn't worry about them right now. I needed to know that Mike was safe and not involved in the robbery.

I backed out of the driveway too fast and was forced to slam on the brakes, almost hitting the mailbox in my haste. The car slid across the slick surface, and I shoved it into all-wheel drive. My breath was coming in heavy, painful gasps. "Dear

God, please let him be okay." I repeated the words over and over in my head, willing them to be true.

Colwestern Mini-Mart was ablaze with light. An ambulance zoomed past me in the other lane, red lights flashing and siren screaming. My mouth went dry as I stared at the sight before me. There had to be six or seven cop cars parked in front of the store, their red and blue lights flashing so intensely that I had to shield my eyes against the brightness. Another ambulance was parked sideways in front of the entrance. Two local news vans were across the street from the store. Why were reporters always the first on the scene?

A policeman was directing traffic in the road. It wasn't Brian or his partner, Adam. I knew most of the cops on the Colwestern force, thanks to my past involvement in several murder cases, but not this man. I rolled my window down as he approached my car.

"Please"—my voice wobbled—"can you tell me—"

He indicated for me to make a U-turn. "Emergency vehicles need to get through here, ma'am."

A horn sounded from somewhere behind me. Having no choice, I turned the car around. I tried to search for Mike's truck, but the blazing lights allowed me to see little beyond them. Crime scene tape had already been draped around the building. With shaking fingers, I continued back the way I'd come. There was a gas station a few feet ahead to my right. I swung the car into the lot and parked, even though the sign said *Customers Only*. Let them tow me.

I slammed the car door shut and ran back in the direction of the market, grateful that at least I had my boots on. Wet snowflakes clung to my face and hair, but I barely felt them as I ran. My stomach rumbled with nausea. The officer directing traffic was talking to a man in an SUV, and I didn't think he noticed me run across the parking lot. I stopped a few feet in front of the entrance but couldn't see anything through the glass windows except the emergency lights reflecting off them. In desperation, I looked around for a familiar face. Brian had to be here *somewhere*.

"Mike's not inside. He can't be." I spoke the words out loud as tears began to sting the corners of my eyes. Another police cruiser pulled into the lot near me, and I spotted a tall, blond man alight from the vehicle while talking on his phone. With relief, I ran in his direction. "Brian!" I screamed.

Brian whirled around at the sound of his name, and I saw shock and confusion register in those brilliant green eyes of his. He placed his hand on my arm when I reached him. "Sally, what are you doing here? This is an active crime scene."

Adam Greensburg, Brian's partner, came hurrying over from the store's entrance. "Hey, Bri, glad you're here. Several of the guys were delayed thanks to a screw-up in directions. There's a fatality inside." He gave me a curt nod and then rushed back inside.

"Oh God," I sobbed and clung to Brian's jacket. "Please help me. I'm afraid that Mike's in there!"

He grabbed me tightly by the wrists. "Sally, what are you talking about?"

Tears crept down my cheeks. "I asked him to stop at the store on his way home. He's not answering his cell. This market is directly on his way. I tried to call you as well. Brian, I'm scared to death my husband is in there!"

"Okay, okay." Brian's voice was calm and steady. He led me to the rear of his vehicle, opened the trunk, and placed a blanket around my shoulders. "Where's your coat? Never mind. Wait for me in the back of my car. I'm sure Mike's fine. He probably stopped at another store. Stay here, all right? As soon as I know what's going on, I promise to come and get you."

"No!" I wailed and shook my head vehemently. From the shocked look on his face, it was obvious I'd surprised him. "You don't understand. I need to know if he's in there. I can't wait, Brian." Without another word, I dropped the blanket onto his car and ran toward the entrance.

"Sally!" Brian shouted and ran after me. I honestly wasn't sure how I planned to get by the burly-looking cop guarding the entrance. He saw me coming from a mile away and put out a hand to stop me.

"Ma'am, where do you think you're going?" he asked sternly.

"My husband might be in there!" I screamed.

Another cop came forward and grabbed me roughly by

the arm. "You need to leave, ma'am," he said. "This is a crime scene."

"Take your hands off me!"

Brian put an arm around my shoulders. "Let her go, Bruce. It's okay—I know this lady. She has reason to believe her husband is inside. I'll take responsibility for her."

Bruce raised his eyebrows in questioning at Brian but didn't argue further. Brian slowly guided me through the vestibule door then gently turned me around to face him.

He swallowed hard and looked directly into my eyes. The cop mask he generally used to disguise his true feelings was gone, replaced by a somber expression. "Sally, you may see some very unpleasant things in there. You don't have to do this. I promise to come and get you as soon as I know if Mike"—he hesitated—"if he's inside."

What was he really going to say? Did he think Mike was the person who had been killed? Furiously I shook my head again, tears blinding my vision. "Please, Brian. Please don't make me stay outside—alone. Don't do that to me."

He stared at me for a long moment, and I noticed emotion flickering in his gaze. Compassion or sadness—I wasn't sure which, but there was no time to figure it out.

Brian reached down and tucked a stray curl behind my ear. His voice cracked as he spoke. "Okay. Stay by my side, and I'll take care of everything."

I held tightly to his arm as we went inside. The first person I saw was a young female employee standing next to the register in a bright blue smock, sobbing and wiping her eyes with a tissue as she talked to a policeman. A woman with two small children was seated on the tile floor in one of the aisles. She had an arm around each child, and they were both crying. Adam had knelt in front of the three of them, talking softly to the kids.

I clutched Brian's hand as we walked on. He glanced sideways at me anxiously then wrapped his arm around my shoulders. "You okay? Can you go on, Sally?"

No, I wasn't okay, but I managed a faint nod for him. Adam's words echoed inside my head. "There's a fatality inside." Who was dead? Where was my husband? Why had something like this happened?

There was another register at the back of the store for the small pharmacy counter, and that was the direction in which Brian and I headed. We passed an aisle end display of cake mixes with various decorations. Bottles of white and pink sprinkles caught my eye and mocked me. It was my fault if Mike was here. Sweat slid down the small of my back. Three policemen were standing in a semicircle, talking quietly amongst each other. On the floor next to them was a black tarp. A puddle of blood had seeped out from one side and formed a long red streak across the white-speckled tile floor.

A cry burst from between my lips. Brian drew me behind him, no doubt his attempt to protect me from the sight, but it was too late. I knew that whoever was underneath that tarp was dead.

A tall, lanky officer with white whiskers that reminded me of Santa Claus greeted Brian and then glanced curiously at me. "Heard the operator gave out the wrong directions. Looks like we're too late for this guy. Shame. A young one too."

Another officer stepped aside, and that's when I saw it. Poking out from underneath the tarp was a piece of seafoam-colored material. A jacket. I gasped out loud. It was the same color jacket Mike had been wearing this morning.

The jacket had been a running joke between us since Christmas. I'd ordered it online as a gift for him and had specifically requested the midnight blue shade since it went so well with Mike's eyes. The package arrived the day before Christmas, and I was annoyed when I saw they'd mistakenly shipped the wrong color. There hadn't been time to return the garment before the holiday, so I'd let Mike open it anyway, assuring him I'd send it back the next business day.

But Mike had only winked, given me a kiss, and slipped it on. "I think I'll keep this one instead. You'll never lose me in a crowded mall again, princess."

A strangled cry escaped from my mouth. I buried my head in Brian's shoulder, and his arm went around me. "What? What is it, Sally?"

I started to sob hysterically. "The—green. It's the same color as Mike's jacket—the one he was wearing this morning."

The silence in the room was deafening. All of the

officers watched me sympathetically and then looked at Brian, waiting for him to make the call. I didn't know what they were thinking about me and honestly didn't care. I wanted my husband. No matter how devastating it would be, I needed to see Mike's face one last time—to kiss his lips and hold him while I said good-bye. With shaky legs I tried to move forward, but Brian wouldn't loosen his hold on me.

"Sally, you can't." His voice was hoarse. "I'm sorry, but this is still a crime scene, and it would be considered tampering with evidence."

My grief turned to anger. "That's my husband lying underneath that tarp. *Dead.* I don't give a damn about police evidence. Don't you understand? He's my entire world." The strength had been zapped from my body, and I fell to my knees on the floor, placing my head in my hands. Why had this happened to him? To us? It was his birthday. Mike was only 31 years old and had so much to live for. How could God be so cruel?

I was dimly aware of Brian squatting down next to me. He gently placed a hand on my shoulder. "Sally, I'm so sorry. I—I don't know what else to say."

My entire body had gone numb. I couldn't look at him. "Why didn't you get here sooner?" I sobbed into my hands. "Maybe you could have saved him."

The silence in the room grew louder. Even though I couldn't see anyone, I knew their eyes were on me. Sorrow and pity for the young widow. If I tried to stand, I feared I might topple over. In my heart I knew this wasn't Brian's fault. No, it was *mine.* I'd asked Mike to come here. At the realization, I wept louder.

"Sally," Brian said softly.

"Please let me see his face."

He placed his palm gently on the back of my neck. "All right, but I need to look first. It might be a—" Brian didn't finish the sentence. "You need to try to prepare yourself for his—for what's underneath the tarp."

I understood what he meant but couldn't bring himself to say. For all we knew, Mike might not even have a face left. I was fully aware of what a gunshot could do, especially at close range.

Could I deal with seeing my husband like that? Did I want to remember him that way? No. In my mind I saw his rugged, tanned face, the black, unruly curly hair that always needed a trim, and those midnight blue eyes, which always stared so tenderly into mine.

"Okay." My head bobbed up and down. "You look first."

Brian gave my hand a little squeeze and got to his feet. I slowly raised my head and watched him. He put on a pair of latex gloves, his eyes pinned on me the entire time. The other officers moved back to make room for him. I noticed another man, with horn-rimmed glasses and a digital camera in his hands, approaching us. One of the officers went over to him and spoke in a low, hushed tone. The man nodded and looked over at me, his expression somber.

Brian's jaw hardened as he stared down at the body. He glanced over at me one last time, and I noticed that his right hand was trembling slightly as he lifted the tarp.

My heart pounded against the wall of my chest and into my ears with such force that I was afraid I might pass out. I'd have to be brave and carry on without him. But how? Another whimper broke from my mouth. I'd loved this man for so long. He was my soul mate, a part of me. I simply couldn't go on without him. All I wanted was to curl up somewhere and die myself.

"Sally," Brian said in a flat, emotionless voice, "it's not Mike."

Relief washed over my body like a tidal wave. Feeling dizzy, I placed my palms flat against the floor in an attempt to keep the room from spinning. One of the other officers came forward and helped me into a standing position. The room tilted to one side as I looked over at Brian with new hope. "You—you're sure?"

He gave a grim nod and then gestured for me to come and stand next to him. On trembling legs, I moved forward.

"It's not a pretty sight," he cautioned. "But I can tell you that it's definitely not Mike."

Sucking in a deep breath, I stared down at the lifeless man who would never see the light of day again. Yes, it was definitely Mike's jacket. The seafoam green was sprayed with blood across the front of it. The body did not belong to my husband, though. This man had carrot-colored hair and a dusting of freckles across his ruddy cheeks. I couldn't see his eyes since his lids were shut, but I knew they were a striking amber color. A bullet hole had been placed strategically in the center of his forehead. There was dried blood in his hair and on his face.

I pressed my face into Brian's jacket, not wanting to see any more. "Oh dear God, no."

Brian stroked my hair gently. "Do you know him?"

"Yes," I whispered. "It's Mike's employee, Trevor Parks."

## CHAPTER THREE

Brian let the tarp gently fall back over Trevor's face. He crooked his finger at the man with the camera who must have been from forensics, indicating that he could come forward. Brian guided me toward the front of the store and sandwiched my hand between both of his. "I'm sorry you had to see that."

Not knowing what else to say, I simply burst into tears again, and he held me against his chest while I sobbed. My emotions were all over the place. I was thankful it wasn't Mike—oh, so thankful—but I also felt guilty. Trevor had been a nice guy, hard worker, and Mike had considered him a good friend. It seemed wrong to experience relief as I'd stared down into his lifeless face. Plus, there was still one huge question left to be answered. I pushed back from Brian and stared up at him. "Where's Mike?"

Brian glanced around the store's chaotic state. "You're positive he was here with Trevor?"

Once again, fear gripped me in a tight hold. "Trevor was wearing Mike's jacket. Maybe Trevor got something on his—they were painting the inside of a house today. Mike was bringing him to our house for dinner, so yes, he was with him. Oh, God. Could the gunman have taken Mike as a hostage?"

Adam came hurrying over to us. "I couldn't help overhearing, Sally. The gunmen got away. There were two of them, both wearing ski masks." He addressed Brian, "From what I've been told, one was about six feet tall, the other about Sally's height. No one here said anything about them taking a hostage, but"—he hesitated for a moment—"I just learned from Bruce that another man has already been rushed to Colwestern Hospital with a gunshot wound to the chest area."

"No." The terror was back, rising in my chest, threatening to suffocate me. "It must have been Mike."

Adam nodded soberly. "I'm sorry, Sally. The description that a witness gave me matches him perfectly. Doesn't he own a Dodge Ram? There's one out in the parking lot, and we haven't located the owner yet."

A high-pitched wail rose from inside me as I rushed for the exit. Brian was quick to grab my arm.

"Let go of me!" In desperation, I tried to shake his hand off.

"Sally!" His tone was sharp, and he tightened his grip. "I'll take you. You're in no condition to drive yourself, especially in this weather." He looked back at Adam. "Is there enough coverage here?"

Adam waved a hand at him in dismissal. "It's fine. Go ahead. We're expecting more units any minute."

Brian ushered me through the crowd of spectators outside. A woman in a brown ski parka rushed up to Brian with a microphone. "Officer, we've heard there's a fatality inside. Can you give us any details?"

Brian only shook his head at the woman and guided me to the passenger side of his cruiser. The cop directing traffic immediately waved him through. Snow was coming down heavier, and the road was barely visible.

For a few minutes, we said nothing. I was lost in my own world of terror and prayer while Brian probably wished he'd never gotten mixed up with me in the first place. To my surprise, he reached across the seat to touch my hand. "Think positive, Sally. He's a tough guy."

"Why did this happen?" The words broke from my lips in an outburst of anger, as if a light switch had suddenly clicked on in my brain. The questions wouldn't stop coming. Why Mike? He'd already been through so much in his life. Why was life so fragile? We never knew what tomorrow might bring. Had I told Mike I loved him on the phone earlier? I couldn't remember. "If I hadn't asked him to stop at the store, this wouldn't have happened to him—or Trevor."

Brian screeched the car to a stop at the curb next to the emergency room and whirled around to face me. Even in the semidarkness, I spotted a muscle tick in his jaw. "Don't you dare blame yourself. This is not your fault. Understand?"

I nodded mutely, a bit shocked by his tone. He came around to my side of the vehicle and helped me out of the car. "Ally's working in the emergency room tonight. Maybe we can use that to our advantage."

Ally Tetrault was Brian's girlfriend. They'd started dating about a year and a half ago, shortly before Mike and I had gotten married. Ally and I had gone to high school together, and although we'd never run in the same circle of friends, I'd always liked and respected her. She'd expressed doubts about her relationship with Brian when they first became a couple, worried that he might still have feelings for me, but I'd been quick to assure her that I had no interest in Brian other than friendship.

A few months back, when Brian had helped me solve the hit-and-run of my upstairs tenant, he'd surprised me with the confession that he was still carrying a torch for me. An uneasy thought flickered across my mind. If Ally saw us in the waiting room together, she might not understand. Or would she? We were all adults, and I couldn't spend any more time worrying about possible hurt feelings. My husband was my only concern right now.

We hurried over to the receptionist desk, where an older woman with salt-and-pepper curly hair was hanging up the desk phone. She looked up and smiled knowingly at Brian. "You just missed her, Bri. She went in to assist Dr. Hanson with immediate surgery. Young guy with a gunshot wound—the result of an armed robbery. Looks pretty bad."

My knees wobbled like Jell-O, and I reached out to Brian, who was quick to put an arm around me in support. He glared at the nurse. "Sonya, I need to know who that man is in there. He may be this woman's husband."

Realizing her mistake, the woman's face turned the color of a forest fire. "Oh my goodness. I'm so sorry. Let me see if they have identification on him yet." She couldn't scurry through the adjoining door fast enough.

"Do you want to sit down?" Brian asked me anxiously. "You look positively green, Sally."

Weakly, I shook my head in reply. I couldn't sit down—

couldn't do anything until I found out for sure if Mike was in the operating room. Deep in my heart, though, I already knew it had to be him. He'd been at the store with Trevor and hadn't attempted to contact me since I'd asked him to pick up the sprinkles. It was time to face the truth here.

Sonya reappeared. She glanced over at the other people in the waiting room and then gestured for Brian and me to come behind the counter. She opened the door for us, and we stood in the small area next to the curtained-off rooms used for emergency room patients. "You're Mrs. Donovan?" she addressed me.

With a sinking heart, I nodded. "The fact that she knew my name reaffirmed my fears. "Is he okay?"

She gave me a small, sympathetic smile. "I don't have a lot of details, but your husband Michael is in surgery right now. It appears that he suffered a gunshot wound to the chest area."

"I need to see him!" I tried to move toward the location of the operating room, but Brian grabbed me by the shoulder.

Sonya shook her head at me. "I'm so sorry. No one's allowed in there during surgery. Please be assured that Dr. Benson is the best we have. Why don't you have a seat in the waiting room? As soon as your husband's out of surgery, the doctor will come and find you."

My husband might be dying, and there was nothing I could do about it. His fate rested in the hands of a man I'd never even met or heard of before. "I can't just sit out there and wait!" I struggled to free myself from Brian's grip. "Don't you understand? I need to be with him!"

"Sally!" Brian's hands tightened around my arms, and I was forced to meet his eyes. There was no anger in them—only pity for me. "There's nothing you can do for him right now." He stared at Sonya. "If Ally comes out, will you tell her to find me in the waiting room?"

Sonya looked from me to Brian and bobbed her head up and down, doing her best imitation of a mechanical man. "Of course, but it's highly unlikely she'll be out until the surgery's over."

"Thanks, Sonya." Brian placed a hand on the small of my back and guided me out the door, past the receptionist desk, and into the small waiting area. He gently lowered me into a metal chair.

I slumped forward in the seat, my head in my hands. "Please tell me this is all a bad dream."

Before Brian could respond, my phone buzzed from my jeans pocket. I drew it out and saw a text message from Gianna. *Where are you? What's happened?*

Oh crap. My family had been coming for dinner. That was over an hour ago. They must be worried sick about me. I dismissed the message and saw that I had ten unanswered calls, five voice mail messages, and several other texts from both my mother and Gianna. "My family," I said dully to Brian. "I forgot to text them. They were coming to my house tonight to celebrate Mike's birthday."

Brian's eyes widened in surprise. "Today's his birthday?"

"Yes." That was when I remembered the fortune cookie message from earlier at the bakery. *Today is a day you'll always remember.* I thought I might be sick. "He has to be okay."

"He will be," Brian assured me. "Mike's a fighter, Sally." There was a small pause before he continued. "And he loves you—more than anything. He'll make it."

We sat in silence for several minutes until Brian spoke again. "Would you like me to call your parents for you?"

Before I could respond, my phone buzzed, and Gianna's name popped up. "No, my sister's calling. Let me take this." I pressed *Accept*. "Gianna?"

"Sal, what's going on?" she asked, the concern evident in her voice. "We've been waiting here for over an hour. Are you sick? Did something happen?"

I cleared my throat, determined not to cry again. "I'm at the hospital. Mike's been shot."

*"What?"* Her voice rose in alarm. "Is he okay? What happened? What hospital are you at?"

"Colwestern. Brian's with me in the waiting room. Mike was shot in the chest during an armed robbery at the mini-mart."

"Oh my God." Her voice trembled on the other end. "I just saw something about the robbery on Facebook. We're all on our way over. Stay strong, honey. We'll be there soon."

With a sigh, I clicked off and shut my eyes. My mind

was preoccupied with Mike and memories of the last time I'd seen him—this morning, before he'd left for work. We'd spent a generous amount of time in bed, and then he'd gone to take a shower and brought me coffee. I'd said I wanted to be a lady of leisure and stay in bed all day with him, and Mike had laughed. He'd held me in his strong arms one last time, and we'd kissed for several minutes before he left. "I love you, princess," he'd told me gently. "This is one very happy birthday boy."

Tears rolled down my cheeks again before I could stop them, and Brian put a hand on my shoulder. "Can I get you anything? Some coffee? Water?"

I shook my head. "I just want Mike."

Another awkward silence, and I exhaled deeply. "I'm sorry about what I said before. This isn't your fault, and I had no right to imply that. Thank you for bringing me here. You're on duty, so I understand if you need to get back to the market."

"Actually, I'm not on duty. I chose to respond when I heard the call. As soon as your family gets here, I'll run back over and see if there's anything I can do. But I don't want to leave you alone." His green eyes watched me intently "Sally, you were upset, and it's understandable. People say a lot of things in stressful situations that they don't mean. As a cop, I see it all the time."

I twisted a tissue between my fingers. "What happened to the gunmen? Have they been caught?"

Brian studied his phone screen. "Adam texted me. We've got an APB out on them, but there aren't any concrete descriptions circulating yet. The surveillance cameras didn't catch much. There's only one, located at the front of the store, which explains why they must have made everyone go to the back and why Trevor's body was—" He stopped abruptly. "When Mike is out of surgery and able to talk, I'd like to have a chat with him."

His statement that Mike would be awake and talking soon gave me profound hope. "Of course."

"What's really weird is that these guys only made off with about fifty dollars," Brian mused as he typed out a text.

I turned to stare at him. "That's *all*?"

He nodded. "Adam talked to the cashier, who confirmed

it. He said the gunmen didn't even seem concerned about the money. Plus, there's a sign displayed in the front window that says there's less than one hundred dollars after six o'clock at night."

"Okay, so what you're actually telling me is that two guys killed a man and wounded another one—my husband, who might be in there fighting for his life—over a crappy fifty dollars?" I was incensed with rage. This made no sense.

Brian gave me a grim look. "It's hard to believe, I know. But there are people out there who kill when there's even less money involved. You, of all people, should know this, Sally."

That was true enough. "Trevor—he has a girlfriend named Tina. They live in an apartment complex on the outskirts of Colwestern. He's got an ex-wife too, but I don't know where she lives."

"We'll find them." His hand closed over mine, and he massaged the palm of it with his thumb. I knew he was trying to be comforting, but the gesture seemed too familiar, and I stiffened slightly. Brian must have noted my reaction because he quickly removed his hand and picked up his phone again.

The clock in the waiting room said eight thirty. Two hours ago, I had been happily planning a birthday dinner for my husband. Now I couldn't even remember if I'd turned the oven off, and Mike might be critically injured—or worse.

"Interesting," Brian mused.

"What?" I asked.

He tapped out another quick text. "Adam told me something else that seems kind of strange. The cashier said that the gunman who shot Trevor seemed especially interested in him from the start. In fact, they charged into the store right after Mike and Trevor came inside. She said that the shooting almost felt…well, personal to her."

I rubbed my arms for sudden warmth. "Are you saying that Trevor and Mike could have been shot deliberately?"

Brian looked at me soberly. "At this point, and considering that there was only fifty dollars taken, we're certainly not ruling it out."

What could I possibly say to that? I was sorry about Trevor—very sorry. He'd been an easygoing guy and a hard worker. He hadn't deserved to die. But all I could think about was my husband now. I slumped forward in my chair.

Brian put his arm around my shoulders. "It's okay, Sally. I promise you, everything will be all right."

Someone cleared their throat, and we both looked up. Brian's girlfriend, Ally, was standing there in a short, dark blue winter coat, her pink scrubs sticking out underneath the hem. From the look on her face, all hell was about to break loose.

Brian removed his arm from my shoulders, and we both rose to our feet. "Mike—how is he? You were in there with him, right?" I asked her nervously.

Ally glared at Brian. Then her gaze met mine, and she spoke gently. "He's still in surgery, Sal. I can't say much about his condition, but he's stable, and I believe the doctor is almost done. I—uh, started to sneeze while I was in there, so of course the doctor ordered me out immediately. Another nurse has already taken my place. I can't be in surgery if there's any chance I'm getting sick. Personally, I think it's only allergies, but you don't argue with Dr. Benson."

Brian slid a sideways glance at me. "Sally, I hate to leave you alone, but I'm going to take Ally home. Then I'll go back and—"

He stopped when he saw Ally's expression. She was an attractive redhead, tall and slender with haunting gray eyes that resembled cold, hard steel at the moment. She pressed her lips together tightly. "I have my own car. Perhaps I'll stay at my mother's house tonight." She turned on her heel and hurried toward the exit door.

Wearily, I sank back down in the chair as Brian rushed out the door after her. *Great.* Not this again. I didn't have the strength to deal with their lovers' quarrel at the moment. A memory stirred in my brain from a few months back when Brian had confessed his feelings to me. *"I love Ally, but I'm not in love with her."* He'd gone on to say that he still hadn't been able to forget about me. Why did life have to be so complicated all the time?

I was somewhat comforted by what Ally had told me about Mike. Stable was a good thing—or at least I thought so. It was the only shred of hope I could cling to. I folded my hands in my lap, closed my eyes, and sent up another silent prayer to God—I'd lost track of how many I'd already said tonight.

The door to the emergency room opened, and my entire family descended upon me. My grandmother was the first person to reach me. She sat down next to me, and I forgot my resolve to be strong, immediately breaking down in her arms.

"Grandma, he has to be okay. He has too much to live for," I wept.

My grandmother held me against her, patting my back and saying soothing words of comfort. The dread lifted a bit from my chest, and I could breathe again. In some ways, Grandma Rosa was my own personal fortune cookie. Her predictions always came true, but unlike the cookies, her messages were never negative.

"He *will* live, *cara mia,*" she promised. "He will live because of his love for you."

# CHAPTER FOUR

---

The minutes on the round, black-and-white wall clock ticked by at an excruciating pace. Brian and Ally had been gone for at least an hour, and I doubted either one would return. Thankfully I had my family to lean on. My father had just returned with Johnny. They'd gone to the gas station to get my car and had brought it back to the hospital's lot. Grandma Rosa sat next to me, holding my left hand, while my mother sat on the other side, patting the right one absently. In the meantime, snow continued to fall outside.

My parents didn't do well with tragic life events. On the other hand, suffering was my grandmother's middle name. She'd lost her own mother at the age of four and watched her husband die following a long, horrific battle with cancer. After a two-day birthing ordeal with my own mother—when it had been touch-and-go for the two of them—Grandma Rosa had been strictly advised not to have any more children. She'd confided to me that her one true love, before my grandfather entered the picture, had never come home from the Vietnam War. To this day she didn't know for certain what had happened to him.

Grandma Rosa told me many times that there were some people in this life who were born to suffer. Undoubtedly, she was one of them, although she'd never come right out and admitted it. My parents, she'd also explained, couldn't handle trauma. My mother had lost a child before I was born—my brother. She and my father never talked about it. In fact, Grandma Rosa had been the one to tell Gianna and me the story a couple of years ago. I wasn't sure if my mother was aware that we knew, but I would never risk upsetting her to find out.

Grandma Rosa was made from unbendable steel and had

once told me that I was cut from the same. After everything that had happened in my life the last few years, she might be on to something. My ex-husband had been murdered, and Mike had been at the top of the suspect list. My former bakery location had burned down, and someone had tried to kill me right before our wedding. Each event had succeeded in making me stronger, but at this moment, I no longer felt like I could conquer the world. Mike *was* my entire world. "If he doesn't make it, I don't want to live."

I hadn't realized I'd spoken the words out loud until Grandma Rosa gave my arm a little shake. "You must never say things like that. Always think positive thoughts, *cara mia*."

She was right. I leaned my head on her shoulder and repeated the words over and over in my head. *Mike's all right. He's going to be fine.*

Gianna walked back and forth across the gray tile flooring so many times that I lost count. Her left hand was placed on her lower back as if it ached, and from the size of her, I had no doubt it did. She wasn't due for another two weeks, but the doctor had told her on her last visit that the baby had dropped and she could go anytime.

I was concerned that the extra stress might harm her or the baby. "Gi," I said quietly. "Maybe Johnny should take you home. You shouldn't get yourself upset like this."

Johnny's dark eyes shifted from me over to his fiancée's face as he waited for her response. He was the grandson of Nicoletta Gavelli, who had been my parents' next-door neighbor for the past 30 years. Nicoletta and I had a love-hate relationship at times, but then again, she did with most people. She'd mellowed somewhat in the last few months—probably from the excitement associated with her first great-grandchild's impending birth.

"Forget it," she said. "I'm fine. Mike's my family too, you know. I'm not going anywhere until we know that—" She swallowed hard. "I mean, until he's awake."

The door to the waiting room opened, and Brian reappeared. A fine dusting of snow covered his dark blue uniform jacket. He gave everyone in the room a curt nod before his bright green gaze settled on me. "Any news yet?"

"No." I clasped my hands together in prayer and stared down at the floor. If we didn't hear something soon, I might go crazy.

The door behind the receptionist's desk opened, and a man in dark blue scrubs stepped out holding a mask in one hand. He glanced around the full waiting room. "Mrs. Donovan?" he called. "Is there a Mrs. Donovan here?"

My heart thumped against the wall of my chest as I rose to my feet. "That's me. How's my husband?"

The doctor extended his hand. "I'm Dr. Benson." He was tall with a thin frame and encouraging, kind blue eyes as he gave me a warm smile. "Your husband made it through surgery very well. He's one tough guy."

My body went limp with relief, and I might have fallen over if Gianna hadn't been there to support me. My grandmother patted my back, and between the two of them, I seemed to gain newfound strength. "Thank God. Can I see him?"

"Mr. Donovan is still in recovery, but I'll have the nurse take you back in a little while. Only for a minute, though. He's sedated. We've extubated him, so he should be able to talk, but he might not make much sense." Dr. Benson cleared his throat before continuing. "He lost quite a lot of blood, but we stayed ahead of it with a few transfusions, and we'll keep him in the ICU until the chest tube is out. I pulled a bullet out of his shoulder, and the scapula was fractured. I'll have him evaluated by an orthopedic surgeon just to make certain he doesn't need to have them set."

"I thought he was shot in the chest?" I asked.

Dr. Benson shook his head. "It might have looked that way when he was hit, but no, it was his right shoulder. Too bad, especially since he's right handed. What kind of work does your husband do?"

"He owns a construction company," I said in a feeble voice.

Dr. Benson frowned. "Well, he's not going to be in any shape to return to work for at least several weeks. I'd say he's pretty much out of any immediate danger now. We're going to watch him for a few days to make sure there's no infection or sudden bleeding."

"Thank you so much," I managed to rasp out, grateful for what he'd done for Mike. I didn't dare say more in case I lost it all together. The no work factor was of little consequence to me, although sitting around doing nothing was sure to make Mike insane. He was going to live—he was going to be all right. That was all that mattered.

Dr. Benson seemed to understand what I was going through. He probably saw this on a daily basis. "The nurse will be out in a few minutes to take you back."

"Hey, Doc." Brian stepped forward. "If Mrs. Donovan doesn't mind, I'd like to have a word with Mr. Donovan as well, about the shooting. It isn't something that can afford to wait."

The doctor glanced from Brian to me. "If Mrs. Donovan is fine with it, I don't have any objection. Like I said, he's been extubated and may complain that his throat hurts, so please try to limit your questions. I'll inform the nurse you'll be coming back as well."

"Pardon me, doctor." Sonya spoke from behind the counter. "Dr. Hudson is on line three for you."

"Thanks. I'll take it in the doctor's lounge." He nodded briefly to us. "If you'll all excuse me, please." He smiled at me again. "I'll be around to check on Mr. Donovan sometime tomorrow."

"Thank God," Gianna murmured, a notable tremor in her voice. She hugged me tightly—as tightly as her protruding stomach would allow. "This is the best news ever."

"There was never any doubt in my mind that he'd make it through," my father bellowed cheerfully "He's part of the Muccio clan. I mean, he's not Italian by birth, but hey…what do they say about the Irish? Besides the drink part, I mean?" He snapped his fingers. "That's it. The luck of the Irish."

"Quiet, *pazza*," my grandmother scolded him. She led me to the nearest chair that I all but collapsed into. Then I started to cry, fat tears rolling down my cheeks as she held me against her.

"There now," she said gently. "What did I tell you? Your man is a fighter. We knew he would come through this fine. Now dry your eyes before you go in to see him, *cara mia*. He won't want to see you carrying on like that. Be strong for him."

"Here, sweetheart." My mother handed me a tissue and blinked back a tear of her own. This was so uncharacteristic of her that it shocked me for a second. My mother always looked at life through rose-colored glasses. "Tell Mike that we all love him."

Gianna pulled out her phone. "Josie texted me. She said she's been trying to reach you—she stopped by the house earlier, but no one was home. She wants to know what's going on."

I pulled my phone out of my pocket and saw that I had three missed calls and six texts from her. "Shoot," I said miserably. "I totally forgot that Josie said she might come by for dessert."

The door behind the receptionist counter opened. A nurse about my age, her long hair the color of copper, looked over at us. "Mrs. Donovan?"

I quickly rose from my seat. "Will you text Josie and explain everything that has happened, Gi?"

"Of course." Gianna's eyes filled as she stared up at my face. "Give Mike a hug from me."

Brian walked across the room to join me. The nurse smiled and held the door open for both of us to follow her. She led us past several blue curtained-off areas to the last one on the right-hand side. "Only for a minute," she warned. "He's very tired from surgery and probably won't make much sense."

"Thank you," I said as she pulled back the curtain. Mike was lying in the bed with his eyes closed, the upper part of his arm and shoulder bandaged and in a sling. His usual tanned complexion was white as powdered sugar. I stared at the machines around him—heart monitor, ventilator, and a blood pressure cuff around his left upper arm—and struggled not to cry again.

I sank into the lone chair next to the bed and reached for his left hand. It was cold and unmoving as I brought it to my lips. "Hi, sweetheart," I whispered. "I'm here and won't leave you. Everything is going to be fine."

Mike didn't respond at first, but then his fingers closed around mine and gave them a little squeeze. A sob escaped from my throat before I could stop it. Mike turned his head slowly, and after what seemed like an eternity, his eyelids fluttered open.

His beautiful eyes were the same as always—that midnight shade of blue—as mesmerizing as the first day I'd laid eyes on him in high school about 15 years ago.

He gave a slow smile as recognition set in. "Hi, princess." His voice was raspy and faint.

Despite my grandmother's warning, tears fell from my eyes before I could stop them. I wrapped both of my hands around his and gently rested my face against it. "Oh, sweetheart. I was so scared, but everything's all right now. You're fine. We're going to be fine." I tried to keep my voice steady.

He sighed and closed his eyes again. "Didn't mean—to—worry. You. Love you."

"I love you too." The lump in my throat wouldn't dissolve, and my voice was clogged with tears. "Everyone's out in the waiting room and sends their love. Grandma, Mom, Dad, Gianna, and Johnny. We've all been so worried." I kissed his hand again. "Especially me."

"Hell of a birthday," he said as a small smile crept across his lips. He withdrew his hand from mine and brought it to his throat. "Hurts. Water?"

"Maybe they'll let you have some ice chips," I said. "Let me find the nurse and ask her."

I started to rise from my chair, but Brian stopped me. I'd forgotten he was there. His eyes seemed different as they looked at me now—there was a haunted quality I hadn't noticed before. Things must not have gone well with Ally.

"I'll ask the nurse for you," he said. "You stay here with Mike."

"Thank you." I wrapped my hands back around Mike's left one and brought it to my heart, vowing silently to never complain about anything in life again.

Mike's eyelids opened, and he stared up at me, his face tight and drawn. "I was—afraid. So afraid."

A chill blew through me, but I tried to make light of the situation. "You? Afraid? That's impossible. You're not afraid of anything." Panic tightened in my chest. I wasn't sure I wanted to hear all the gruesome details about the robbery and shooting yet.

"When I lay there—after getting shot," he murmured. "Before I blacked out. So afraid. Afraid—I'd never see you again."

I kissed his hand again and tried to keep the emotion out of my voice. "Well, you're not going anywhere, Mr. Donovan. Except home with me in a few days."

He smiled up at me, but a troubled look came into his eyes. "Trevor. Where—is—how is he?"

Oh no. I was ashamed to admit I'd almost forgotten about the poor man and his fate. "He didn't make it, sweetheart. I'm so sorry."

Mike closed his eyes tightly and drew a deep breath. "No," he whispered. "Didn't deserve it. Didn't deserve to die—like that."

The curtain opened behind me, and Brian stepped back into view. Mike's gaze wandered over to him, and he looked confused, as if he didn't recognize him at first.

"Hey, Mike. How are you feeling?" Brian asked.

"Been better," he croaked out.

"Sweetheart, Brian wants to ask you some questions, but we know your throat hurts, so you can just nod or shake your head. Okay?"

Mike kept staring at Brian. "You found them? Those SOBs—killed Trevor. Good guy. He was a good—friend."

Brian's expression was grim. "Not yet. That's where you come in. Is there anything you can tell me about the gunmen? Features that stand out? Piercings, scars, tattoos, shaved heads?"

"Ski masks. Couldn't see faces." Mike licked his dry lips.

The nurse came into the room with a plastic blue cup and spoon and handed them both to me. "Only a few," she cautioned. She checked the monitor, glanced at Mike, smiled, and left us alone.

I spooned some of the chips into Mike's mouth, and Brian and I waited until he was able to continue. "One guy was tall—taller than me. The other was short—like my princess. Taller guy had tattoo."

Brian looked confused. "If they were wearing masks and jackets, where was the tattoo?"

"Wrist." Mike tried to shift in the bed slightly, but it was impossible with all the machines he was hooked up to. "Coat sleeve pulled up when—he pointed—gun. Weird-looking—

cobra with red eyes—like blood. Never saw one like it."

Brian whipped out a small pad of paper from his breast pocket and made some notes. "Do you remember what their voices sounded like?"

"Little guy didn't talk." Mike looked at me, and then his eyes moved to the cup in my hands. I immediately gave him another spoonful. After he swallowed, he went on. "Taller guy was big, muscular. Deep voice. Like a smoker."

"Sweetheart, no more," I pleaded. "You need to save your strength."

Mike continued as if he hadn't heard me. "Came inside—right after we did. Almost like they were waiting for us." He grimaced and turned his head slightly, obviously in pain. "Need to fry for what they did. Trevor—didn't deserve this—to die."

It wasn't enough that Mike was in physical pain, but he was in emotional pain as well. I knew Trevor was more than just an employee to Mike—they had been friends. It had been great for Mike to finally have someone he could depend on to help him with his business too.

"We're going to do everything we can to catch those scumbags," Brian promised. "Which one shot you? The tall guy or the short one?"

"Tall guy," Mike croaked out. "Short guy got Trevor first. I jumped forward when he shot him—don't know what I was thinking. Gut reaction, I guess. Think I scared him—he made a squeaking noise like a mouse. Must have surprised him. Then the tall guy—he got me. Don't think he meant to—"

Brian looked intrigued. "How do you know he didn't mean to?"

In annoyance, I stared at him. "Brian, no more. Please."

"He swore as I went down," Mike said. "Then stared at me and said, 'Look what—what you made me do.' Then they left." He paused and closed his eyes. "Kind of like they had it in for T-Trevor right from the s-start."

I recalled what the cashier had told Adam. "Sweetheart, the cashier in the market said that it seemed like Trevor and the robbers might have known each other."

The room was silent, except for the beeping of the

machines. "Yeah," Mike finally said. "When the little guy—he turned the gun on Trevor, tall guy said something. Real strange." He paused, as if trying to remember. "Saw his mouth move—the cutout in the mask. Guy gave Trevor an evil smile. And Trevor, he said, 'Don't do this. You know you don't want to. We'll work it out.'"

A shiver ran down my spine as I waited patiently for him to go on.

Mike looked at the cup in my hands, and I gave him another spoonful. "Tall guy said something like, 'You know what we want. You won't get away with it.'" Mike paused for breath, and his face contorted with pain.

Brian and I exchanged a confused glance. "What happened after that?" he asked Mike.

Mike's forehead wrinkled. "Little guy pointed the gun at Trevor's head—" He turned to look at me, his beautiful blue eyes filled with grief as they met mine. "Then—he pulled the trigger."

# CHAPTER FIVE

---

Brian left a few minutes later, after promising to keep me posted on any new details with the robbery. He seemed suddenly cold and distant, and I wondered if he felt like he'd intruded on an intimate moment between Mike and me. I'd been so concerned about my husband's welfare that I hadn't even asked about him and Ally. It was probably better to stay out of their business anyhow.

I'd gone back to the waiting room to sit with my family so that the nurse could check Mike's vitals and get him ready for the move to the ICU. It was after midnight, and everyone looked exhausted. I begged Gianna to go home with Johnny. She'd been hesitant at first, but then finally relented.

"What about you?" Gianna asked as she pulled me into a hug. "Are you staying here tonight?"

I nodded. "The nurse said I can stay in Mike's room. They promised to come and get me once he's all settled in the ICU."

"Sal." Johnny gave me a kiss on the cheek. "Can we get you anything before we go? I know the cafeteria here is closed, but I can run down the street and grab you a coffee. There's a mini-mart open until one. Or how about something to eat?"

I shuddered at the word *mini-mart*. "Thanks, Johnny, but I'll be okay. I can't even stomach the thought of food right now."

"*Cara mia*, you must eat," Grandma Rosa said sharply. "You cannot get sick as well. I will be back in the morning and bring you both something special for breakfast."

"Thanks, Grandma." She knew that I never had an appetite when I was worried or upset. I was beyond thankful that Mike was out of immediate danger, but other concerns had already started to crowd my brain. I tried to tell myself that they weren't important, but they must be dealt with. Mike was under my health insurance provider. We were the only two on it since Josie had coverage through her husband's employer. The monthly premium was a small fortune to maintain, and it had a high deductible. I wasn't even sure how much of the claim they would cover, but I knew it wasn't higher than 80 percent.

With Mike out of work for several weeks, it was going to be tough for us to manage. Business at the bakery had been up and down as of late. Thank goodness I had some savings and knew Mike had a decent amount in his business account as well. We'd discovered long ago that you had to put money aside when business was going well *and* when it wasn't. Our work would never be a steady, 365-days-of-the-year thing.

I swallowed hard, hating to ask for help. "Grandma, there's no way I can go to the bakery tomorrow. I don't want to bother you, but—" I stopped abruptly. "I can't put all of this on Josie's shoulders. Is there any way—"

"Of course," she interrupted. "I will be glad to help."

"No," Gianna broke in. "I'm officially on maternity leave as of today. I can help Josie."

Johnny shook his head. "No, sweetheart. You should stay off your feet until the baby comes. I won't have you carrying those heavy trays around."

"He's right," I agreed.

Gianna gave her fiancé a scornful look. "I'll sit down when I get tired. At least I can wait on customers for Josie and answer the phone. It will be fun. Plus I'm really craving cookies these days."

My father, who had been silent up to this point, gave a hearty laugh. "From the looks of you, my sweet girl, you're craving everything these days." He turned to my mother for confirmation. "Isn't that right, Maria?"

*Ouch. Bad choice of words, Dad.* Gianna had always been slender and was self-conscious about her weight these days. I watched her lower lip quiver for a second while Johnny gave my father a murderous glance. Last I'd heard, she'd gained sixty pounds during her pregnancy, which was too much for one baby. Still, my father needed to learn to think before he spoke. In his sixty-seven years on this earth, he'd never learned to do that and probably wouldn't anytime soon.

My mother came forward and put an arm around my shoulders as she addressed Gianna. Her long dark hair brushed against the side of my face. For as long as I could remember, Maria Muccio had had a perfect, size-four figure and gorgeous face to match, even now at the age of fifty-four.

"Gianna, your father is only kidding." My mother frowned at him, something she rarely did, and then turned to me. "We're going to leave, sweetheart, but call if you need anything. What about Spike?"

Oh crap. I'd forgotten about our poor dog. He had a doggie door in the kitchen, which led to a small, fenced-in yard, but I couldn't leave him alone all day and night. I rubbed my eyes wearily. "I fed him earlier tonight but don't know what time I'll be going home tomorrow. You're allergic to dogs, though. Maybe I—"

"We'll stop and pick him up," Johnny volunteered. "Spike can stay with us. He'll be good company for Dante." Dante was a beagle-mix puppy that he and Gianna had adopted a few months ago. In fact, Dante and Spike had had a play date together last week. Despite his age, Spike tolerated the puppy well.

After Johnny and Gianna had left, my grandmother turned to me, her eyes anxious. "*Cara mia*, you cannot stay here around the clock. You will need your strength for when Mike comes home. I will plan on being here for a few hours so that you can go home and get some rest."

"I can come too," Mom volunteered, but I noted the somewhat panicked look in her eyes. My mother hated hospitals, and so did my father. They loved Mike as a son—there was no doubt in my mind about that. They didn't do well with blood, needles, and other realities of life. I'd always hated hospitals myself but had been admitted so many times in the past few years that I'd learned how to deal with my phobia. My parents were different from most people's parents, though. Life was always a party, and that did not involve sickness in any way.

"It's not necessary, Mom." I noticed how her expression immediately changed to one of relief. Then I squeezed my grandmother's hand. "You don't have to come either."

"I know I do not," she said. "But I am coming anyway. Now are you sure you do not want me to stay here with you tonight?"

"No, but thanks." I gave all of them a kiss and clung to my grandmother for a few extra seconds. "I'm fine. I only want to be with Mike."

She nodded gravely. "I understand, *cara mia*. Try to rest if you can. I will be here at nine o'clock. Remember the saying. Things always look lighter in the morning."

"I think you mean brighter, Grandma."

"That is good too."

When they opened the door to leave, Brian was standing there, cell phone pressed against his ear. I was surprised to see him back. My parents and Grandma Rosa nodded to him. He put the phone away and started toward me. I noticed my grandmother raise one eyebrow in my direction as she shut the door.

Brian handed me a bottle of water. "Sorry, the cafeteria's closed, but I can try to find another place if you really need a caffeine fix."

I removed the cap and guzzled half the bottle down in one gulp. "This is fine. I hadn't realized how thirsty I was—thanks."

He shot me a worried look. "You look exhausted, Sally."

"You don't exactly look rested either." I finished off the drink.

Brian smiled. "Yeah, but that's an on-the-job hazard for me. Do you need a ride home?"

I shook my head. "Thanks, but my car's in the lot. I'm staying here tonight anyway."

His face flushed, and he looked away. "Oh, right. I should have guessed that. Uh—I'm glad Mike's okay, Sally. Really, I am. He was very lucky."

Unlike Trevor. Brian didn't say the words, but he didn't have to. I sighed. "I appreciate all you've done." He continued to stand there, and I sensed there was another matter on his mind. "Did you want to talk to me about something? Do you have more details on the robbery?"

He sat down next to me. "We located Trevor's girlfriend, Tina Landon, and gave her the news. Adam and I went over together to their apartment. Tina took it pretty hard. We stayed with her until her girlfriend got there. Tina also told us where to find his ex-wife, Erica. Adam and I went to see her as well, but a neighbor said she's been out of town for the last couple of days. We're going to try again tomorrow."

His news surprised me. "I didn't know that Trevor's ex-wife was local. Mike said that Trevor moved here last summer. That was when he answered Mike's ad in the paper for help. He was new to the area and desperately needed the job."

"Did he tell Mike where he moved here from?" Brian asked.

I paused to think. "Maybe Virginia? I can't remember." Then I noticed the grave look on Brian's face. "Is there something else you're not telling me?"

He turned towards me until his knee was touching mine. "Sally, I have a strange feeling about this. From what Mike told us earlier, and everything the cashier relayed to Adam, it makes me think that this robbery might not have been *just* a robbery." He blew out a breath. "I wonder if it might have been staged to take Trevor out."

My blood ran cold. "You mean the gunmen were acting out a performance?"

He nodded. "I ran a check on Trevor but didn't find any arrest records. Still, it's possible that he might have been involved on some level with these guys. Maybe he had an item of value that belonged to them. Or he was fooling around with one of their girlfriends, I don't know. Without knowing exactly who these guys are, it's going to be difficult to figure out the motive." He ran a hand over his unshaven chin. "I'd like to talk to Mike again tomorrow, after he's gotten some rest."

"I'm sure that won't be a problem."

"You should get some rest too." His voice became husky as he placed his hand on top of mine, and I immediately stiffened. The color rose in his cheeks and he drew his hand away. "Sorry."

Since the situation was already awkward, I decided to go for broke. "Is everything okay between you and Ally?"

That got a slight smile out of him. "Things are never okay between Ally and me. You, of all people, should know that."

What was that supposed to mean? "I don't understand."

He reached over and tucked a stray curl behind my ear before I could stop him, and his finger brushed against my cheek. "Brian, please, don't—"

"Sally, I'm thinking about going back to Boston."

"For a visit?" Brian had transferred to the Colwestern force from Boston almost three years ago, shortly before I'd returned to town after my divorce. All of Brian's family still lived there, including his father, a retired chief of police. I'd never met his family, but they seemed like a close bunch. I assumed that his father becoming a cop had led to the career choice for him.

"No," he said quietly. "I'm thinking about going back there to live—permanently. My father still has ties to the department, and one of the detectives is planning to retire next year. I've already taken the exam and did well. Dad thinks there's a great chance I could have the position. Until that happens, I could serve as a cop on their force."

"Oh." I hated to see him leave Colwestern but didn't say so. Brian was more than just a police confidant who had helped me out of some scrapes in the past. He'd become a good friend—someone whose opinion I valued—and he was easy to talk to. Mike had been jealous of him in the beginning, knowing that Brian was interested in me romantically, but eased up once we'd confessed our love for one another. Mike knew that he could trust me, and I had no interest in any other man.

"Well, if you think it's best for your career, then I'm happy for you," I said carefully. "Of course, I'm sorry for all of us, though. When will you and Ally be leaving?"

He stared into my eyes for a long time before he answered, the gaze so intense that my face started to heat from the contact. "Ally won't be going with me. I—I'm planning to break up with her before I leave."

This was worse than I'd expected. "Brian, it's none of my business what's happening between the two of you, but I hope that the incident earlier tonight didn't make her worried that—" I stopped, fully aware of the green eyes with golden flecks that were pinned on mine. "I wouldn't want her to think that there was something going on between the two of us."

He laughed then—a bitter, sarcastic sound that left my insides hollow. I'd never seen him react this way before. Sure, steam poured out of his ears when I tampered with an investigation or questioned a suspect he'd warned me to stay away from, but this was different.

Brian rose and stood in front of the window, staring out into the semidarkened parking lot, hands perched on his slim hips. The snow had finally stopped, and it looked picturesque outside, like a winter wonderland. He waited a few seconds before he spoke again. "Of course it's you, Sally. It's always been *you*. But don't worry. Ally doesn't blame you for any of this—not like she did before. She knows that you're in love with your husband." His voice was barely audible now. "Ally knows you're in love with Mike and he with you." He lowered his tone, and I barely caught the next words. "And she probably knows that I love you too."

Sickening dread swept through me. "Brian, please don't—"

"No," he interrupted and turned around to face me. "It's not fair to do this to you now, after everything you've been through tonight, but I can't help myself."

Uneasily, I glanced around the room. We were alone—even the nurse behind the receptionist counter had disappeared. With resignation, I gripped the sides of my chair for support. "Say what you have to, then."

Brian walked toward me, his Greek god-like face stricken with visible grief. He knelt next to my chair. "I've loved you since the first day I saw you in the bakery." A smile formed on his lips, as if he was replaying the memory in his head. "I remember how your dark eyes were shining with happiness as you waited on customers and those gorgeous curls bounced on your shoulders. How you spoke so sweetly to everyone, even the customers who were rude. I've tried to forget about you—God, how I've tried! But it's as if fate always draws me back to you, like when you get involved in the middle of a murder for what—oh, I don't know, the hundredth time? I feel like someone's trapped me in a version of *Groundhog Day*." He stared down at the floor, his breathing becoming rapid and loud. "There's no way out for me."

If I'd thought it wasn't possible to feel any worse than I already did, Brian had proved me wrong. Without meaning to, I was ruining his life. I put my face in my hands and refused to look at him.

"Don't cry, Sally. I can't bear it." When I uncovered my eyes, he had already risen to his feet and was facing the window again. "I have a confession to make."

My shoulders slumped forward heavily. Hadn't he just made one? I didn't know how much more I could handle tonight. "What is it?"

Brian's voice was barely above a whisper. "Please don't hate me, but for a brief second tonight—when we saw Mike's jacket under the tarp, I—"

He didn't finish. There was no need to. I knew what he was going to say, and it sent a wave of shock ricocheting through my body. "You thought that if Mike had—I mean, was gone, you might have a chance with me."

He turned around to meet my eyes but made no attempt to approach me this time. "I'm sorry. It's sick, I know. I don't want anything to happen to your husband, I swear. Mike's a good guy, and I like him. Really, I do. When I saw how broken up you were earlier at the market—when you thought he'd died—and then when you sat next to his bed and kissed his hands…" His voice trembled, and he forced a laugh to the surface. "Boy, what a schmuck I am. I never realized how much you loved him before tonight. Or maybe I just didn't want to."

"It's okay," I said dully, but knew it never would be between us again.

"No, I've been fooling myself," he admitted and stared down at his hands. "I can't live like this anymore. I can't even have a normal relationship with another woman. Every time I'm with Ally, I see your face."

The words froze me into shock. Brian had bared his soul to me, and I didn't want this burden on my shoulders. "I've never led you on." With great effort, I tried to keep my voice calm. "You know that I've always loved Mike. Even when I was married to Colin—"

"Damn it, Sally, I'm aware of all this. Don't you get it? That's why I have to go away. I can't be around you anymore. I thought it would get better after a while, but now I know it never will." His eyes had dulled and become watery. "I'll never get you out of my heart."

My stomach filled with dread. What could I possibly say to that? He already knew how I felt. Mercifully the awkward moment was interrupted by Sonya reappearing.

"Mrs. Donovan? Your husband's all settled in ICU on the second floor," she said cheerily. "You don't have to call on the phone when you get up there. Another nurse will be waiting to take you back."

"Thank you." I hoisted my purse over my shoulder while Brian walked with me to the door. We stood there in uncomfortable silence, waiting for the other person to speak.

Brian went first. "Give Mike my best, okay? I'll stop by tomorrow to talk with him further. Probably early afternoon." He cleared his throat. "I figured you'd want to know, in case you'd rather not be here at the same time."

My brain was a mass of jumbled confusion while every other part of my body ached from weariness and the ordeal of tonight. How had everything gone so wrong so quickly? There was nothing I could say to make it right between the two of us—perhaps ever again. "Brian, I'm so sorry. For everything."

Brian stood in the doorway and gave me a small sad smile that tugged at my heart. "Don't worry, Sally. I promise to never mention this again, and I'm a man of my word. Thanks for listening."

He let the door close quietly behind him.

# CHAPTER SIX

---

"Princess."

"Hmm?" I turned on my side but couldn't manage to get comfortable. I tried to stretch out, but there was no room. Boy, we needed a new mattress.

"Your grandma's here." Mike's voice was raspy and sounded far away.

Why was my grandmother in *our* bedroom? And why did the room smell so funny? Slowly I opened my eyes. Mike was lying in a hospital bed with a sling on his right arm and looked pale and tired. Everything came back to me in a rush as I quickly uncurled myself from the fetal position in the chair.

Grandma Rosa was standing at the opposite side of Mike's bed, unpacking a bag of goodies. She offered me a cup of coffee and a croissant, but I shook my head.

Mike took the croissant and bit off a large piece of the pastry. "Thank goodness for you, Rosa. I hate hospital food," he said as he chewed.

"Small bites," I said anxiously. "What about your throat? Is it okay for you to swallow that?"

Grandma Rosa waved her hand impatiently. "He is fine. The injury was not to his throat. He will have some soreness for a day or two, but let the boy eat what he wants."

I took a cup of coffee from her and held it to Mike's lips. He drank from it gratefully and then kissed me. His lips were cracked and dry, but I didn't care. They tasted like heaven to me.

"The nurse came in earlier while you were asleep," Mike said. "They gave me a swallow test with water to make sure that I could take solids." He bit off another piece of the croissant and gave me that sexy, lopsided grin of his. Such a beautiful smile and one that, after last night, I hadn't been sure I'd ever see again. "I passed with flying colors," he bragged.

"Yes, I can see that." I leaned over the bed and gave him a soft peck on the lips. "Did you get any sleep?"

"Some," he said, but his response didn't fool me. Mike had dark circles of weariness under his beautiful eyes, which regarded me with affection. I almost wept as I ran a hand through his thick mass of curly black hair and sent a silent prayer of thanks up to God. I kissed him again, more passionately this time, forgetting my grandmother was there.

"Now that's more like it," he whispered. "I feel better already."

Grandma Rosa cleared her throat. "Ahem. Now you children behave while I am here. What is the saying? Get a hotel."

I laughed. "It's get a *room*, Grandma."

"Whatever." She offered me a blueberry muffin, but I shook my head. My appetite had disappeared. Instead, I poured myself a cup of water from the little blue pitcher next to Mike's bed.

My grandmother's wise, dark eyes, which never missed anything, examined my face closely. "You look terrible, *cara mia*."

"Gee, thanks," I said lightly.

She didn't laugh. "I do not mean that you look unattractive. I meant that you look ill—very tired. Are you feeling okay?"

I ran my hand over Mike's forehead, which was a bit warm to the touch. "I am now."

He started to say something, but I put a finger over his lips. "Are you sure your throat doesn't hurt? I feel bad that you had to spend so much time talking to Brian last night."

"A little," he admitted, "but it's better than it was." He fumbled with the lid on the coffee cup with his left hand and would have knocked it over if my grandmother hadn't grabbed it in time. He sighed. "This is going to be fun."

"Well, that's why I'm here," I reminded him.

My grandmother sat down in the other chair and removed her crocheting from a canvas tote bag. "Go home and take a shower, *cara mia*. Have a nap. I will stay with Mike."

"No, I want to wait for the doctor."

"The nurse said he won't be around until this afternoon." Mike's eyes were anxious as he watched me. "You need to rest, baby. Would you take care of something else for me while you're at the house?"

"Of course. I'll bring you clothes, razor, and toothbrush. Is there anything else you need?"

He shook his head and gestured to the sling on his right arm. "This is going to limit what I can do for a while. I won't be able to go back to work until I'm healed." He muttered a curse word under his breath and then glanced sheepishly at my grandmother. "Sorry, Rosa."

She waved a hand dismissively. "I have heard it all before, dear boy. Sally's grandfather loved to fuss all the time. Very nasty habit."

Mike smiled at her. "That's cuss, Rosa."

She nodded. "I like that too."

I held out the blueberry muffin my grandmother had offered me to Mike. "Something tells me that you're not going to be an easy invalid to take care of, my darling."

Grandma Rosa grunted. "No patience. Your grandfather had none either. God rest his soul." My grandmother had been a nurse many years ago, before she'd met my grandfather. For the last year of his life, he'd been bedridden with cancer. She'd faithfully taken care of him and sat by his side until he'd passed away, at the young age of fifty-three. I was too young to remember, only being two years old at the time.

Mike took my right hand in his left one. "I was hoping you could pay some bills for me. I had been planning to do it last night after the party. I've let things go the last couple of weeks, and now they're in danger of being late. But if you're too tired, they can wait till tomorrow."

"Don't worry, I'll pay them." Mike was a meticulous businessman. Like me, he prided himself on paying all vendors on time. We didn't like to owe people money.

"You know where I keep everything, right? My password for QuickBooks is our wedding anniversary date. And the invoices to be paid are inside a manila folder in the main desk drawer. You can use my business debit card to pay them. It's in my wallet." He looked around the room. "Although I have no idea where that is."

"Brian gave it to me last night. Oh, and Johnny got the extra set of keys from our house and drove your truck home. It's in the garage, waiting for its owner."

He pursed his lips together. "Yeah, well, it won't be seeing me in action for a while. Look, baby, you're tired, so it can wait till tomorrow."

"That's okay. I'm happy to do it. I'm sure it won't take more than a few minutes." I didn't want Mike to worry about anything while he was in the hospital, but I knew my husband. A proud man, his brain was already working overtime, thinking about possible past due notices that might hurt his excellent credit.

Mike glanced over at my grandmother and then hesitated for a moment before he spoke again. "I'm not going to be bringing in any money for a while. There should be enough in the account to cover the current bills, and I don't want to be charged interest." He closed his eyes and sank back against the pillows. Fine lines were etched into his forehead, and I wasn't sure if they were from worry or pain. Maybe both.

"They're not late yet, right? My vendors give me thirty days to pay." Mike and I preferred to stay out of each other's business affairs whenever possible. We were both a bit bossy and headstrong when it came to our respected professions.

"That's right, thirty days. No, they're not late. There's at least a couple of days left. I can't believe I let them go this long, though."

I rubbed his forehead, which was still warm. "It's hard to remember everything, especially when you're working 16-hour days."

He brought my hand to his mouth and kissed it. "And you don't have any spare time to spend with your beautiful wife who never complains."

"Well, you'll make up for it now," I teased. "I'll be seeing a lot more of you for quite a while."

Grandma Rosa looked up from her crocheting. "Are you two going to be all right? Do you need any money?"

"No." Mike's tone was sharp. He closed his eyes for a moment, then opened them and stared at my grandmother with obvious regret. "I'm sorry, Rosa. I didn't mean to be rude. But you know how I feel about borrowing money."

Grandma Rosa had once put up bail money for Mike when he'd been arrested for Colin's murder, and he'd insisted on paying her back in record time. He was too proud and independent to borrow, no matter how badly we might need the funds.

She frowned at him. "Bah. We are family. You should not feel that way. But I will respect your wishes." She took up her crochet hook again.

"We'll be okay." I massaged Mike's hand between mine. "As long as we have each other, that's all that matters." I had vowed silently last night that if Mike lived, I'd never ask God for anything again. Or at least not for a long time. "I'm just thankful to have you here with me. You gave me such a scare last night." There was a sudden catch in my voice. "You could have easily—" I couldn't go on, but there was no need. He realized what I was going to say.

Mike bit into his lower lip. "I know, baby. And I can't believe that Trevor's gone." Grief and sadness mingled in his eyes, and I longed to kiss them away. I couldn't even begin to imagine the horror that Tina, Trevor's girlfriend, was going through. It could have been me instead of her planning a funeral today. That was when Brian's words from last night came rushing back to me. "How much do you know about Trevor's personal life?"

"Not much," he admitted. "He and his wife divorced last summer, right before he came here. They were living in Virginia at the time. He told me it was amicable, but he needed to start over in a new town, new state. He's got a sister who lives in Colwestern. That's why he decided to come here."

"But, sweetheart, his ex-wife is here—in Colwestern. Brian went to her house last night, and she wasn't there."

Mike raised his left eyebrow. "Erica's here? In town? That's strange. Trevor never said a word about it. She must have followed him."

"Do you know who he worked for before?" I asked.

He frowned and stared up at the ceiling. "I can't remember the name of the guy, but I've still got the notes from my phone conversation with him at home. They're somewhere in my desk. The guy was a solo operation like me."

Thoughts crowded my brain, and they were not pleasant ones. What if Trevor had been shot deliberately? Who wanted him dead, and why? Had he done something terrible, like take someone else's life? His death might have been payback. I wanted answers but wasn't sure where to find them.

Grandma Rosa sipped her coffee with one eye on me. I found myself wondering if she had somehow clued into my thought process. She always knew more than she let on and now pointed at the door as if reading my mind. "Go, *cara mia*. It sounds like you have many things to do."

\* \* \*

I sat down behind the heavy oak desk in our spare bedroom and pressed the *On* button for the laptop Mike and I shared. Mike used both the desk and the computer more than I did. I wasn't a fan of social media and only used the laptop if I wanted to Google a recipe. A payroll service provided checks for Josie and our bakery driver bi-weekly, while Mike handwrote checks for Trevor. I did most of the shop's finances from my cell phone in the bakery because it was more convenient, while Mike preferred to use our spare bedroom. He had no on-the-job office, while I could easily sit down in my shop and go through sales receipts. I'd been debating putting a desk in the vacant apartment upstairs over the bakery and turning that into an office.

We both used the same accountant for our taxes, but Mike's system was entirely different from mine. He used a QuickBooks program to keep track of jobs, materials, what he owed vendors, and his bank account balance.

Mike often talked about the various jobs he was working on so that I'd have an idea of where he was on a day-to-day basis. When we were alone together in the evening, he preferred not to talk about his work though. On the other hand, I often regaled Mike with tales of my customers and their antics. He especially enjoyed the stories of Mrs. Gavelli and her irritation over the messages in her fortune cookies.

    My husband went wherever there was work to be found but didn't travel out of state. He could perform any job asked of him—from laying a foundation to installing a new roof. Mike preferred not to be separated from me overnight, and the feeling was mutual. We both figured we'd already spent too many years and nights apart.

    I tried to keep between five and ten thousand in my bakery account at all times, but it wasn't easy. Like the construction industry, there were certain times of the year that business in the bakery was more profitable, such as holidays and summertime, with its graduation parties and weddings. There wasn't a certain pattern, though. I also made a note to call my health insurance provider and find out how much of Mike's hospital stay would be covered. I didn't want any more surprises.

    The invoices had a *To Be Paid* scrawled on the outside cover of the manila folder. It looked like Mike completed four different jobs in the past month or so, and most likely, they were all ones that Trevor had done since Mike had still been involved in the house restoration. A set of kitchen cabinets, carpeting, and sheetrock for one job. I noticed another invoice for the exact same things and hoped the supply company hadn't charged him twice. I looked at the balance in his checkbook and saw that it read fifty-five hundred dollars. That seemed like a low figure—I knew Mike usually kept between ten and twenty grand in his account. He must have been paid for the renovation job as well, which would have added a significant amount. This didn't make sense. I glanced at the invoices in my hand, fervently hoping there was enough to pay them.

    I added the bills together on the computer's calculator. There was enough money, but after paying all of them, the balance in his account would be less than a thousand dollars. I glanced at the two Home Depot bills that were identical to each other and reached for my cell. If there had been a duplicate bill printed by mistake, that would clear up at least two thousand dollars. No location or authorization were on the invoices, so I would need to match them up to the correct job. When I reached customer service, I asked if they could email me the work orders for each slip, and they promised to do so within the hour.

While waiting for the work orders to arrive, I went into the bathroom to take a shower. The hot spray felt wonderful and invigorating, but as I wrapped myself in a giant pink towel, exhaustion hit me like a ton of bricks. I got into our comfortable bed with my phone and scrolled through my unread texts and voice mails. I hadn't talked to Josie since before the shooting, and there were five texts from her. Gianna had filled her in, but I felt terrible for not responding myself. I typed out a message as I struggled not to fall asleep.

*I'm fine. Came home to take a nap and pay some bills. Grandma's with Mike. I was so scared he wouldn't make it. Feel like the luckiest girl in the world today. Will stop over at the bakery before I go back to the hospital. Thanks for the prayers. Love you.*

The bakery must not have been busy because I got an immediate response. *You do what you have to. Get some rest, girl. We're fine here. Take care of your man and let me know if you need anything. Love ya, partner.*

For some reason, the simple message brought tears to my eyes. I was so fortunate to have my family and Josie. Sure, my parents were a little wacko, but they'd been wonderfully supportive and caring last night. And Grandma Rosa had been my rock as always. Yes, I was definitely the luckiest girl in the world today.

I set the phone on the pillow next to me and closed my eyes. Even though I was exhausted, sleep did not come easily. In frustration, I punched the pillow and turned onto my side. The house seemed eerily quiet without Spike. My heart started to pound in my ears, and I sat up in bed with a start. What was the matter with me? Mike was going to be fine. Hopefully he'd be home in a couple of days. I needed to rest while I had the chance. Between taking care of him and running the bakery, things were going to be very hectic for the next few weeks. With a sigh, I finally let myself sink into a state of unconsciousness.

A pinging sound awakened me. I opened my eyes and realized it was the email on my phone. I'd only been asleep for a half hour, but at least it was something. Yawning, I stretched and pulled myself into a sitting position as I checked my messages.

Home Depot had sent two separate emails for each work

order. I sent the documents to the printer and waited patiently for them to roll out. To my disappointment, the invoices were for two separate locations—the first one had an address of 26 Fairlawn Avenue. Upon delivery it had been signed for by Trevor. The other location was for 55 Reynolds Way. This work order had also been signed for by Trevor.

With Mike being so preoccupied with the restoration, I knew he'd come to rely heavily on Trevor these past few months, so why did seeing his signature on the work orders bother me? Maybe it was because I'd never heard Mike speak about either one of these jobs? My mind wasn't a steel trap every day, but Janice Trembley, my godmother and good friend of my parents, had lived on Reynolds Way for many years. She'd moved across the country last summer to be with her boyfriend in Oregon. If Mike had mentioned the job to me, I would have remembered it for the street name alone.

Something here wasn't adding up. I didn't want to upset Mike with a lot of questions, but uneasiness settled in the bottom of my stomach. Had Trevor deliberately tried to keep the details of these jobs a secret from Mike? If so, why? What was he hiding?

I glanced at my watch. Almost twelve thirty. If the bakery was still slow and Gianna was feeling okay, I wondered if Josie might accompany me on an impromptu road trip to Reynolds Way.

## CHAPTER SEVEN

It had been less than twenty-four hours since I'd been inside my bakery, but it seemed more like a week instead. The last time I'd been here, I was full of excitement about the family dinner that I was throwing in honor of Mike's birthday. Cripes. Nothing ever went exactly as I planned, but last night's events had taken the cake, so to speak. Once Mike started to feel better, I still wanted to have the special dinner for him. Maybe it might help erase some of the horror from the evening before.

Gianna was sitting at one of the little white tables by my front window, a tray of fudgy delight cookies in front of her. She was reading a copy of the *Colwestern Journal* while she munched away. I smiled as I watched her. She looked adorable—a small smear of chocolate on her chin, and her cheeks flushed pink with what I thought was happiness. I couldn't wait to spoil my nephew when he arrived. Gianna and Johnny knew the sex of the baby, and she'd let me in on the secret but had not told anyone else, wanting it to be a surprise.

Gianna looked up at the sound of the bells and struggled to her feet—not an easy task for her these days. "Sal," she breathed. "How's Mike?"

I wrapped my arms around my sister and kissed her cheek. "He's much better this morning. Grandma stopped by with some food, and he didn't have any problems eating. She's with him now. I want to get back this afternoon before the doctor comes by."

"Thank God." Gianna sat back down and pointed at the newspaper. There was a picture of Trevor on the front page. It looked like a driver's license photo. Above it was a shot of the Colwestern Mini-Mart with police cars and EMT vehicles lined up in front, accompanied by the headline, *Local Man Shot and Killed During Robbery.*

"Gosh, Sal," Gianna murmured. "That poor man. He was only thirty-eight years old. It says that he had an ex-wife and a girlfriend he was currently living with. No mention of any children." She looked at me sadly. "I keep thinking how it could have been—"

"Yes, I know." Wearily, I sat down next to her. The thought that it could have been Mike had run through my head at least a hundred times since last night. I yawned and rubbed my eyes. "Gi, can we please change the subject?"

"Of course," she said soothingly and gave me a wan smile. "Josie said you were stopping by. That was right before Dad called and wanted to know if you were here. He asked if you'd come by the house later this afternoon with some fortune cookies. He said he doesn't have time to drive over here himself—major happenings at Coffin Central, I guess."

Gianna's new name for our childhood home made me wince. I wasn't sure what major happenings meant and probably didn't want to know. "He does remember that my husband almost died last night, right?"

She shrugged. "I don't know what he remembers some days. His mind is a unique piece of work. But he did say to tell you that he has a present for Mike. Something that will keep him busy while he's in the hospital. God knows what."

My father meant well in his own way, so how could I refuse? "All right. I need to borrow Josie for a little while, if you're okay with that. Then my plan is to run back to the hospital for a bit and hopefully get to speak to the doctor. Then I'll bring the cookies to Mom and Dad's."

"Take all the time you need," Gianna assured me as she bit into another cookie. "It's been dead here all morning."

The word dead covered a lot of territory in my world these days. In this case, though, we needed business to pick up—especially since Mike was going to be out of work and our income cut in half. "So, what's Dad up to now? Is he buying another coffin or going on a book tour with Stephen King?"

Gianna's mouth twisted into a wry smile. "Doesn't he wish. But who knows? I can't keep up with the man, Sal. He's got ten times the energy I do these days."

"Yeah, tell me about it." I glanced around my cute but empty shop, with its blue-and-white-checkered vinyl floors, the beige walls with silver-framed artwork, and the little white tables accentuated with the crocheted tablecloths from my grandmother. "No customers at *all*?"

"We had a few first thing this morning. I'm guessing the storm last night didn't help, and we're supposed to get more snow later." She pointed out the window at the snowflakes that had already started to descend from the sky. "If this winter doesn't end soon, I'm going to do something drastic."

I reached over and rubbed her stomach. "It will. Hey, how's our little guy doing?" I wasn't sure why they insisted on keeping the baby's sex a secret. I certainly couldn't have done it. Maybe they were afraid that if Nicoletta knew, she'd harass them even more—although I wasn't sure that was possible. She'd declared that if the baby was a boy, she wanted it named after her husband, Alessandro. In the meantime, Gianna also had my mother calling every day, asking if there was a wedding date set yet. My sister saw drama unfold in the courtroom daily, but this had to be far worse for her. She tried to put on a brave face, but I suspected she was a hot mess on the inside.

Gianna smiled fondly. "He's quite the kicker, that's for sure. Johnny thinks he's going to be a quarterback."

As if on cue, Gianna's stomach vibrated against my palm, and I gasped. "Oh my gosh, he's saying hello to his auntie!"

She grinned at me, but her eyes were anxious, and my heart went out to her. "Gi, what's wrong?"

Gianna glanced toward the back room, but Josie was out of sight. "Can you keep a secret?"

"I'm already keeping one, remember?" I said playfully, but her comment made me nervous since I couldn't handle any more bad news right now. "Is everything all right with the baby?"

She nodded. "He's fine. I'm the one who has the problem." She blew out a breath, and I watched her stomach expand even further. "I'm scared. Not about the labor—well, maybe a little. But I'm scared about everything else. That's why I can't stop eating. I'm afraid I won't be a good mother, not like you will be someday." Her cheeks turned pink, and she stared at me sheepishly. "Oh Sal, I'm sorry. I shouldn't have said that."

"It's okay." Everyone knew I was the one who had wanted children, not Gianna. Her pregnancy wasn't planned, and she'd had a hard time accepting it at first. The truth was, I had too. That no longer mattered, though. I was thrilled she'd made her peace with the pregnancy, and I couldn't wait to meet my beautiful nephew. "You're going to be a wonderful mother. Plus, you've got Grandma and me to help, and Johnny of course. Even Mom and Dad."

She raised an eyebrow at me. "Sure, Mom and Dad can help with the baby. I mean, we turned out somewhat normal, so I guess they did something right."

I laughed and squeezed her hand. "I'm sure it's natural to feel like this. You and Johnny will make awesome parents. Everything will be fine—wait and see."

She leaned forward to give me a tight hug. "Thanks, Sal. I needed to hear that."

Josie emerged from the back room, wiping her hands on a dishtowel, and wrapped her arms around me. "Sorry, I was on the phone. Thank God everything's okay. Mike's out of danger, right?"

I nodded. "He's doing well. Talking nonstop this morning. I'm sorry I didn't text you back last night. Things were so crazy."

"You already apologized. Stop worrying about me, hon." Josie stopped to adjust her long auburn hair, which was pulled back in a ponytail. "I've got to whip up a batch of raspberry cheesecake cookies. Mabel Patrick is having a seventieth birthday party tomorrow night, and her kids just phoned in an order for a last-minute cookie basket." She glanced at Gianna, who had answered a call on her cell. "Come into the kitchen with me for a second."

"Sure." Something was bothering my best friend, although I wasn't sure what. Perhaps lack of business? The weather? We'd been through both before. The bakery had up and down days like any other type of business. With Mike out of work, I might have to think of some more creative ways to bring in money. A cookie sale? We rarely did that, but maybe the time had come.

Josie tossed three bricks of cream cheese into the steel mixing bowl along with six eggs, flour, vanilla, sugar, and frozen raspberries. "You know how much I love Gianna, right?"

Uh-oh. "Yes..."

She glanced out the doorway into the storefront. Gianna was still talking on her phone. "Sal, this isn't working."

I filled a plastic bag with fortune cookies for my father. "All right, I know she's moving slow, but that's to be expected. She's about to have a baby."

"That's not it. The problem is that she's eating us out of profits." Josie started the mixer and raised her voice slightly to be heard over the whirring. "Every time she sold a cookie this morning, she took one for herself. She's polished off at least a dozen of the fudgy delights. All that sugar isn't good for her or the baby."

She had a point. I too was worried about Gianna's health and hoped that our talk might help ease her some of her concerns. It didn't help that Nicoletta stopped by their house almost every day with genettis, biscotti, or various dishes of pasta. "This baby gonna know it a hundred percent Italian from day one," she'd grunted.

Josie removed the steel bowl from the mixer and stirred the contents with a spatula. A sweet smell drifted into the air, and I sniffed it in rapture. "This isn't the Gianna I know," she said. "Maybe something else is bothering her."

"Gianna's going to be okay," I said. "It's her first baby. Don't you recall how nervous and scared you felt right before you gave birth?"

"Not really," she admitted. "Rob and I were living with his family back then because he'd gotten laid off. I was more concerned that I might strangle him and his parents before the baby got here."

You had to admire Josie's candor. She made Gianna's issues seem like a walk in the park compared to what she and Rob had gone through. "Would you mind if we left her in charge for a while? She said it was fine with her, and I could use your help."

Josie covered the mixing bowl and put it in the fridge. "Sure, I can finish these later. Unless Gianna eats the uncooked dough while we're gone."

"Stop it." I grabbed a sugar cookie off one of the nearby trays and took a bite. It was delicious, but my appetite had disintegrated since last night. I hoped it would return soon. With a sigh, I dumped the rest of it into the garbage.

Josie shook her head at me. "You never eat when you're upset. It must balance out all those times when you eat an entire cheesecake of your grandmother's since you don't have a weight problem."

"I'm at least fifteen pounds heavier than you," I pointed out.

She shrugged. "What can I say? I do so much baking that it kills my appetite for sweets."

How I wish I had that problem. "Will you come with me? To do a little sleuthing?"

Josie's eyes gleamed. "You're looking for the gunmen, aren't you? I had a feeling that you were up to something."

"I'm not sure. Something doesn't add up from last night. Brian and Adam talked to the customers and employees at the mini-mart, and along with information Mike added, it's possible that Trevor could have been killed on purpose."

"Get out!" Gianna was standing in the doorway, rubbing her belly, cookie crumbs all over her chest. "Were they trying to kill Mike too? And why?"

"We don't have all the details yet," I confessed. "But Mike said that the gunmen acted like they knew Trevor. They talked to him before they shot him."

"Maybe they were following Trevor," Josie suggested. "What if he and Mike did a job for them and screwed it up?"

This almost made me laugh. "My husband does *not* screw up jobs, Jos. And I've never heard of anyone shooting someone for putting in a leaky faucet." I clenched my hands at my sides. "This does make me wonder how much Mike knew about Trevor, though." Maybe Trevor had been involved in something shady. Would he have tried to involve Mike as well? But if my husband had known, he would have fired him immediately. Mike had no tolerance for that type of behavior from an employee. Plus, he had a business reputation to protect.

"There are a few job sites that Trevor ordered parts for. One is a house over on Reynolds Way in Colgate." I turned back to my sister. "We'll only be gone about an hour. Twenty minutes there and back and a few minutes to check out the house. Are you sure you don't mind staying here alone? I could call Mickey and see if he can come in to help for a while." Mickey was our part-time delivery guy but in a pinch, he would wait on customers, too.

Gianna frowned and shook her head. "Don't bother. I'm fine." She watched me thoughtfully. "Sal, do you think Trevor could have been stealing money from Mike?"

My sister, always the attorney. While she defended her clients to the best of her ability, she also knew that sometimes they didn't tell her the complete truth. Like Grandma Rosa, though, she usually managed to worm it out of them. Gianna had learned to never let her guard down, and in a sense, so had I after all the near brushes with death I'd experienced. "It's...possible. Mike's invoices and work orders have left me with some serious questions to be answered."

Josie grabbed her jacket off one of the brass hooks on the wall. "Your partner in crime is here and ready to assist." She narrowed her eyes at Gianna. "The sugar cookies on the trays need to be frosted when I get back. They're for a delivery, so please make sure that they stay untouched."

Gianna's mouth fell open in surprise, and she put her hands on her hips. "What exactly are you trying to say?"

I grabbed Josie's arm and pulled her toward the back door. "Ah, Josie means don't let Mickey eat them if he comes in. He's addicted to sugar cookies. Thanks, Gi!"

As soon as we were in the car, I turned to my friend. "Please don't upset her. She's an emotional roller coaster these days."

"Well, she's almost as big as one too," Josie remarked, and then her face reddened. "Hey, I don't mean to be mean, Sal, but let's face facts here. She's not going to have a 60-pound baby. It's not easy taking all that weight off."

I glanced at Josie in her size six jeans and said nothing. Josie had never gained more than twenty pounds with any of her pregnancies. Normal weight gain was between 25 and 35 pounds for most women. Josie was the type you didn't even know was pregnant until she was about eight months along.

It wasn't fair to make comparisons between the two women. Josie didn't have an easy childhood and had become a mother at a young age. Her pregnancy wasn't planned, same as Gianna's. But she'd never had the support that Gianna did. My parents had been forced into a shotgun-style wedding when my mother became pregnant with my brother, who had died at birth. The irony of the situation wasn't lost on me. I was the only one who would have gladly welcomed a pregnancy, planned or not, even during my first marriage to cheating Colin. That's how desperate I'd always been to have a baby.

"She has a lot going on in her life, and it doesn't help that Mrs. Gavelli is ticked about her and Johnny not setting a wedding date yet. My mother keeps hinting at it too."

"Yeah, I know. Nicoletta as a grandmother-in-law is the stuff nightmares are made of." Josie checked her phone. "What are you hoping to find at this house? From the information I can see on Google Maps, it looks like this is a regular residential neighborhood."

"Yes, my godmother lived there for years. I honestly don't know what I expect to find." What was Trevor hiding? Had he done the entire job without Mike's knowledge?

We pulled onto Reynolds Way and found number 55 at the end of the road. The house appeared to be new. It was an attractive, light blue Cape Cod with red shutters and built-in flower boxes, which I imagined would be pretty in the summer. A silver Honda Civic was parked in the driveway and I pulled up behind it.

Josie's blue eyes became large and round. "What are you doing? Are we actually going to the door?"

I shut off the engine. "I need to find out what's the deal between this house and Trevor."

The snow had stopped for the moment, although we were supposed to get a few more inches later. I tried not to let the weather bother me. There were more important things to worry about.

We climbed the two concrete steps of the small porch,

which had been cleared of snow. A dark blue, straw welcome mat was positioned in front of the door. I rang the bell. After a few seconds, a young woman with long, black hair opened it, keeping the chain in place as she peered out at us. "Sorry. We don't allow solicitors here."

"We're not selling anything." I had to stop and think about what to say next. *Excuse me, why was Trevor Parks signing for supplies at your house? Supplies that my husband paid for?*

Josie, sensing my hesitation, jumped right in. "Um, we were driving by and admiring your house. I've actually been looking for one just like it."

The woman's rounded face creased with suspicion. "Okay, what is this? Are you real estate agents? We moved in last month, and we're not looking to sell. Sorry to disappoint you."

"Hold on." I held up a hand. She looked annoyed but propped a hand on her hip, waiting for me to proceed. "Okay, I'll level with you," I lied. "My mother's a real estate agent, and she had a client who wanted this house. They thought the winning bid belonged to them, and then suddenly my mother was told by the owner that it was no longer available."

The woman looked at me like I was a moron. "That's impossible. This house was custom built for my husband and me. We bought it from the man who actually built it."

"Was his name Trevor Parks?"

She shook her head. "I don't know anyone by that name."

This didn't make any sense. "What about Mike Donovan of Donovan's Construction? Did he do any work on the house?"

Her nostrils flared, and I knew the questions were starting to irritate her. "No. I've never heard of him or his company. Are you in construction too?"

I shook my head. "I'm Mike's wife—Sally Donovan. I own a bakery in Colwestern."

"Oh, sure. Sally's Samples, right? Great cookies. That place is always in the newspaper. Lots of weird stuff going on there."

Tell me about it. "Would you give me the name of the

company that performed the work on your house?"

"We bought it from a man named David Webb. He built the house himself. It was finished in January, and we moved in last month."

It seemed like we'd reached a dead end. "Oh. Well, I guess we misunderstood." I was about to thank her for her time when I noticed the *Colwestern Journal* still sitting in the mail slot next to the door. "One more thing, and then we'll be on our way. Can I show you a picture of someone—in your newspaper? Perhaps you could tell me if it's the same man, David Webb?"

She let out a small sigh of exasperation but undid the chain on the door. She was dressed in a black T-shirt and matching yoga pants, her wispy hair pulled back from her face in a ponytail. A white hand towel was wrapped around her neck, and it looked as if we'd disturbed her exercise routine. "What's really going on here?" she demanded.

"We need to ask this David guy some questions," Josie said. "He may have been involved in some shady dealings."

I pulled the paper out of the box. The woman waited for me to locate the picture, tapping her foot against the dark blue carpeting with a steady beat. I pointed at the picture of Trevor on the front page. "Is this the man you bought the house from?"

She studied the photo of Trevor closely and bit into her lower lip. I flashed Josie a triumphant smile. *Bingo. We have a winner.*

To my surprise, the woman shook her head. "No. It's not David."

The wind quickly went out of my sails. "Are you sure?"

"Positive." She folded the paper and stuck it underneath her arm. "This guy definitely worked on my house, though. I never knew his name, but I remember David once referred to him as his business partner."

## CHAPTER EIGHT

Josie watched me anxiously as I steered my car through the busy early afternoon traffic. "Sal, are you okay?"

I stopped for a red light and gripped the steering wheel tightly between my hands for support. "No, I'm not okay. How am I supposed to tell my husband that I think his one employee—a man he trusted and thought of as a friend—might have been going behind his back and stealing from him? Was Trevor building other houses with Mike's money?"

"You don't know for certain," Josie remarked. "Maybe Mike knew about the job. Laura said that her husband was more involved in the details of the house than she was. She only stopped by a couple of times while the work was going on, and that's when she saw Trevor. Maybe Mike was there as well, working on the house, but she never met him. It might all be legit."

I had my doubts. From what Mike had told me, Trevor didn't have two nickels to rub together. Yet this David Webb guy had referred to him as his business partner? Laura Pusatere, the woman we'd spoken to, told us we could talk to her husband, Evan, if we wanted more information. Evan worked as a manager at the local Ford dealership and usually wasn't home until after seven o'clock at night. She mentioned that he had a contact number for David. I didn't understand exactly how he fit into the picture. She also told us that Evan had tried to call David last week and he'd never returned the call. That didn't come as a total surprise if he and Trevor had been ripping people off together. He'd probably skipped town.

I pulled my car into the alley behind the bakery. "I'm going to have to tell Mike and don't want to do that right now.

He's in a lot of pain, and this won't help his recovery." Regardless, he'd be even more upset if he discovered I'd tried to keep it from him. The sorrow I'd experienced for Trevor before was quickly turning to anger. "Why would he take advantage of Mike like that? Mike was good to him. He even gave Trevor an advance on his pay a couple of times. The gunmen who killed him—could they have been in on it with Trevor as well? Was this David guy one of them?"

Josie turned to face me. "It's possible, I guess. Where would you even start to look for answers? Does Brian have any ideas?"

I hesitated, searching for words. "I'm not sure that Brian will be working on this case any longer. He may be going back to Boston soon, so it's probably best that I don't bother him."

She watched my face carefully for a moment, and then hers dawned with recognition. A small smile played on her lips. "Shut up. He's still in love with you, isn't he? I knew it! I thought that living with Ally meant that he'd moved on and—"

"We're so not talking about this," I said evenly. "It's his life, and I don't want to be involved."

She cocked her head to the side and studied me. "Hate to say it, but you're already involved, love, whether you want to be or not."

My entire life was a mess. "I need to get back to the hospital. Somehow, with or without Brian's help, I've got to track down Trevor's relatives and start talking to them. I'll start by making a visit to see his girlfriend, Tina." I hated to disturb the woman, especially right after her boyfriend had been killed, but I had to know what was going on.

"Let me know when you're ready, and I'll go with you. I don't want you going there alone." Josie pulled me into a warm hug.

"That would be great. Maybe after you close the bakery tonight? I'll have to see how Mike's feeling first, though." I closed my eyes with my head still on her shoulder. No matter what happened, I could always count on Josie. "Thanks for taking care of the bakery." After a few seconds I raised my head again and looked her straight in the eye. "And please—try not to insult my sister. It would be nice if you'd refrain from mentioning how big she's getting."

Josie blew out a sigh. "Okay, I'll be good. Promise." She got out of the car, and I waited while she unlocked the back door. She blew me a kiss before she disappeared inside.

Snowflakes started to fall from the sky again as I pulled into the hospital's parking lot. Cripes. Could we have one lousy, stinking day without snow? I slammed the car door in annoyance and desperately tried to pull myself together. It wouldn't help Mike to see how upset I was. The goal was to get him out of the hospital and home to me as soon as possible.

When I entered his room in the ICU, he was sleeping. Grandma Rosa was sitting next to him, crocheting something that looked like a tiny white sweater—most likely for Gianna's baby. She looked up at me and put a finger to her lips.

"The nurse said that the doctor will be in very soon," she whispered. "He had some type of emergency, and his rounds got delayed. The nurses have looked in many times, but your poor husband has been very uncomfortable. They gave him something for the pain, and he finally went to sleep a few minutes ago."

The sight of my big, strong husband looking frail and ill was new, and one that I hoped I'd never have to see again. I wanted desperately to put my arms around Mike and hold him, but he needed his rest. Plus, if I woke him, I'd have to tell him about Trevor, and that was one conversation I didn't mind delaying.

Grandma Rosa watched me thoughtfully. "What is wrong? Something is bothering you, *cara mia*."

I glanced over at Mike. His face was peaceful, and the lines of worry that had been present earlier had faded. His chest rose and fell at a steady pace while his right arm looked painfully awkward in the sling. "I can't talk about it now. Maybe later."

She nodded, as if she understood. "You have found out something that will make Mike very upset."

I honestly didn't know how she did it. Grandma Rosa had always had some type of sixth sense about her, as if she could predict the future. Unlike my fortune cookies, she did it in a nicer way, though.

Before I could say anything further, there was a tap on the door, and Dr. Benson came in. He looked less disheveled than last night, dressed in everyday black trousers and a white polo shirt. He nodded to my grandmother and smiled at me. "How's our patient doing today? My apologies that I couldn't get here any sooner, but I'm certain the nurses took good care of him."

"He's been in a lot of pain," I said. "When can he go home?"

The doctor looked down at the chart in his hands. "Possibly tomorrow, or maybe the day after. I understand that he just had Percocet. That should make him sleep for a while. Dr. Snail, our orthopedic specialist, stopped by to see him earlier. His shoulder won't have to be set, but he recommends physical therapy when Mr. Donovan is released. He'll let you know his recommendation—once or twice a week and probably for at least two months. We can give you the names of some excellent therapists in Colwestern to use. Of course, you'll want to see which ones your insurance will cover first."

"Oh, sure." The chance that my basic health insurance policy even covered physical therapy was slim. A wave of despair washed over me. "Thank you, Doctor."

"I'll stop by again in the morning to see how he's doing." He gave me another encouraging smile and was gone.

Mike sighed and stirred in the bed. Unable to help myself, I leaned over and kissed his forehead. He opened his eyes and smiled up at me sleepily. "Am I dreaming, or are you really back?"

I laughed and kissed him again. "Go back to sleep, sweetheart. Is the medication helping any?"

He gave a slight nod. "Makes me tired. Did you get a chance to pay the bills?"

Always business first with my guy. "Yes, everything is taken care of. Uh, Mike."— Since he'd given me an opening, I decided to take it—"did you happen to do work on a house located at 55 Reynolds Way?"

His eyes remained closed, and for a moment, I thought he'd drifted back off to dreamland. Finally, he shook his head. "Colgate, right? Your godmother—didn't she live there?"

"Yes. Did you help to build a new house on that street? Or maybe put a foundation in?"

Mike shook his head again and then opened his eyes. He pinned me with that penetrating dark blue gaze of his. "Never done work there before. Why are you asking?"

"No reason." Shoot. Why had I bothered to say anything? Mike couldn't—and shouldn't—have to deal with this now. He had to focus on getting better first. "I think Home Depot sent you the wrong bill, that's all." I never knew when to quit. Now I was lying to him. What a great basis for our marriage.

Grandma Rosa glanced up at me sharply but said nothing. She always knew when I wasn't telling the truth. I remembered that one fateful time at the age of eight when I came home with a candy bar from the local store. My new friend Josie had dared me to take it, and I'd desperately wanted to impress her. My grandmother had seen the offensive Kit Kat sticking out of my jeans pocket and asked where it had come from. I lied that Josie gave me the money to pay for it. Five minutes later Grandma Rosa had me back at the store apologizing to the owner and returning the candy bar. She then told him that I would be back in the morning to sweep the entire parking lot. After that day, I'd never again taken anything that hadn't belonged to me.

Mike looked suspicious at first, but then his eyes glazed over, most likely from the medication, and he closed them again. "Love you," he said sleepily before he drifted off.

I released his hand and turned my face away from my grandmother. She could read it too easily.

Grandma Rosa stood and patted me on the arm. "Let us go down to the cafeteria for a minute, *cara mia*. I could use a cup of John."

"It's Joe, Grandma."

She made a face. "Whatever."

We silently rode the elevator to the cafeteria in the basement. Grandma Rosa watched as I selected a carton of milk from the cooler and gave me a questioning look.

I paid for our drinks. "Since Mike's accident, everything has been upsetting my stomach. I can't eat, sleep, or concentrate on anything—especially now."

She gestured to a nearby table and sat down. "Tell me, *cara mia*. What else is wrong?"

I twisted the napkin between my fingers. "Trevor was

stealing from Mike. I found some work orders among his papers that led me to a house over on Reynolds Way. Josie and I went there today and talked to the owner. The woman remembered seeing Trevor working on it, but not Mike. Another man by the name of David Webb sold them the house, and I'm thinking that he may have been in on this with Trevor."

Grandma Rosa clasped her hands in her lap. "Oh, my dear, no."

A lump formed in my throat. "He was stealing from us, Grandma. Stealing from Mike's business. This was all a game to him. He didn't care about Mike." I bit into my lower lip, resolving not to cry again. After the last 24 hours, I wasn't sure I had any tears left.

My grandmother pursed her lips as she sipped her coffee. "It is sad when you cannot trust anyone in this world. How I long for the days when I was a young girl. Everything was so much simpler back then."

"How am I going to tell him?" I managed to choke out. "This is going to hurt Mike, and he doesn't deserve any more pain. I'm so angry, Grandma. I should be sorry that the man is dead, but all I feel right now is rage towards him and what he's done to us. There's hardly any money left in Mike's account and—"

I stopped myself right there. I didn't want her to think I was fishing for a loan. She already knew our feelings on the topic, and as far as Mike was concerned, the subject was closed.

"How much money did he take from you?" she asked gently.

I shrugged. "No idea. But I intend to find out."

"Let Mike handle it," she said. "You need to tell him, my dear."

"No, Grandma! Not yet. Plus, there's more. Brian and I both think that Trevor was intentionally shot and killed last night. Was he involved in something else illegal? What other things did he do to Mike that we don't know about yet?" My voice grew louder, and a couple at a nearby table turned to stare at us.

"Calm down, *cara mia*," she said sharply. "It is natural that you are angry. This man has done a terrible thing to your husband—and to you as well. But this is Mike's business. You should tell him what happened right away and let him finish going through the paperwork himself."

"Grandma," I protested.

She cut me off. "He is a proud man. How do you think it will make him feel—to learn that his wife discovered the deceit before he did? He is going to feel like a fool that he did not notice this himself."

My grandmother had a point. I sat there, stirring my straw around in circles, and said nothing.

"You must tell him, my dear. Let Mike decide how he wants to handle this." She glanced at her watch. "I can stay with Mike for a while longer. Please go home and get some sleep. It is plain to see that you are exhausted. You cannot help your husband get better if you are sick too."

I rose to my feet and dumped the rest of the milk into the trash. "I have to run over to Mom and Dad's first. He's already texted me three times today about needing emergency fortune cookies."

She placed her forefinger at the side of her white hair and made a circular motion. "That man is a nutsy cookie. He should have come to get them himself, but they have visitors. You go, my dear. I will stay here with Mike."

"What visitors?" Maybe he'd invited a group of morticians over for a beer. Nothing surprised me with my parents these days.

Grandma Rosa rolled her eyes toward the ceiling, something she rarely did. "You will have to go and see for yourself."

"Wonderful." I wasn't sure I had the strength to deal with my father's latest antics. "Does it have anything to do with the book?"

"Of course," she said. "When does it not? But that reminds me of something else. I am going to move in with you and Mike for a while so that I can help you take care of him when he comes home."

My mouth dropped open in amazement. "Grandma, it's wonderful of you to offer, and we'd be happy to have you, but it's not necessary. We'll be all right."

"Yes," she said. "You will, but I am a far better nurse than you, *cara mia*. Plus, you have a business to run. Mike will need someone to cook for him and help change bandages while he gets his strength back. I know you want to be with your husband, but you also need to be at the bakery." Her warm brown eyes regarded me fondly. "I understand that money is tight."

I swallowed hard. "We'll manage."

She patted my hand. "I know this. And I know you, *cara mia*. You will not rest until you find out who did this to your husband."

"He almost died last night." Tears sprang into my eyes again. "His employee was killed, and I'm certain it wasn't a random shooting." A terrifying thought seized me. "Those men who killed Trevor—what if somehow they're also privy to Mike's private information? Bank account or credit card numbers?" Dear God. Could they have somehow managed to get his social security number as well? "I have to find these guys."

My grandmother nodded. "It is settled then. I will move in when Mike comes home."

"Grandma, I appreciate this more than you know. But you have a life too." I'd love having her there and knew that Mike would too. Mike had never known his grandparents and adored my grandmother like she was his own. Still, I felt like I depended on her too much of the time. My entire family did.

She laughed. "*Cara mia*, it is fine. This will be like a vacation for me."

"A vacation? What are you talking about?"

Grandma Rosa smiled. "Anytime I can have a few days away from your parents, it can be considered a vacation."

It was hard to argue with that logic.

# CHAPTER NINE

On my way out of the hospital's main doors, I ran straight into Brian. My head was down as I attempted to pull on my gloves, and I wasn't watching where I was going. After I brushed against his coat, he stooped down to pick the gloves up off the floor then pinned me with that brilliant green gaze of his. Talk about your awkward moments.

"Hi, Sally. How's Mike doing today?" he asked.

"Better, thanks," I said. "Were you planning to talk to him? They gave him something for the pain, and he's asleep."

Brian stroked the unshaved stubble on his chin. "Oh. Well, I don't want to disturb him. I guess I could come back later."

"Okay. If you'll excuse me, I have to—"

"Do you have a minute to talk? It's about the robbery," he added quickly.

So, he didn't intend to chat about yesterday's heartfelt discussion, for which I was eternally grateful. I couldn't worry about Brian right now. There was too much else going on in my life. "No problem."

We stood in the hallway by the emergency room entrance. A nurse walked past us and smiled at Brian.

"Hi, Julie," he said.

"I don't think Ally's here yet," Julie said as she gave me a questioning look.

Brian cleared his throat. "Yeah, right. She's working later tonight. Thanks."

After Julie had walked on, I leaned against the wall. "You must know all the staff here."

Brian gave me a wan smile. "Pretty much. The nurses at

this hospital are a tight bunch. I get the feeling that I'm talked about a lot and may not have many fans left after they hear about the powwow Ally and I had last night."

It sounded like they hadn't made up yet, but I didn't dare ask. "Getting back to the robbery. Did you find the gunmen?"

He shook his head. "The car they were seen leaving in, a 2005 Buick Regal, was abandoned a few miles from here. Turns out it was stolen from another grocery store last night—probably right before the heist, we're guessing."

"A dead end." I shut my eyes and sighed. "I might have a lead."

The hallway was so quiet that you could have heard a pin drop. After a few seconds I opened my eyes to find Brian watching me intently, the way a cat does a mouse before it pounces. "Please go on," he said.

I blew out a breath. "Well, I haven't told Mike this yet, but while I was going through his bills earlier, I became suspicious about a couple of things, so I asked for work orders from the supply places. To make a long story short, it looks like Trevor was doing his own construction jobs, specifically a new home at 55 Reynolds Way in Colgate. He was kind enough to let Mike foot the bills for the supplies as well."

Brian's eyes resembled shiny headlights in size. "Wow. Sally, I'm sorry this is happening to you guys. We're trying to find out about Trevor's past, but Tina either doesn't know anything or is staying mum. We were finally able to reach Erica, his ex-wife, by phone, and she was shocked to hear the news. She's headed back to Colwestern tonight. She was not happy to learn that the wake is already scheduled for tomorrow and no one had bothered to consult her."

"Well, they're not married anymore, so I can't imagine why she thought she'd be asked." No one had asked for my opinion when Colin had died, five months after our divorce was finalized. "Who arranged it?"

"Tina did," Brian replied. "Apparently the two women don't get along. No surprise there. I already know what you're thinking, Sally, so don't go there. The service is private—for family members only. You won't be able to get in."

That was fine with me. I'd been to enough funerals over

the past couple of years. "I'd like to stop and see Tina, either tonight or tomorrow, and at least offer my sympathy." *And to see if she was in on the scheme with Trevor. And David.*

Brian's mouth twisted into a frown. "I thought you didn't know her."

"Did I say that?" I gave him a small impish smile, but he clearly wasn't falling for it.

Brian pursed his lips. "Sally, I've lost track of how many times I've told you this before, but you need to stay out of police—"

"Look," I interrupted. "Trevor cheated my husband, Brian. If there's a chance that the gunmen who killed Trevor were in on it too, they might have access to Mike's personal information. And what if they do this to someone else?"

A sudden gleam came into Brian's eyes. "I know this is personal, but does Mike have a lot of money in his bank account? Maybe he could leave a couple of hundred for bait, in case they try to make another withdrawal? Then we'd have an opportunity to catch them."

"Trevor's already taken care of that." My tone was bitter. "All Mike has left is a few hundred bucks."

Brian looked sympathetic. "God, I hate to see innocent people taken advantage of like this. If you know Tina, I can't stop you from going to see her. But my advice is to be careful about what you say. She might be in on it as well."

"Yes, I've thought of that. At least it gives me a place to start."

Brian stared down at the floor. "Do you know if Mike got any references for Trevor when he hired him?"

"Yes, there was one man. Mike has his information at home, but I haven't gotten around to finding it yet. Can I text it to you later?"

He nodded. "Please. As soon as possible." Another awkward silence stretched between us.

I cleared my throat. "When are you leaving for Boston?"

The lines around Brian's mouth tightened. "I don't know for certain yet. Maybe a week or two. I'm staying at the Colwestern Hotel until then."

This wasn't what I wanted to hear. "A hotel?"

"Ally and I had a huge fight last night. I told her I was going back to Boston and that we needed to take a break. She, in turn, told me to get out of the apartment and never come back."

My heart sank at the news. "I'm so sorry, Brian."

"It's not your problem, Sally." He looked into my eyes, and the sadness that I saw in them made me want to weep again. "This is all my own doing."

Without another word, Brian turned and walked out of the hospital. Guilt spread through my body as I stared after him. Yes, it was my problem—my fault. At least it felt like it. I had ruined Brian's chance at a permanent relationship with Ally. He'd pretty much told me last night that he couldn't have the one thing he wanted—me.

Perhaps no one could have everything that they wanted. I'd wished in vain for a child for many years. Before I married Colin, he'd told me that he didn't want kids—ever. I was certain he'd change his mind, but it hadn't happened. As a little boy, Mike had wanted a real family. Instead, his own father had abandoned him when he was five years old, his mother died of cirrhosis due to alcoholism, and his stepfather was abusive. Josie had longed to be a pastry chef in Paris but had gotten pregnant before she could finish culinary school. My father wanted to be a mortician, then a hearse driver, and now a New York Times best-selling author. Okay, so maybe he wasn't the best example to use when compared to everyone else's dreams.

I waited a couple of minutes until I figured Brian had driven off, and then I left the hospital. As I drove to my parents' house, I found myself wishing, of all things, that I could be more like them. Despite their strange behavior, they were good people. My mother and father loved each other, my grandmother, Gianna, and me. They adored Mike and Johnny and were excited about becoming grandparents. Despite all of this though, they did what they wanted, no matter how crazy or outlandish, and always seemed to have a good time. Maybe they were doing life right, while the rest of us were doing it wrong. It seemed to work for them, so who was I to judge?

There was no room in my parents' driveway since a television van occupied most of the area, with another unfamiliar vehicle parked behind it. For a brief second, I thought about leaving the fortune cookies in the mailbox and running away as fast as I could. The media was most likely there to talk about Dad's book, and I wanted no part of it.

While I debated what to do, someone tapped on my car window and I jumped. A leathery, lined face stared in at me. Nicoletta Gavelli was dressed in a black coat and hood that resembled a shroud. *Great.* If I left, she'd tell my parents. After my breathing had returned to normal, I waited for her to step away from the car before I opened the door.

Nicoletta's dislike of me had been cemented when she caught Johnny and me playing doctor in her garage. I'd only been six years old at the time, and he'd lured me in there with promises of ice cream after we'd played a "new, fun game." Nicoletta had immediately branded me a hussy, and now, 24 years later, not much had changed. Over the years, I'd learned that her bark was worse than her bite and that she was often snippy with the people she most cared about.

My grandmother had once told me that I resembled Nicoletta's daughter, Sophia, who'd died of a drug overdose when Johnny was five. She thought Nicoletta might have associated me with Sophia in some ways and acted mean to cover up her true feelings. Who knew? The one person who could put Nicoletta in her place and get away with it was my grandmother. She was truly a miracle worker.

Nicoletta grunted at me. "Your papa—he really off his rocker now."

"What's going on?" I asked.

She turned her back on me and started up the driveway, gesturing with her bony finger for me to follow. I was worried about her trudging up the icy path in those black Birkenstocks she always wore, but she managed it better than I did.

"Your papa hire publicist for this *pazza* book of his." *Pazza* meant crazy in Italian. "They get him television interview. He walk around like he some big star." She puffed out her chest in an exaggerated manner. "Think he too good for the rest of us. Come. You see."

"Maybe we shouldn't interrupt if they're taping," I said, not wanting to see.

"Bah. They sit around and talk about coffins. Your papa

say Josie make cookies shaped like them. This I gotta see. He tells them book signing to be at your bakery. It good you here then." She gave me a sly smile. "They wanna talk to you."

"Oh, darn," I said. "I need to get back over to the hospital. Will you tell Dad that I'll stop by later and—"

But it was too late. The front door opened, and my father stuck his head outside. He grinned and waved at me. "Baby girl, come on in! We need you!"

This day was getting longer and weirder by the moment. Defeated, I started toward the house when Nicoletta touched my arm and spoke gruffly. "Your man. How he feel? Johnny say he lucky to be here, not dead like other guy. The good Lord watch over him."

I was touched that she'd asked about Mike. Nicoletta was difficult to read at times, and although my grandmother insisted that she truly liked and cared about me, I wasn't always convinced. "He's in a lot of pain, but I'm just thankful that he's alive."

Nicoletta's coal-colored eyes softened for a second. If I'd blinked, I might have missed the stark, raw emotion in them. She grunted and nodded. "I glad he be all right. Too bad about his worker, but I no trust that man—not ever. Shifty eyes. Maybe he rob stores too."

Puzzled, I stared at her. "What do you mean? Trevor fixed your water heater." And we'd charged her next to nothing. She couldn't have heard anything about Trevor's scam yet. "Did he say something offensive when he was at your house?"

She gave me a sour look. "I not meant that time. He have shifty eyes when I see him before." Her gaze zeroed in on the plastic bag in my hand. "You give me fortune cookies, and I tell you more."

The woman always had an ulterior motive. With a sigh, I opened the bag and watched as she selected three cookies. Two she put into her coat pockets, and the other one she cracked open in front of me. I prayed she'd get a good message for once.

Nicoletta read the strip of paper aloud and then waved it at me like a fan. "Ha. It say, 'You are the sunshine of your neighborhood.' What you think about that, Miss Hot Shot Baker?"

No way. "Let me see that." Yes, that was exactly what the message said. Wow. I guess these messages were not as reliable as I'd once thought. "Where did you see Trevor before?"

"When Ronald and I go to eat at Casa Diner. Couple of weeks ago." Ronald Feathers was Nicoletta's eighty-something-year-old main squeeze. He was hard of hearing, probably one reason he found Nicoletta so appealing. "We drive out of lot, and I see him waiting next to garbage dumpster. Another man drive up in car. Trevor hand him something through window."

"Did you see what it was?" I asked excitedly.

"Envelope," she said simply. "Probably have drugs or money inside. You young kids all a bad lot."

What if the man driving the vehicle have been one of the gunmen? It was entirely possible. "Did you get a good look at the guy driving? What kind of car was it?"

She paused to think. "He wear dark sunglasses. Have dark hair. Nice car. One of those fancy ones. They call them beamers, no? Stupid name."

"A BMW," I said more to myself than Nicoletta. "What color?"

"It black. Good color," Nicoletta said approvingly as she pulled her shroud-like hood of the same color around her face and tapped the side of her head. "Your papa's favorite—the color of death. He missing something upstairs that one."

There were days when I didn't think Nicoletta was playing with a full deck either, but I refrained from saying so. At least this was something to go on. Should I tell Brian?

Nicoletta started in the direction of her house.

"Aren't you coming inside?" I asked.

She shook her head. "No way, Jose. You spend too much time with crazies, you become crazy. Tell your parents stay away from baby Alessandro when he come. They make him crazy too."

*Jeez Louise.* I thought I had my hands full, but Gianna might have me beat.

My father gave me a kiss on the cheek as I hung up my coat. "How's Mike doing, baby girl? We're going to stop and see him later."

"He's better today, thanks."

He rubbed his hands together gleefully. "Good. That's what I want to hear. I'm bringing him an autographed copy of my book tonight. Some light reading for him. Now come on inside and meet Jerry." He led the way to the dining room while I followed, mystified. My mother was seated at the cherrywood dining room table next to a man who looked vaguely familiar. Another man was adjusting the lens on a television camera with the words *Buffalo News Channel 11* on it.

My father pointed to the man at the table, who was busy texting something on his phone. "Look! It's Jerry Maroon, the star anchorman from Channel 11!"

I gave the man a polite nod while I tried to think up an excuse to get the heck out of here. I'd been on television twice before. Both had been baking show appearances with Josie, and they'd turned out to be embarrassing ordeals, with one even deadly. I had no interest in a repeat performance.

Panicked, I waved the plastic bag at my father. "Dad, I'm dropping off the fortune cookies you wanted. I can't stay—I need to get back to the hospital."

My mother rose from her seat at the table and trotted over to me in her tiny silver stiletto sandals. She was wearing a strapless, maroon-colored dress with sparkles that I'd never seen before. I had to wonder if she'd worn it because of Jerry's last name. Anything for attention with her.

She put her arms around my shoulders and gave me a kiss. "Hello, darling. How's Mike? We're going to stop and see him tonight."

"He's doing much better," I said, "but still in a lot of pain."

Jerry finished his text and came around the table to greet me. He'd always seemed taller on television, but in person, he wasn't much bigger than me. Jerry was in his midthirties with a definitive swagger about him and a thick head of prematurely gray hair. His curious green eyes examined my face carefully, as if he wanted to know every detail about me.

He held out a hand. "Jerry Maroon from News Channel 11. The best station in all of New York State, in case you were wondering." He shot me a supercilious grin, his white teeth gleaming from the lights above. "Are you the daughter who's the attorney or the one who makes the coffin cookies?"

For the first time ever, I was tempted to lie about my profession. "Sally Donovan. I own Sally's Samples."

"Right. The coffin cookie lady." Jerry pursed his lips. "Sally's Samples… Didn't the *Colwestern Journal* rename your bakery Sally's Shambles because there's always something interesting going on there? Hey, been locked in any freezers lately?"

*Cripes.* Did this guy know my entire life history? Nervously I stared over at the camera. "That thing isn't on, is it?"

"Hey," my father bellowed as he cut a slice of cheesecake from the china serving plate in the center of the table. "Want one, baby girl? How about you, Jerry?"

We both shook our heads. It was hard to believe that I wasn't hungry for cheesecake, especially Grandma Rosa's. Her ricotta-filled one was my favorite. "Thanks, but I had a late lunch," I lied.

Jerry continued to watch me intently. "Mrs. Donovan, err—can I call you Sally?"

"Please."

He edged closer to me. "How's your husband doing? Terrible thing about that shooting. Trevor Parks worked for Mike, right?"

Was there anything this guy didn't know about me, except maybe my shoe size? Perhaps Mom and Dad had already filled him in on Mike, but I was doubtful. This guy reminded me of a bloodhound, constantly sniffing around for information. "He's doing better, thank you."

"I was at the mini-mart last night," he continued. "I saw you leaving with a blond-haired cop. Pretty sure it was Officer Brian Jenkins. He's the one who found you the time you got locked in the sauna with your friend, right?"

Damn, this guy was good. *Too good.* "Yes, that's right."

He grinned. "I'd love to do a live interview with your husband when he's feeling up to it. We could run it during the noon and six o'clock news hours."

"But mine will get televised first, right?" Dad looked worried as he stuffed a large bite of cheesecake into his mouth and then dribbled crumbs onto his new jacket. He'd received it in the mail the other day from a vendor who was looking to advertise on his blog. It was made of a black mesh-like material and had *Father Death* embroidered on the upper left-hand pocket in a bloodred color. That was the name of my father's embarrassing, yet prosperous, blog.

"Of course," Jerry said in a condescending tone, as if he was speaking to a five-year-old. "Dom, the interview about your book signing and blog will air during tonight's news. You're going to have a sellout crowd for the signing next week, mark my words!"

My father beamed at me. "Better have Josie double that cookie order, baby girl," he said.

I winced inwardly. I hadn't even filled Josie in on the infamous coffin cookies yet. When she found out, she might ask for *my* head on a cookie platter.

Jerry folded his arms across his chest. "So how about it, Sally? Would your husband be willing to talk to me and tell the world everything that happened last night?"

I started to shake my head. "No, he'd never—" Then a light switch clicked on in my brain. Maybe this was the opportunity we needed. If the gunmen were watching, we might be able to set a trap for them and somehow convince them that we knew their identity or another key factor about them.

"Would you happen to have a business card?" I asked Jerry. "I'll be in touch as soon as I talk to my husband."

# CHAPTER TEN

Mike slept most of the night while I dozed in the chair next to his bed. He'd told me to go home and get some rest, but I refused to leave him. Yes, I was tired, but I didn't want to be alone in our house either. As I watched him slumber, I kept thinking about Trevor. Tomorrow I had to tell my husband the truth—that the man he'd trusted was in fact stealing money from him.

Josie had texted earlier, and the message had not been a happy one. *Bakery fridge died. Had repairman out this afternoon. He can't fix it. We need a new one. I'll bring in a small portable one from home, but it won't be enough. Need to get something else right away.*

Another thousand dollars I couldn't afford to spend right now. I gritted my teeth in exasperation and texted her back. *Great. Any more good news?*

*Well, since you asked, Mrs. Mitchell canceled the order for her daughter's wedding.*

There went another three hundred dollars out the window. *Did she say why?*

*The groom was having an affair with the maid of honor, bride's BFF. Guess everyone knew about it except for the bride. And Mrs. Mitchell. You coming in tomorrow?*

I sighed in despair. From the way things were going, I'd have to stop in at some point. *Yes. For a little while. I'm also planning to stop and talk to Trevor's girlfriend, Tina.*

Josie must have guessed how I was feeling, because her next message was, *Don't worry, girlfriend. Things always seem worse than they appear.*

*Hey, that sounds like a good fortune cookie message,* I

texted back. At least she'd managed to bring a smile to my face. Still, I had a strong urge to smack my head against the wall. As Grandma Rosa often said, "It never rains, but it snows." Her unique phrasing worked well with the type of weather we often experienced in Colwestern.

Panic set in, and I wondered how Mike and I were going to pay our bills. I'd respect his wishes and not borrow money from my parents or grandmother. If necessary, we could take out a home equity loan. We owned our house free and clear since Mike had inherited it after his mother's death. But with our car loans, credit card payments, and other everyday bills, things would still be a bit tight. I'd taken a minute to call my health care provider earlier, and as I suspected, they only covered eighty percent of Mike's hospital bill, plus we also had to pay a five-hundred-dollar deductible. His physical therapy would need to be paid for out of pocket as well. We needed nothing short of a miracle now.

Exhaustion finally won over, and I dozed off. When I opened my eyes, sunlight was streaming through the blinds of the hospital room. Mike was sitting up in bed, staring blankly ahead at the television, which wasn't even on. He continued looking at the screen, his face tight and drawn.

Worried, I leaned over the bed to kiss him. "Good morning, sunshine."

He didn't respond.

My chest tightened with fear as I watched him. "Are you in a lot of pain?"

In response, he handed me the cell phone that he'd been holding in his lap. "What's really going on, Sal?"

The look in his midnight blue eyes was intense and scared me. "I don't know what you're talking about."

"Jenkins left me a voice mail asking if I remembered the name of the guy who'd given Trevor a reference." Mike's tone was icy.

Crap. I'd forgotten to check on that last night for him. "Did he say why?"

Mike's dark steady gaze observed me thoughtfully. "Yeah, Jenkins said the police wanted to talk to him, to find out what else he knew about Trevor. Why are the police checking into Trevor's past if he was a victim?"

Good old Brian. He couldn't wait for me to check on the reference? One stinking day? What was really going on? Was he sorry about what he'd confessed the other night and trying to hurt me as result? If so, he'd succeeded.

"Sweetheart." I cupped his cheek with my palm. "I wanted to wait until you were feeling better before we got into this."

A muscle ticked in Mike's jaw. "Got into what? Sal, what's Trevor done? Did these guys shoot him intentionally?"

"It looks that way. The police believe—based on the information you gave Brian and what the cashier told them—that yes, the gunmen knew Trevor. And it gets worse." I exhaled sharply. "Trevor was stealing from you, Mike."

Mike's eyes resembled cold hard steel. "What are you talking about?"

The lump in my throat wouldn't dissolve. "Trevor was ordering supplies on your dime and having them shipped to other job sites. Remember how I asked you about that house on Reynolds Way?" When he nodded, I continued. "Josie and I went to check it out. There's a newly constructed house sitting there. Some guy by the name of David Webb sold it to a young couple, and the woman who lives there remembers seeing Trevor working on the house. He must have been doing it on the weekends or at night after he left your—"

Mike cut me off and looked away. "No. You have to be wrong."

My heart ached as I watched his expression. It was like being beaten on the inside. "I asked for the work orders to be emailed, and Trevor's name was on them. I don't know how much he took yet, but there's not much money left in your business account."

He said nothing, so I reached out to put my arms around him. To my surprise and shock, he stiffened at my touch. "Sweetheart, it could have happened to anyone. Please don't—"

Mike still wouldn't look at me. "Sal, I think I'd like to be alone for a little while, if you don't mind."

His words stung like a wasp. My husband was a proud man, and I'd known that hearing these words would prove difficult. If he'd yelled, screamed, or thrown something at the wall, it would have made me feel better. Anything would be easier to take than this brooding silence.

I tried to understand this from Mike's perspective. He'd been taken advantage of his entire life. When we met at sixteen, he'd been terribly insecure and jealous as a result of his upbringing. While we were dating in high school, he'd never hesitate to punch any guy who looked at me the wrong way and then ask questions later. Over the years he'd learned to control his anger, and I was proud of him for that. But it hurt that he was pushing me away. He needed someone to help him through this.

"Okay." My voice trembled as I backed out of the room, afraid that I might start to cry. "I'll be back about lunchtime, all right?"

He gave a quick nod and kept staring at the wall. My eyes filled with tears as I shut the door behind me and hurried down the hall. Once I was alone inside my car, I allowed myself a good cry.

My phone buzzed as I started the engine, and I glanced down at the screen, hoping it was Mike asking me to come back. Instead, Brian's name popped up. Anger coiled in my gut. "Yes?" I asked coldly.

He hesitated. "Everything okay, Sally?"

"No, everything is not okay," I huffed. "Why did you leave Mike a voice mail about the reference for Trevor? I told you that I would ask him."

"There was no time to waste, Sally," Brian explained. "We need to follow up on any leads as soon as possible. Those guys could still be in town."

My temper flared. "Thanks to you, I had to come out and tell Mike about Trevor stealing from him—from us. He's ill and needs his rest, Brian. I wanted to wait a day or so before springing it all on him. How could you do this to me?"

Silence followed, and I knew very well how. This was Brian's way of getting back at me—his attempt at revenge for ruining his relationship with Ally. I had never led Brian on or tried in any way to make him care for me. Why would I, when there was only one man I'd truly ever loved?

Brian sidestepped my question. "I called to tell you that

Trevor's obituary is in the paper this morning. Like I said before, the service is private, but I'm trying to find out when it's going to be held. There was no time listed in the paper. If you're planning to see Tina today, maybe she'll give you details."

"Thanks for the tip." The words and sarcasm freely rolled off my tongue together.

"Sally, wait!" he said. "Don't hang up yet. I really am sorry. Please call me after you've seen Tina and let me know how it goes. What else have you got planned?"

Even though I was still furious with him, and despite what I'd told Josie, I needed Brian's help to find these guys. "I met a news reporter yesterday—Jerry Maroon from Channel 11. He wants to interview Mike about the shooting. He's allowed to speak to the media, right?"

"We can't stop him," Brian replied. "But why would you want to subject yourself to such an ordeal? It might hurt business in your bakery, and I'm guessing you can't afford that right now. Plus, every nut in the state will be calling you, claiming to have a lead."

He had valid points. "I don't care about that. I want the gunmen to see it so that we can set a trap for them—you know, by letting them think Trevor told us some important details about them."

A stunned silence met my ears. "Sally, you tried something like this once before, and it backfired. If I recall, it almost got you killed. This is way too dangerous."

"If Mike agrees, you can't stop us."

Brian swore on the other end of the phone. "Sally, please think about this first. We can't provide around-the-clock protection for you and Mike. He's not even in any condition to protect *you* right now."

"We'll take care of each other." My tone was defensive. "Thanks for your help, but I need to run."

"Sally, listen to me! Don't—"

I clicked off before he could finish. Maybe I'd been too hard on him, but he'd put me in an awkward position with my husband. I was beyond tired and depressed, and let my head rest on the steering wheel for a minute. If only we could go back forty-eight hours in time. Life had been so perfect then.

A man in a white van pulled up to the curb and proceeded to fill the newspaper vending machine. After he drove away, I got out of the car, the icy wind whipping my hair around and leaving me gasping for breath. Would spring ever get here?

I inserted coins for the paper and then hurried back to my car. I thumbed my way over to the obituary section and shuddered inwardly when my eyes connected with Trevor's face, smiling back at me. It was the same picture that had been in the paper the day before—his driver's license photo. I read the short paragraph that followed with interest.

*Trevor Zachary Parks of Tully, New York, age 38, died suddenly on March 23, 2019. Born in Roanoke, Virginia, he was the son of the late Steven and Emily Parks. He is survived by his brother, Curtis Parks of Virginia, a sister, Morgan Parks of Colwestern, his fiancée, Tina Landon of Tully, and his former wife, Erica Parks of Colwestern. Services are private and to be held at the convenience of the family. Those wishing to remember Trevor and assist with the cost of the funeral can contribute to a GoFundMe account that has been set up in his name.*

The link to the fund was included. Disgusted, I crumpled the paper into a ball and threw it into the back seat. As I drove out of the lot, I mulled over the few interesting tidbits of information I'd learned from the paper. Trevor's siblings, who I presumed were in town for his service, might know something about his dishonest hobby. It was interesting that Tina was listed as his fiancée, when Mike had told me Trevor had no intention of ever getting married again. The mention of the GoFundMe account made me physically ill. I had no issues with people who used the funds to raise money for worthy and honest causes, but according to my calculation, Trevor had taken more than enough money from my husband to cover his own funeral expenses.

Trevor and Tina lived in Tully, a small industrial type of town that bordered Colwestern. Their home was on the right-hand side of an older duplex. I'd never met Tina, but Mike had stopped there one time on a Sunday to let Trevor borrow some tools while I'd waited in the truck. Trevor hadn't talked much about Tina to Mike—or at least I didn't think so. When he'd come to our house for dinner last month and the subject of marriage came up, he'd murmured that once was more than enough. It made me wonder what had happened with his ex, Erica. She was next on my list to visit.

A rusted station wagon was parked next to the curb in front of the duplex. There was no driveway or garage. I climbed the creaky steps of the porch, the aging boards groaning under my weight. The mail slot on the right bore the name Parks/Landon on it, written with a black Magic Marker.

As I knocked on the door, I surveyed my surroundings, noting that the duplex was sorely in need of repairs. The vinyl siding was peeling, and the shingles of the asphalt roof were worn and tattered. I found it ironic that a construction worker like Trevor was living in such poor conditions, especially when he could afford to make repairs, thanks to what he'd stolen from us.

The door opened a crack, and a slim blonde woman peeked out from the other side. Her eyes were red rimmed, as if she'd been crying. "Yes?"

"Hi. Are you Tina Landon?"

A frown spread across her thin, angular face. "Who wants to know?"

I extended a hand. "I'm Sally Donovan. Mike's wife. He was Trevor's—"

"Oh!" Recognition dawned on Tina's face. She shut the door, undid the chain, and opened it. "Sorry, I don't think we've ever met."

"We haven't. I'm so sorry about Trevor." My voice sounded hollow with the lie.

She blinked back tears and nodded. "Thank you. Would you like to come in for a minute? I have to leave soon. Trevor's service starts in an hour."

Ah. She'd just given me the information I was looking for. "Thank you." I stepped into the small entranceway and glanced around at the interior of the home. The main room to the left doubled as both a living and dining room, with a gray couch, matching armchair, and a walnut dining table and four chairs that were stuffed into a corner. A staircase to my right most likely led to the bedroom and bathroom. Directly in front of me was a small kitchen, where I could see a sink piled high with dirty dishes.

Tina was about my height and slim as a pencil, with a brittle air about her that warned she might shatter into pieces at any moment. She was dressed in black slacks and a matching sweater. A brown wool coat was draped over a chair in the entranceway. The entire place was dark and depressing. "Don't you have anyone staying with you at this—difficult time?"

She shook her head. "My family isn't local."

"How are you getting to the service?"

"I have a friend who's picking me up. She should be here soon." Tina glanced at the plastic, round clock that hung on the wall. "How is your husband doing?"

"He's much better today, thank you." I bit into my lower lip and took the plunge. "I was wondering if I could ask you a few questions about Trevor."

Her eyes narrowed. "What kind of questions? Did he owe your husband money?" Before I could reply, she went on. "I know he gave Trevor an advance on his pay a few times. Sorry, but I don't have anything to give you."

It was interesting how money was her first thought. Maybe this wasn't the best time to bring up the fact that her boyfriend had been embezzling from Mike, but I needed to get to the bottom of this. "As a matter of fact, he did owe Mike money. Trevor was stealing from his business. Did you know anything about it?"

Her face grew pale. "Oh, gosh, no. He never talked much about his work. I don't know anything, honest."

She didn't seem surprised by my remark, so I continued. "You weren't in on it with him?"

Like a faucet, tears streamed out of her eyes. "How can you ask me such a thing, today of all days? My fiancé just died. At least your husband is still *alive*."

The anger within me died temporarily at her words. She was right, of course. I couldn't be positive if Tina was guilty, but this certainly was not the best time to be asking her such a thing. "I'm sorry. That was tactless of me. I know your life has changed drastically in the last 48 hours, but so has mine. At first, I even thought it was my husband who had been killed instead of Trevor. Believe me, I understand how you feel."

"No, you don't." Tina's mascara ran down her face in streaks. "Maybe Trevor and I rushed into this too soon. I guess I didn't know him as well as I thought I did. But I can't believe he'd steal." She hiccupped back a sob. "He warned me that he didn't want to get married again. It was too soon. They only divorced a few months ago. Erica did a real number on him."

"Do you know her?" I asked.

Tina's nostrils flared. "I've only seen her a couple of times, but the woman hates my guts. Trevor and I were in Sam's Sammywich Shop one night when she came in with Trevor's brother. I think they're dating. Pure spite, if you ask me. Both of them."

Interesting. "Trevor and his brother didn't get along?" He was another one I'd have to find a way to speak to.

"Curtis has always been jealous of Trevor. They almost got into a fistfight that night. Sam told them to get the hell out or he'd call the cops."

"How long have you and Trevor been together?" I asked.

"Only a couple of months," she said. "He and Erica were already divorced when we met. I don't know much about the rest of his family. Trevor was close with his sister Morgan, but not Curtis. Guess they've never gotten along. Their father died a few years ago in a car accident, and their mother had a sudden heart attack shortly afterward. But that Erica—" She sucked in a sharp breath. "She wanted every last cent she could get out of Trevor. He was paying her alimony too. It's a good thing they never had kids, or she would have drained him dry for them as well. Maybe that would explain why he lifted a few bucks from your husband."

I pursed my lips in annoyance. "It wasn't just a few bucks. He took thousands of dollars that didn't belong to him."

Tina's eyes widened at my words, and then she stared down at her hands. "Look, I'm sorry, but I can't help you. I don't even know how I'm going to pay next month's rent. If you'll excuse me, I have to fix my makeup before Jenna gets here."

"Could I come back to speak with you at another time?" I asked.

The look that Tina gave me clearly said no—she didn't care to see my face again—but she nodded. "Yeah, I guess that would be all right. But I've told you everything that I know. You should talk to Erica."

"Is she going to the service as well?" I asked curiously.

She shrugged. "Who knows with that woman? She was a gold digger. Anything to make Trevor's life miserable." A lone tear rolled down her left cheek. "Despite what you say he might have done, I know the facts. Trevor was a good man. He loved me, and we were going to be married."

I drew my eyebrows together. "Trevor told Mike and me that he didn't plan on getting married again."

Tina stuck her chin out in defiance. "Maybe not. But I happen to be pregnant with his child, so he didn't have much choice."

## CHAPTER ELEVEN

---

"Next time, will you please come and get me before you go off snooping on your own?" Josie made a sharp turn into Starbucks's parking lot. "We're partners—not only at the bakery but in our crime-stopping business. Understand?"

I suppressed a giggle and reached into the bucket on my lap to select a drumstick. "So we not only have a bakery, we have a crime-stopping business too?"

After my visit with Tina, I had gone back to the bakery. I'd needed to sit for a while and digest the information she'd given me. I'd then called Mike and talked to him briefly. He'd said that if things continued to progress well, the doctor would let him go home tomorrow. Grandma Rosa was there, and Mike told me I didn't have to hurry back. He said that he was tired, but I knew in fact that he was angry and felt like he could no longer trust anyone. The thought of him in so much physical and mental pain made my heart ache.

I wouldn't be able to rest until I'd discovered who had shot my husband and helped Trevor rip him off. I had high hopes of getting our money back but knew that might be impossible.

Josie ignored my question. "We're lucky we still have a bakery. Your sister was back at it again this morning, except that she only ate a half dozen fudgy delights this time. Maybe she's decided to go on a diet."

I exhaled sharply. "Okay, let it go. She's under enough stress with the baby coming and our mother and Mrs. Gavelli grilling her about wedding dates." Gianna had seemed a little better today and insisted that Josie accompany me to Trevor's service. She'd assured us that she would be fine until we returned.

Hunger had finally caught up with me, so Josie had stopped at Chuck's Country Fried Chicken. We'd gone to the drive-thru window and ordered a bucket of extra crispy plus two small containers of mashed potatoes. The Starbucks lot where we were now parked was directly across the street from the funeral home. I longed to go inside the building, but the service was private after all. I still wasn't sure how I planned to connect with anyone—maybe waylay them on their way out?

"I think the whole David Webb thing could be a dead end," Josie said as she selected a chicken wing.

"Why do you say that?" I spooned some potatoes into my mouth.

Josie wiped her hands on a napkin. "Because Laura Pusatere said that she'd let you know if they saw him again. Seriously, what are the chances of that? David already got his money from the house. We don't have a definitive description of him or even know what kind of car he drives."

It was like looking for a lone chocolate chip in a bakery display case. "Well, we have to start somewhere. Mrs. Gavelli saw Trevor meeting a man in a black BMW a few weeks back. It might have been David Webb. Maybe he'll show up at Trevor's service to see what's going on?" It wasn't likely, though. We may have hit a bump in the road.

Josie shrugged. "It's possible. I can't believe that Tina chick is pregnant. Do you think she planned to trap Trevor?"

I wrapped the remains of my piece of chicken in a napkin and sucked at the straw in my soda. "Trevor didn't want to get married again, so yeah, I think she might have." Still, what did it matter now? She would be raising a child on her own. I wondered why Trevor hadn't told Mike about the baby. There was so much we still didn't know about this mystery man.

I thought back to the few times I'd met Trevor. He'd always been pleasant and made polite conversation with me, asking about the bakery and so forth. He and Mike got on well together. My husband knew many people and was well liked in town, but didn't have many male friends besides Josie's husband, Rob. He'd always been somewhat of a loner.

Nausea stirred in my stomach. Trevor hadn't given a damn about Mike's friendship, the tools Mike had lent him, or advances on pay he'd received. Why did people do such hurtful things and take advantage of one another? Was everyone always looking out for number one?

Josie and I sat in silence for the next several minutes as we watched the funeral home for any signs of life. The service had started almost an hour ago, and I figured someone had to be out soon.

As if reading my mind, Josie sighed and looked at her watch. "It's four o'clock, Sal. Should I text Gianna and tell her to close up in case we don't get back in time?"

"Please." I kept my eyes glued on the building.

Josie's fingers flew over the keyboard, and then she put the phone away. "How long are you planning on staying here?"

"As long as it takes."

A rapping on my window startled us, and we both shrieked. My father was waving at me from the other side of the glass. "Hi, baby girl," he shouted. "Hello, Josie. What are you two doing here? Coffee run?"

"Good God," Josie said in disbelief as I rolled my window down. "Your parents are everywhere."

Yeah, no kidding. "Dad, what are *you* doing here? Mortuary convention at Starbucks?"

He beamed. "Nah, but it would make a great location. Those morticians can guzzle down a lot of java, let me tell you." He held up a duffel bag. "I'm dropping off some copies of my book at Phibbins Mortuary. Eddie Phibbins requested them. He's going to put a couple out with the mass cards."

The whole world had gone mad. "Isn't he the owner? The same guy who once fired you for driving his hearse and talking to the mourners too much?"

My father waved a hand in impatience. "Ah, that's all ashes over the ocean. I don't hold grudges. Besides, I'm a celebrity now. It's natural that everyone would want a piece of me."

Give me strength. "There's a private service being held inside, Dad. I don't think you can just walk right in. It's for Trevor Parks. You know, the guy—"

His face sobered. "Yes, I remember. I'm sorry, baby girl. By the way, your mother and I thought that Mike looked much better when we stopped in to see him last night. I believe your grandmother was headed over there this morning."

"Yes, she's at the hospital with him now," I said.

"Are you still going inside?" Josie asked him in surprise.

"Certainly." Dad puffed out his chest. "Eddie knows I'm coming. We'll sit in his office and chat about my book. I'm sure he'll want me to sign them."

This might be the opportunity I was looking for. "Hey, Dad. Could you do me a favor?"

"You bet. Anything for my baby girl."

"I'd like to talk to Trevor's brother and sister but don't want to interfere with the service, since it's private and all. I don't know what they look like or if they're even here for that matter. Do you think Eddie would help us out?"

He nodded happily. "Why sure. I'll text you and let you know what I find out. It's the least I can do when you're making 500 coffin-shaped cookies for me." He whistled cheerfully and started across the street. An elderly man opened the door as he approached the entrance of the funeral home.

Josie waved a hand in front of my face. "Um, what does he mean, 500 cookies? And who is making them, pray tell?"

"Oh, didn't I tell you?" I tried to laugh it off, but Josie wasn't smiling. "Dad needs 500 cookies for his book signing."

"How the heck am I supposed to make 500 cookies?" Josie exploded. "And shaped like coffins? What am I, the baker of doom and gloom?"

My phone pinged at that moment, and I glanced down, grateful for the distraction. It was a text from my father.

*Only five people here for the service. Trevor's girlfriend, her friend, Trevor's ex-wife, his sister and brother. I guess Jerry Maroon stopped by to try to talk to the family earlier. Sorry I missed him! Eddie had to tell him to leave.*

The so-called star anchorman was relentless. I texted my father back. *Is there any way you can let me know when they're about to wrap up?*

Dad shot back an answer. *Service is over. The brother and sister are leaving now. Should be coming out the front door soon. Said something to Eddie about wanting coffee.*

Jackpot. *Thanks, Dad. I owe you.*

His reply came back within seconds. *Maybe you should add another 100 cookies to that order.*

Me and my big mouth. "Trevor's brother and sister should be coming out of the building any second," I said to Josie. "Sounds like they're going to Starbucks."

She threw me a shrewd look. "You're the boss of this operation, Sal. I've never seen you so determined. You always want to get to the bottom of a crime, but I guess this one is a bit too personal."

"Yes, it is," I said sadly. "Mike was almost killed, and now his business has taken a hard blow. I want to find out exactly what is going on and who was involved with Trevor."

We watched as the front door of the funeral parlor opened and a woman emerged, followed by a man. They looked to be in their early forties, and both were petite in height. Trevor himself had also been on the short side, only a few inches taller than me. The woman had dark hair styled in a curly bob and was wearing a black, belted trench coat. Curtis had red hair and, even at this distance, looked shockingly like Trevor. My heart gave a jolt as they got into a black SUV and quickly drove out of the lot. "Here we go."

As my father had indicated, the couple turned into the Starbucks lot and immediately went inside the building. I opened my car door and looked expectantly at Josie. "Are you coming with me?"

Josie beeped the minivan locked. "As if there was ever any doubt."

We got in line behind the sister, who ordered two lattes. The man was seated at a table in the corner of the room, texting away on his iPhone. I handed Josie a ten-dollar bill. "Get whatever you want."

"What about you?" she asked.

"My stomach's in knots. I'll hold off for a while."

With some hesitation, I approached the table. Again, I was struck by the likeness to Trevor—even more so up close. They could have been twins. Same red hair, freckles, and wiry build.

The man must have sensed that he was being stared at because he suddenly looked up at me. "Help you?" His tone was not especially friendly.

"Hi," I managed to squeak out, as if meeting a celebrity for the first time. "Are you Curtis Parks?"

He put the phone down on the table and raised an eyebrow at me. "Who wants to know?"

I extended my hand. "You don't know me. My name is Sally Donovan. Your brother worked for my husband at Donovan Construction."

Curtis stared at my hand for several awkward seconds then grudgingly brushed a few fingers across it. "What can I help you with?"

"I'm sorry about your brother. I can't imagine what—"

"Save it," he interrupted. "Just get to the point. You don't care that Trevor's dead. You're here because you want something, so don't beat around the bush—come right out and say it."

His rudeness shocked me, and I heard myself babbling as I often did when nervous. "My husband was with Trevor when he was killed. He was shot too."

"Sorry to hear that," he muttered. "But that's not why you're making small talk, is it?"

A demure woman's voice sounded from behind me. "Curtis, what's going on?"

I turned around to see Trevor's sister standing there with a cardboard tray between her slim hands. Curtis jumped up and placed it on the table, then gestured toward me as he selected his latte. "This woman's husband is the one who Trevor worked for."

"Oh." Her blue eyes widened as she scanned me up and down. "I'm Morgan Parks, Trevor's older sister."

"Sally Donovan. Nice to meet you." At that moment, Josie walked toward us, Starbucks cup in hand topped off with a tower of whipped cream. "This is my friend and partner, Josie Sullivan."

Josie nodded at them while Curtis guffawed. "Partner in what? Crime?"

Ah, if he only knew.

"Oh, I know who you are," Morgan spoke up. "I live in Colwestern. You own Sally's Samples, right?"

I studied her for a second. Morgan looked vaguely

familiar, but I didn't remember ever seeing her in the bakery before. "Have you lived in town long?"

"A couple of years," she said. "I'm the one who convinced Trevor to come stay with me for a while after things went bad with his ex-wife. He needed a new start, and I told him it was a lovely little town."

Curtis glared at his sister. "Morgs, there's no reason to tell this woman anything. It's obvious she's on a fishing expedition."

Morgan wrinkled her brow. "I don't understand."

Curtis eyed me suspiciously. "What's Trevor done, Mrs. Donovan? Because you certainly aren't here to pay your respects."

This guy had a major chip on his shoulder. Curtis must have known what his brother was capable of, otherwise he wouldn't be acting this way. I gestured toward the two empty chairs. "May we join you for a minute?"

He rolled his eyes but removed his coat from the chair so I could sit down next to him. Josie sat across from me, next to Morgan. "Get to the point. I have things to do."

I tried not to let his sour manner bother me. "I don't know how to tell you both this, but Trevor was embezzling from my husband. He stole thousands of dollars from him."

Morgan gave a little cry of surprise, but Curtis's face remained stoic. "And? Anything else?" he demanded.

"Isn't that enough?" Josie snapped back at him.

I shot her a warning look. "It's my belief that whoever killed your brother might have been in on it with him. I want to track down these people and make sure they get what's coming to them." *And save my husband's business in the process.*

Curtis leaned back in his chair and studied me, as if seeing me for the first time. After a few seconds, he chuckled. "Thanks for the laugh, lady. I needed one today."

"Curtis!" Morgan gasped. "Why are you being so rude to this woman?"

He glared angrily across the table at his sister. "Why? Gee, Morgan, I have no idea. Maybe because Trevor never cared about anyone but himself? Maybe because he did the same thing to you? Stole money out of your bank account and was forging checks with your name on them? He didn't give a—"

"Stop it!" Morgan pleaded. She looked as if she was about to cry. "I asked you to never bring that up again. I forgave Trevor for that a long time ago."

Curtis scraped his chair against the floor as he got to his feet. "I'm going to finish my coffee in the car. When you're done talking to Nancy Drew and company, I'll drive you home." Without another word he looked down his nose in disgust at Josie and me, pushed the door to the coffee shop open and walked outside.

Morgan watched her brother get into the SUV and then turned back to me, her eyes filled with unshed tears. "Please forgive Curtis. He doesn't usually act like this."

"You mean he's human after all?" Josie blurted out.

"Jos," I warned.

Morgan stared at me sadly. "Curtis has never forgiven Trevor for what he did to me. He wanted me to press charges, but I refused. A week later, our mother died of a sudden heart attack. Trevor had always been Mother's favorite, and Curtis was jealous. He said that Trevor was the one who killed her. At the funeral, he even started a fight with Trevor. At her *funeral,* for God's sake!" Her lower lip trembled. "He hit Trevor in the face several times before the undertaker and some friends finally pulled him off. Things haven't been right between the two of them since." She hiccupped back a sob. "And now they never will."

My heart went out to her. I'd known families with bad blood between the siblings before, but this was taking it to a whole new level. Could Curtis have hated his brother enough to kill him? Or was there a bigger motive? Was there any chance Curtis had been in on Trevor's embezzlement scheme too?

"This has to be a very emotional day for you, and I'm sorry to intrude," I said. "I had hoped that maybe you or your brother might be able to point us in the right direction. I want to find who did this to Trevor as much as you do."

She twisted a napkin between her two tiny hands. "Trevor was my baby brother. Sure, he did some rotten things, but I still loved him. When he met Tina, I told him maybe he should think about staying near Colwestern and starting over. It's my fault he was killed."

"You can't blame yourself," Josie said. "You didn't tell him to get involved with people who'd end up killing him. Any idea who the gunmen might have been?"

She shook her head with regret. "I don't know if Trevor knew them personally. He never talked about any friends to me. I tried to stay out of his business—you know, the divorce with Erica and then when he moved in with Tina. He seemed happy, so I minded my own business."

"He never mentioned anyone else?" I asked.

Morgan glanced at me sheepishly. "He did talk about your husband a couple of times. He said that Mickey was a great guy."

"Mike," I corrected.

"Sorry." Her face reddened. "Trevor said he owed Mike a lot since he gave him a job." A tear trickled down her cheek. "About a week ago, he called me out of the blue late one night. He didn't sound like himself. Trevor went on to say that Mike was going through some stuff, and he felt bad for him. I didn't know what he meant and didn't think about it any further, nor did I ask for details. Hey, I thought that he meant Mike was going through a divorce too or maybe he had a sick kid at home—something like that."

Trevor must have been referring to the embezzling part. It was the only thing that made sense. Did this mean that Trevor had a conscience after all? "Is there anything else you remember?"

Morgan wiped her eyes with a napkin. "Trevor said he'd done some terrible things that he wasn't proud of. I thought he was referring to stealing money out of my bank account. Then he mentioned he'd be moving on soon." She blew out a breath. "Trevor said he was afraid he'd eventually have to pay for what he'd done."

# CHAPTER TWELVE

"Okay, so I was wrong," Josie admitted as we watched the SUV speed away. "We found out more than I thought. So where to begin? Curtis hated his brother's guts and may have been dating his ex-wife. Trevor stole money from his sister and, from what Morgan said, knew his life was in danger and was planning to leave town. It makes sense that he was taking money and materials from Mike's business to profit himself and that David Webb guy. Trevor Parks was one busy guy."

We were sitting in Josie's minivan, still pointed in the direction of the funeral home parking lot. The past couple of days had caught up with me, and I could barely manage to stay awake. "Maybe I should go back to the hospital." My grandmother had called a little while earlier saying that she was leaving and Mike would be alone. Shortly afterward, Johnny had texted to say that he was stopping by to see Mike. Maybe he could lift his spirits. My heart ached when I thought of him lying in that hospital bed alone, feeling betrayed. I'd asked Mike if he wanted me to come back, but he hadn't responded yet. Hopefully that meant he was sleeping.

"Sure. I'll take you back to the bakery to get your car." Josie had started to put the van into drive when the front doors of the funeral home opened and a petite woman hurried down the steps. Josie nudged me in the side. "Who do you think that is?"

The woman had shoulder-length, dark hair covered with a blue knit cap and looked to be about our age. Her coat was the same light blue as the cap, and she had paired it with a plaid skirt and white boots. She almost looked like she was attending a party instead of a funeral service. This had to be Trevor's ex-wife.

We watched as the woman hurried over to a gray Chevy truck and got behind the wheel. Josie raised an eyebrow at me, having an idea what was running through my mind. "Your call."

"Follow her," I said.

Josie pulled out onto the main street. The truck was going over the speed limit, but Josie had a lead foot, and we managed to keep her in view.

"Erica lives in Colwestern, so hopefully she's not going far. It sounds like she moved here after Trevor left Virginia. Maybe she wanted to keep him in her sights." I was curious as to why they had divorced. Had Trevor been unfaithful?

"Sounds like one of those clingy females who can't accept that the relationship is over," Josie grumbled as she took a left onto a one-way residential street. "I hate women like that. They can't live without a man." She rolled her eyes in dramatic fashion. "Whatever will I do without a big, strapping male to take care of me?"

"Well, you have five in your life," I teased.

She gave me a sly wink. "Yeah, but that's different. *I'm* the boss and take care of all of them. You can bet that they know it too—especially Rob."

There was no doubt in my mind that they knew it. Rob was no wimp, but he knew better than to mess with Josie. Every male in that house needed her, and they weren't ashamed to admit it either. "You're so lucky," I said softly.

Josie knew how much I loved and envied her those beautiful kids. She reached over to pat my hand. "Hey, it's going to happen for you guys too, Sal. Don't give up hope."

I said nothing as we watched the truck pull into the driveway of a small gray ranch home with a stone façade. Erica got out carrying a black, leather bag in one hand and a manila envelope in the other. She fumbled with the key to the door for a minute. I noted the address on the mailbox—3244 Burbank Street. Did Erica have any money of her own, or had she been relying on Trevor to pay her alimony? Was she grieving her ex or secretly glad to be rid of him?

Josie pulled her van over to the side of the road and turned to look at me. "What do you think, partner?"

I eased myself out of the van. "Well, she might shut the

door in our faces, but it's not the first time that's happened to us, right?"

The driveway was slippery and covered with a slick coating of flakes from the earlier morning's light snowfall. Spring was officially here, according to the calendar anyway. Some days I wondered why I'd ever moved back from Florida. It was a big state, and I could have managed to stay away from my ex-husband. Then again, if I hadn't come back to Colwestern, I might never have found Mike again.

A dog barked from inside the house as we got ready to knock. A curtain on the inside of the door moved slightly to one side. The woman peeked out at us and then opened the door a crack. "Yes?"

"Hi, are you Erica Parks?"

Her brow wrinkled with suspicion. "Are you a reporter?"

I shook my head. "My name is Sally Donovan, and this is my friend Josie Sullivan. Your husband, Trevor—"

"Ex-husband," she corrected me.

"Sorry about that," I said. "Your ex-husband worked for my husband, Mike, at Donovan Construction."

She blew out a sigh and held the door wide open. "Oh. I think I know what this is about. Would you like to come in for a minute?"

Surprised at her cordialness, Josie and I stepped inside. A small living room was directly in front of us, with a baby gate separating it from the kitchen. On the other side of the gate, a white poodle looked over at us and started to yip yap. He jumped around in circles while barking, trying to leap over the obstacle but not even coming close. He bared his teeth at us and tried to look fierce, but it was almost comical.

"Donny!" Erica clapped her hands together. "Go to sleep!" The dog obediently trotted back over to his bed on the floor and climbed into it, his beady eyes still fixed on us.

I glanced around. It was a cute house, similar in size to mine. A narrow stairway led to what I assumed were bedrooms on the second floor. Everything was immaculate.

Erica pointed to a brown couch decorated with white flowers. "Please sit down."

Still in our coats, we accepted the invitation while Erica

took a seat in a recliner across from us and rubbed her eyes wearily. "It's been a long day. Trevor's service was this afternoon." She glanced up at us then as her face dawned with recognition. "Did the funeral home give you my address?"

"No. Mike mentioned where you lived once. Trevor must have told him." I was surely going to hell for all these lies.

She looked surprised. "Really? I wasn't aware that Trevor still talked about me. He stopped speaking to me altogether when he moved out. If he owed your husband money, I can't help you. I just got a job as a secretary for a local office supply company and am only renting this place."

"I'm sensing a pattern here," Josie mused. "Money is the first thing everyone thinks of when Trevor's name pops up in conversation."

Erica frowned. "What do you mean, *everyone*? Who else have you talked to? I don't even know what you're doing here."

As much as I loved Josie, sometimes I wished she had a little more tact. "Erica, I'm not sure if you know all the details about the robbery, but my husband was with Trevor when he was killed. In fact, he was shot himself. We found out that Trevor was stealing money from my husband's business account the last few months. Thousands of dollars."

She sucked in a deep breath. "Oh, no. I was afraid he might do that again."

Josie and I exchanged glances. "Again?" I asked. "Trevor's done this before?"

A muscle worked at Erica's jaw as she stared down at the floor. "He took money from his sister a few years back. She told me all about it. He stole from my father too. There are probably others. Your husband wasn't the first."

"He probably wouldn't have been the last either," Josie said grimly. "Did you move here to get back together with him?"

She choked back a laugh. "Hardly. After Trevor moved out, I discovered that he took several pieces of my jewelry. These were items that my parents gave me over the years, and Trevor knew that they were valuable. Of course, when I confronted him, he denied taking them. What am I, an idiot? He probably hocked them or gave them to that bimbo he shacked up with. So how could I make his life miserable? I decided to move near him." Her mouth quivered into a small smile. "Tina can't stand the sight of me."

And vice versa. "What happens to the money in his bank account? Does it go to you?"

She looked at me like I had two heads. "What money? Trevor never had a dollar to his name. We had to declare bankruptcy a couple of years ago. Tina told his brother, Curtis, at the service today that there's less than five hundred dollars in his bank account. Oh dear, what's little miss tramp going to do now? Find some other guy to steal away from his wife?"

Tina had said they'd met in a bar one evening after Trevor moved here. Someone was obviously lying, but who? "Wait a second. Trevor left you for Tina?"

Her lips clenched together. "Yes. Do you know how that makes me feel? After eight years of marriage, that's how he treats me—the little regard he had for our marriage. It's obvious he never cared about me."

"But I thought he didn't meet Tina until you guys were separated," Josie remarked.

"Is that what she told you?" Erica's voice rose. "Well, it's a lie. He came out here to visit his sister last summer and met Tina in a bar one night. He got drunk and slept with her. The next day he called and told me he wanted a divorce."

Was she telling the truth? I honestly couldn't tell. "Someone mentioned that you and Trevor's brother were an item. Was that to get back at him?"

She stared at me in disbelief. "I don't know what all of this has to do with your husband's business."

"Is there a chance that Curtis could have been in on Trevor's embezzlement scheme?"

Erica looked stunned. "Doubtful. They didn't like each other, so it seems crazy to believe that they'd be working together."

"Not as crazy as you might think," Josie put in.

Erica bit her lower lip. "In answer to your earlier question, no. I wasn't fooling around with Curtis. We never got along. Then again, he's never gotten along with anyone except Morgan. You want to know what I believe is going on?"

"Yes," Josie and I both said in unison.

"I think that Tina was carrying on with Curtis behind Trevor's back."

If she was correct, maybe Tina and Curtis had been in on it together to kill Trevor. Curtis could have been one of the gunmen and this David Webb character the other. But why would they want him dead? He must have cut somebody out of their share of the so-called business. It was the only thing that made sense. "Did Trevor ever mention a man named David Webb?"

She shook her head. "Trevor didn't have many friends. I always thought it was a shame that he and Curtis never got along. My own family back in Virginia is a tight-knit bunch. Nothing like the Parks' family tree. Curtis caused a huge scene at our wedding. He got drunk and tried to grope one of my bridesmaids. I can't stand the sight of him, and it wouldn't surprise me if..." She trailed off and then stood. "Look, if you'll excuse me, I have things to do."

This was the sign that we'd overstayed our welcome. Josie and I both rose to our feet. I was leaving here with no answers, and it frustrated me. Either Tina or Erica was lying to me. And where did Curtis and Morgan fit in? "Thanks for your time. Oh, did you and Tina speak at the service today?"

Erica's nostrils flared. "No. I avoided her like the plague. She and her girlfriend left before I did. I wanted to talk to the owner and make sure he knew that Tina was to get the bill for Trevor's service. He was busy talking to some weird old guy who had books about death. I kept waiting for the nutcase to leave since this was a private matter." She rolled her eyes. "Some people get so turned on by death, you know? I don't get it. The guy was definitely a fruitcake."

Josie coughed and stared down at the floor. Heat burned my cheeks. *Dad strikes again.* I should have said something in my father's defense, but what was there to say? He *was* weird.

"Can you give me the name of Trevor's former employer in Virginia?" I took out a pad of Post-it notes and a pen from my purse. "Why did he leave their employment?"

She shrugged. "After he hooked up with Tina, he called his boss and said he wasn't coming back. That's the way he was about everything—irresponsible."

"Do you have contact information for his previous boss?" I had a hunch that she'd say she didn't have a number or couldn't find it.

Erica surprised me when she rose from her chair, went to the kitchen, and leaned over the baby gate. Donny watched her expectantly from his round, plush bed on the floor. She lifted her purse from the counter and grabbed her phone, scrolling through a list of contacts. "Roberts Construction. Alden Roberts is the owner." She rattled off a phone number and then looked at me strangely. "I received a voice mail earlier from an Officer Jenkins who said he wanted to come by and talk to me. Is he going to ask me the same questions as you? Do you think that Alden might have been one of the guys at the mini-mart who killed Trevor?"

Her question startled me. I hadn't been thinking about a former employer as Trevor's killer, but had to admit it was possible. Perhaps Trevor had stolen from Alden before he'd taken off and the man had wanted revenge. What if I'd been mistaken and the gunmen weren't even in on the larceny charges? There was a good chance I might be going in the wrong direction. I'd have to ask Brian to check this guy out.

Erica's phone pinged with a text, and she mouthed a quick *sorry* to us as she hastily typed out a reply. My mind was jumbled with all that I'd learned. Curtis had hated his brother. Morgan, who professed to have loved Trevor, was also a victim of his. A possible disgruntled former boss, two gunmen, and a pregnant fiancée rounded out the bunch, along with an ex-wife scorned. Where did I go from here?

Erica put her phone down and walked us to the front door. "It was nice meeting you both." She jotted down a number on an index card and handed it to me. "Here's my cell. If I can do anything else to help you catch Trevor's killer, please give me a call." She smiled at me. "I saw your husband having lunch with Trevor about a month ago. I was never formally introduced to him, but he looked like a nice guy. Very attractive too." Her face reddened suddenly. "Sorry, perhaps I shouldn't have said that."

"It's all right." Women were always attracted to Mike—this was nothing new. I'd gotten used to the sly winks and smiles as women checked him out, even if he was holding hands with me out in public. Sure, it was annoying, but we were secure enough in our relationship that I'd learned long ago not to let it bother me.

"How's he feeling?" Erica asked.

I placed the card in my purse. "Better, thanks. He'll be going home from the hospital tomorrow morning."

Her lower lip trembled. "I'm sorry for what's happened, but you have to know that your husband is the lucky one here." She stared over at Donny, who'd resumed barking, as if knowing his owner was in distress. "I did love Trevor once, but he destroyed it. Tina wasn't the first woman he cheated on me with. Despite all the pain, though, I'm still sorry he's dead and keep thinking about all the good times we shared. Does that seem strange to you?"

"Not at all." I hadn't realized it before, but Erica and I shared a common bond—a cheating ex-husband who'd been murdered. "I was married to a cheater once. He was killed too, so I understand exactly what you're going through."

Her eyes widened. "Really? What are the chances? How did you get through it?"

I didn't want to get into the whole scenario and tell her how Mike had been accused of Colin's murder and then left town, insisting that I was better off without him if he ended up going to prison. Despite that, our love for each other had seen us through. "With Mike's support. I hope you have someone you can turn to at this awful time."

A tear trickled down Erica's left cheek, and she nodded. "I do. I recently started dating another man, and he's been wonderful to me. It might be the real thing." She dabbed at her eyes with a tissue. "Hey, sometimes true love doesn't always happen the first time around, you know what I mean?"

I smiled and laid a hand on her arm. "That's what second chances are for. Another opportunity to get things right."

## CHAPTER THIRTEEN

———

I spent another restless night in Mike's room while he seemed to sleep enough for the both of us. He'd said very little to me when I'd returned. Johnny had been with him and in the process of telling some jokes. It was obvious my husband was tired and in pain. The nurse had given Mike something to help him sleep, and he'd drifted off soon afterwards.

I watched him breathing for a long time, his chest rising and falling in a rhythmic pattern. The lines of worry had returned to his handsome face and bothered me to no end. Mike was upset that I hadn't told him about my findings, but there was more to it than that. He was worried about the future and the possibility of his business going under. I kept thinking about the bills that were piling up. I'd told Josie to go ahead and order a new fridge since I didn't have time or want to be bothered with it. *Cripes.* Less than three years old. It could only happen to me. Grandma Rosa once told me how she'd had the same fridge for over twenty-five years. How cheaply did they make appliances these days?

I must have fallen asleep at some point because I was awakened when something touched my face. My eyes opened, and I stared up at Mike, standing over me in his hospital gown and gently stroking my hair.

Blinking, I sat upright and yawned. "Is everything okay? Are you in pain? You shouldn't be out of bed, sweetheart."

He cupped my cheek with his left hand and leaned down to kiss me softly on the lips. "Sal, I'm sorry. I wasn't angry with you yesterday, although it must have seemed that way. I could never be angry at you, baby. But I am angry at the world—at everything that's happening to us."

Relief swept over me. "It's okay. You work so hard and

didn't deserve to have this happen," I said sadly.

"It's not just me. We're a team, remember? Whatever happens to one of us happens to the other one too." His voice grew soft." You know that I love you more than anything in this world."

My eyes grew moist at his words. "Me too." I got up out of the chair and helped him back into bed. When he was settled against the pillow, he reached up with his good arm and drew me close, placing his mouth over mine. It was a long time before we came up for air.

Mike smiled wickedly and patted the space next to him on the bed. "There's enough room in here for two. And you could lock the door."

I shook my head and laughed. "Listen to you. You almost got killed a couple of days ago, and already you're thinking about romance." I pulled the sheet up around him. "You'll be home in a few hours, and we can be naughty then."

"But just think," he teased. "How many opportunities do you get to play doctor in a real hospital?"

Erica's words from the previous day came back to me. Yes, I did know how lucky I was. Things weren't looking wonderful, but we had each other, and that was all that mattered.

"It's a tempting offer," I admitted. "But we'll have to play when we get home. And as soon as you're up to it, I'd like to still have that birthday dinner in your honor—well, a belated one, that is."

He sighed. "I'm really not in the mood for a celebration, Sal."

"It will do us both good," I said firmly. "We have a lot to celebrate. Things could have been so much worse. We'll get through this, sweetheart, and then things will be better than ever. You'll see."

\* \* \*

We arrived home shortly before noon to find Grandma Rosa waiting at the front door. Despite Spike's advanced age, he started barking and danced around in a circle when we got inside the house.

Mike laughed and stooped down to pet him. "The big guy missed us."

"Johnny dropped him off a little while ago," Grandma Rosa said. "He played very nicely with Dante too. It is good that Gianna and Johnny have been training the little doggie."

Johnny and Gianna had recently started taking Dante to puppy school. The last time they were at my parents for dinner, they'd mentioned how he was "tops in his class." Nicoletta, who had also been present, wondered out loud why they had time to take the dog to school but couldn't seem to set a wedding date yet. Johnny and Gianna had left shortly afterward.

Once Mike was settled in our bed, I grabbed his prescription pain killers out of my purse and noticed that there was a voice mail on my phone. I retrieved it and found that Laura Pusatere had called. She was brisk and to the point. "I might have some information that can help. Call me at your convenience."

Exhausted from the morning's activities, Mike had already started to drift off. He refused the pill and asked for a kiss instead. Afterward, I went into the spare bedroom where Grandma Rosa was staying to call Laura so that I wouldn't disturb him.

She came on the line immediately. "I told Evan about your visit. He tried calling David, but the number's no longer in service."

No surprise there. "Well, thanks for letting me know."

"Hang on a minute," she said. "Evan mentioned that when he first went to see our house—without me—he asked David if he had any other homes for sale. David told him that he was starting construction at a home over on Fairlawn Avenue soon. He said it was still in the development phase then, but I'm guessing there must be something up by this time."

I wrinkled my forehead at the name. This was the other home on the work order that I hadn't checked out yet—26 Fairlawn Avenue. "Is that in Colgate too?"

"Yes, it is," she said. "Probably about a fifteen-minute drive from your bakery."

"When did he first tell your husband about it?"

Laura paused for a moment. "David first told Evan about

it sometime in January. We signed the papers on the twenty-fourth. Since it was brand-new and we paid cash, we were able to close in only a couple of weeks. David had the building permit when we first met him and obtained the Certificate of Occupancy once the house was finished. There was no reason for us to think anything was wrong." Her tone sounded concerned. "Evan wants to know what's going on. Did they do something to the house that we don't know about?"

"I don't think there's anything structurally wrong with your home," I said with all honesty. "We believe that David was embezzling money from other businesses—including my husband's—to build these houses. The man who did the construction work was in on it too."

She sucked in a sharp breath. "The one who was killed?"

"Yes. Was anyone else involved with the transaction? Did you have a real estate attorney?"

Laura sounded surprised by my question. "Sure we did. We're not stupid. Evan doesn't like to take chances with that stuff. Our attorney arranged for the transfer of title. We also had all the proper inspections done—structural, termite, and radon. Everything passed with flying colors. Since we paid cash, there was no need for a bank." She paused. "David didn't tell us that he wanted a cash payment until after we'd seen the house. It wasn't mentioned in the ad online."

"Weren't you at all suspicious?" I asked.

"Not really," she replied. "Like I said, we were convinced the house was structurally sound. He was offering a twenty percent discount to anyone who paid cash. We assumed he needed the money as soon as possible. Let's face it, the housing market hasn't been the greatest in New York State this winter."

That was true enough. Josie and Rob had recently listed their home in hopes of buying a larger one, but they'd had no bites so far.

"Oh, I totally forgot," Laura murmured. "Evan said that David once told him that when the house on Fairlawn sold, he was going to be moving on. Not sure what that meant."

I had a fairly good idea. "So he may not even be in the area anymore." If David had been one of the gunmen, why stick around? "Most likely he was going to try to find another honest business owner to scam."

"I'm sorry," Laura said. "If we hear from him, I'll be sure to let you know."

"Thanks for your help." After I disconnected, I sat there with the phone between my hands, debating what to do. There was a chance that the house on Fairlawn hadn't sold yet, so it was worth checking out. I dialed Josie's cell. Gianna had offered to help in the bakery this afternoon if I needed her. Although I hadn't planned to take her up on it, Johnny's school was closed today, and she said he would help too.

"Yo, girlfriend," Josie said. "It's dead here. Don't worry about coming in."

That was not encouraging to hear. "Gianna and Johnny will be there shortly. Want to do a little detective work with me? I might have a lead on this David Webb guy."

"Absolutely," she said. "I'll be waiting for you."

I went into the kitchen and found my grandmother stirring something in a large steel pot on the stove. Smells of oregano and basil wafted through the air, and my stomach began to growl. I reached down to pet Spike, who was snug in his bed next to the stove. "That smells wonderful."

"Pasta fagioli." She smiled at me. "Mike's favorite."

My grandmother was truly amazing. "I'm going out for a couple of hours to run some errands. Mike's asleep."

Grandma Rosa gave me a sharp look. "Errands, bah. What you really mean is that you are going to snoop." She offered me a taste, but I shook my head. Grandma Rosa sighed. "You need to eat, *cara mia*."

"I had a bagel at the hospital this morning." I grabbed my coat off the back of one of the dining room chairs. "Do you need anything while I'm out?"

Grandma Rosa shook her head. "No, I am fine. Do not worry about Mike. I will look in on him in a little while."

I gave her a kiss on the cheek, and she patted mine in return. "Tell Josie I said hello."

She'd already guessed that Josie would be accompanying me. There were days when I was certain my grandmother was psychic. Or maybe she knew me better than I knew myself.

There was no time to waste if I was going to find the men responsible for shooting my husband and helping Trevor carry out his scheme. The more days that passed, the more of an opportunity for these gunmen to get farther away. True, I didn't even know if this David Webb was linked directly to Trevor's killing at the mini-mart, but I had a strong suspicion that he was.

Josie had a copy of the real estate section from the paper when I picked her up. "We may have hit the jackpot," she said as she got into the car. "It says that there's an open house at 22 Fairlawn Avenue from noon to two today." She checked her watch. "It's exactly 1:30. We should make it in time."

I stopped for a red light. "Is it listed for sale by owner or with a broker?"

Josie squinted down at the paper. "It's with a broker. Some place called Hospitable Homes."

In confusion, I drew my eyebrows together. "I thought they went out of business."

"Not the local office. Their branch in the Albany area closed down a couple of years ago," Josie explained as she rustled the pages. "I remember reading about it. A real estate agent was found murdered at that office. One of the female coworkers found her body, and the killer then tried to frame the agent for it."

I shuddered. It sounded eerily familiar to some of the experiences I'd been through. This woman and I needed to talk and compare notes sometime. "Well, it can't be the right house if it's with a broker. Besides, I thought weekends were the most popular days for an open house?" Today was only Thursday.

"Yeah, I've heard that too," she admitted. "But if David knows there's another one going on in the same neighborhood, he might take full advantage of the free advertisement. He could hold one and then sell it under a fictitious company name."

*If* the house hadn't already sold, that is. "It feels like we're looking for a needle in a haystack, but we don't have much else to go on right now." I flicked the blinker to turn right on Fairlawn and spotted the open house sign in front of number 22. There were three cars in the driveway, but none of them were BMWs.

"Want to go in?" Josie asked.

"Let's check out the rest of the street first." There was a fork in the road after the home for sale, and I maneuvered my car to the right, which turned out to be a dead end. The very last house on the left-hand side had a generic *For Sale* sign on its front lawn. The house appeared new and was the same design as Laura's, except this one was a beige-colored Cape Cod with an attached one-car garage. *Pay dirt.*

Josie bounced in her seat excitedly. "This has to be it."

I pulled my car across the street and parked it in front of a brown raised ranch house. Underneath the *For Sale* for the Cape Cod, someone had written, *Open House from 12-2 pm on Thursday.* There was no phone number or agent name listed on the sign. How interesting. It looked like David—if that was even his real name—was attempting to lie low.

There were two cars in the driveway, and one was a black BMW. Praise Mrs. Gavelli. "I think we've found our guy," I whispered.

"Should we call Brian?" Josie wanted to know. "Could he at least bring him in for questioning?"

"I'm not sure." While we chatted, a young couple emerged from the house, each one carrying a toddler in their arms—twins from the look of their matching pink jackets. They were adorable, but I was more interested in the man standing behind them.

The couple waited for him to lock the door. He was tall, well over six feet, with broad shoulders apparent through the black overcoat that he wore. My pulse quickened as I watched him. I didn't have much to go on, but the description of the car that Mrs. Gavelli had given me matched perfectly. One of the gunmen had been taller than Mike and prominently built. If he had a cobra tattoo on his wrist, like the one Mike had seen, there might be probable cause for Brian to arrest him or, at the very least, bring him in for questioning. But how could I manage to see his wrist?

We watched as the man shook hands with the couple and they exchanged a few words. He waved to them as their car pulled out of sight, then got into the BMW and zoomed down the street. I placed the car in drive. "Sit tight," I warned Josie and accelerated.

Her mouth fell open. "Are we going on a high-speed chase? You're going to follow him?"

"Get Brian on the phone. I'm not about to lose this guy. It may be our only chance to snag him." The couple had already turned off to the left, while David was gunning it down the main road that branched off to the right. With the highway in the other direction, he was clearly headed into the center of town. Did this mean he'd stop soon? We started to pass strip malls, hotels, and a couple of bars. Maybe David was holed up in a hotel somewhere.

"What should I tell Brian?" Josie clutched her cell in her hand. She leaned over in my direction and gasped. "Holy crap, Sal. You're going seventy in a forty-mile-an-hour zone. You're going to get a ticket for sure."

"Good," I breathed heavily. "Then the cops can pick this guy up. They sure haven't done much so far."

Josie waved me off. "Oh. Hi, Brian, it's Josie. What's that? No, Sal just said that her Pop wasn't doing much today."

I struggled not to roll my eyes. Josie went on to tell Brian about our chase as I watched the BMW make a left-hand turn into the paved parking lot adjacent to a one-story building with gray, clapboard siding. I drove into the next lot, which happened to be a McDonald's, and then waited there until he'd gone inside, not wanting him to see us pull in right behind him. Once David was out of sight, I drove back into the other lot.

Josie stared at the lit-up sign on the building and gulped. "That's right," she said into the phone. "He's stopped, and we're going to follow him inside."

I also stared at the sign and cringed. Of all places, why did he have to come here?

"The address?" Josie was still talking to Brian. Her eyes went wide with alarm as they focused on mine. "Uh, we're at Bottoms Up." She let out a small sigh. "Yeah, that's right. The strip club."

# CHAPTER FOURTEEN

Bottoms Up had a storied and sordid reputation to go along with its name, which pretty much said it all. Like my bakery, the club always seemed to be in the news. Fights over strippers, strippers fighting amongst themselves, and a robbery attempt once engineered by a stripper were just some of the headlines I recalled. The club claimed that it was strictly an entertainment venue, but everyone knew that there were back rooms where the "dancers" provided other things for the male population in return for extraordinary amounts of dough.

My skin started to crawl as I stared at the building. The sign displayed next to the road featured an outlined silhouette of a woman bending over—*way over*—as she served up a drink on a tray.

I cleared my throat. "Ah—I've never been in one of these places before."

"And you think I have?" Josie cocked an eyebrow at me.

"No!" I said quickly. "But—didn't you tell me that Rob—um, he had his bachelor party here, right?"

Josie's nostrils flared. "Don't get me started on that. When I found out about the so-called *party*, I almost knocked his head through a wall. But he swore to me that nothing happened, and I believed him. I've always been able to tell when he was lying anyway." She calmly pulled out a compact to check her hair, then glanced over at me slyly. "Has Mike ever been here?"

My cheeks burned at the question. "He's never mentioned it." Still, what did I know? It wasn't a question that came up at the dinner table. We were apart for ten years after high school while I'd been dating and then married to another man. I'd never asked Mike about the women he'd dated during that time because, truthfully, I didn't want to know. Plus, if he'd been lonely for female companionship, all he had to do was walk down the street. Women flocked to him wherever he went. As Grandma Rosa often said, "Why buy the cow when you can have the butter for free?"

"Honestly, I can't see Mike in a place like this." I quickly changed the subject. "What did Brian say?"

Josie opened her car door. "He's in the middle of an investigation right now. There was a break-in a few streets away from the bakery. He said he'll get here as soon as he can."

"You're kidding, right? Can't he send someone else?" I asked in alarm. Lord knows I didn't want to wait for him *inside*.

She came around to my side of the vehicle. "He didn't come right out and say it, but I'm guessing he thinks this might be a wild goose chase. Brian probably doesn't want us wasting someone else's time on the police force. He said to sit tight and keep this guy in our sights until he gets here." Her lips twisted into a sneer. "Then he said, and I quote, 'Try to be inconspicuous and don't do anything stupid.'"

"Great," I muttered under my breath. We had no choice but to go inside. How the heck would we make ourselves inconspicuous? Two young women going into a strip club in the middle of the day. No, that didn't look weird. "God, I hope no one thinks we're part of the entertainment."

Josie locked her arm through mine as we climbed the steps, our boots thudding loudly on the concrete. "Try to think of it as a compliment. We're over thirty, remember? Our best years are behind us."

"Jeez, I was hoping that I still had a few good ones left," I remarked as she opened the door.

The main room of the club was poorly lighted, most likely on purpose. To our left was a three-sided oak bar, where a couple of patrons were seated. There were mismatched plastic chairs and tables scattered over a black-and-white-checkered floor. It was obvious no one came here for the décor.

The customers were busy watching the lone woman dancing on the crudely constructed wooden stage to my right. There were two shiny poles, about six feet apart from each other, and the woman was busy shimmying up and down one. She had nothing on save a pink G-string. *Ew.* I gasped and quickly swerved my head in the opposite direction. "This is embarrassing," I said to Josie in an undertone.

She smiled hesitantly in return. "Just act like you're having fun. Come on. Maybe the bartender can give us some information."

A heavyset man behind the bar was polishing glasses while he watched a small television that was perched on the edge of the counter. David Webb was nowhere to be seen. Another man sat alone in a darkened corner of the room, sipping a beer while he watched the woman perform. He never took his eyes off her, and the creepy expression on his face made me think he was either a serial killer or a pervert. Maybe both.

"Hey, beautiful ladies." One of the patrons at the bar winked at us and twirled his handlebar mustache while he spoke. He looked close to my father's age. "Want to join us for a drink—and whatever?"

"When hell freezes over," Josie spat out.

The bartender laughed out loud at Josie's comment. He had greasy, sparse hair and small dark eyes set close together. When he flashed us a sly smile, I couldn't help thinking how he was similar to the club—seedy looking and dark. Despite his appearance, he was surprisingly cordial. A nametag on his black polo shirt identified him as Stony.

"That's what I'd expect one of the dancers from The Fuzziest Navel to say. Hello, ladies. Want a drink before your shift?"

"Oh, we're not—" I started to say before Josie kicked me in the shin. "Ouch!"

Josie ignored me and smiled coquettishly at Stony. "Hi, sweet thing. Yeah, dancing does make a girl thirsty. Rum and Coke for me, please, and a ginger ale for my friend." Josie knew I didn't drink. "She never has hard liquor before a shift because it makes her extra giddy with the customers."

Oh, this nightmare needed to be over soon.

Stony started to prepare our drinks. "You ladies must be the ones that Roger hired for tonight's private party. He's not expecting you for a couple of hours, though. He just phoned and won't be here until four o'clock himself."

"Roger—he owns the place now, right?" Josie asked carefully.

"Yeah, for the last ten years," Stony said. "Ever since he bought it from Old Lady Wilson's family after she croaked. Remember? Choked to death on her prime rib one night."

Holy cow. Old women owned strip clubs? What was happening to this world? Did she come here to watch the dancers perform? Did she—*no*. I needed to remove that mental image from my brain. For some strange reason, I tried to imagine Mrs. Gavelli at a strip club. Nope, that wasn't working for me either.

"We always like to be early so that we can check the place out first," I explained. It might be easier than I thought to snoop around and locate David. "Uh, is it okay if we go into one of the back rooms to wait until Roger gets here and tells us what we need to do?"

Stony shot me a puzzled look while my shin took another beating from Josie. "You ladies should already know what to do. Same thing you do at The Fuzziest Navel. Lap dances, pole dancing, and you know—whatever else you work out privately with the customers."

I started to cover my mouth in horror, then faked a cough at the last second. There was no way in hell I was giving some sleazebag customer a lap dance. I wasn't even sure that I knew how. This was so not my area of expertise.

"Cool." Josie winked at Stony. "Yeah, we know what to do. But we would like to freshen up first. Oh, and by the way"—she looked around the room and lifted her nose in the air—"what happened to that hot guy who came in right before us? He looked like my type."

"If you mean that he's got money, then yeah, you've pegged him right." Stony chuckled in an undertone and gave her one of those looks that said she wasn't fooling him. "David's a regular here. He's in the private back room, waiting for Indigo to finish on stage and give him a lap dance. Unfortunately, Indigo isn't feeling well. Wants to go home. She must really be sick if she doesn't care about losing out on a pile of money."

If I had to wear that disgusting G-string in front of leering strangers, I'd be sick too.

Stony stroked the unshaven stubble on his chin

thoughtfully. "Say, do one of you ladies want to step in? I'll tell Roger about it when he gets here, but I'm sure he won't have a problem."

Josie gave a nervous laugh while my insides froze in panic. "Sure thing. Ah, David—he looks familiar. Is his last name Webb by any chance?"

Doubt registered in Stony's eyes. "We never ask their last names. They're here to have fun and forget about real life for a while." He leaned forward on the bar. "Have you entertained this guy before?"

"Not me," Josie admitted. "But I think a friend of mine has. Her name is Coco."

She was so much better at this lying gig than me. "He has a deep voice, right? Like a smoker's?" I asked.

Stony nodded and grabbed a notepad that was sitting next to the register. He pointed to his nametag. "I'm Stony, by the way. Roger didn't leave your names, so go ahead and give them to me."

My mind was drawing a blank. I'd never thought about stripper names before. What was a good one to use—Shauna? Candy? Maybe Bambi?

Josie kicked my shin again, and I was positive it was black and blue by now. "I'm Cinnamon," she giggled. "And this is my friend, Sugar."

The customer who'd tried to pick us up threw back his head and laughed. "Did you ladies work at a bakery in a previous life?"

Josie impishly batted her eyelashes at the man, but I watched her hands ball into fists at her sides. "It's Cin for short. As in sinfully delicious."

Okay, now she'd gone a bit too far.

"Nice." Stony laughed as he wrote the names down, then gave the customer a scornful look. "Wes, how stupid are you? You know that strippers never give their real names." He glanced up at us. "You brought your G-strings, right?"

Oh. My. God. How were we going to get out of this mess? There was probably a greasy pole in the seedy back room waiting for me to slide off it. Or with my luck, I'd try to wrap my leg around the pole and both would break in the process. Where was my mother when I needed her?

"Ain't got mine," Josie said cheerily. "The dude I was with earlier wanted to keep it for a trophy. Got any extras lying around?"

My stomach flip-flopped as I listened to her. Josie seemed to be a natural at this whole stripper lingo thing, which was making me a bit uncomfortable.

"Roger won't put up with a customer doing that here," Stony assured her. "Those outfits cost money, especially with all that glitter glued on them. Yeah, you'll find a couple of extras in dressing room A." He glanced at Josie then at me. "I'm not sure if the ones in there will fit Sugar, though. She's got a little more meat on her bones than most of the other ladies. No offense, honey."

Stony had succeeded in lighting a fire under me. "What does *that* mean?" I asked in a shrill voice. It was one thing to refuse to wear a G-string but quite another to be told that I was too fat for one. "That was totally uncalled for."

Stony held up a hand in defense. "Hey, no need to take it personally, love. I'm sure David will prefer you to saggy Indigo. You're the type he goes crazy over. He loves cute-looking brunettes, especially those with a little extra beef on them."

"That's not beef, it's cheesecake," Josie whispered to me.

"Wow, that's cold," I snapped back.

Indigo walked off the stage and toward us. She had light brown, feathered hair and a face with such tightly stretched skin that I figured she must be one of Botox's biggest supporters. It was difficult to ignore the fact that she was still topless, and Stony's remark about her sagging body parts seemed to be correct. Embarrassed, I averted my eyes.

Indigo accepted the glass Stony slid across the bar to her. "Stone, I gotta go. I think I'm coming down with the flu. Chastity should be here soon. Is it okay if I head out?"

"No problem," Stony assured her as she drank down the contents of the glass in one gulp. It smelled like straight vodka to me. "These two ladies can cover until she gets here."

Indigo glanced casually at Josie, and then her eyes scanned me up and down. She exhaled sharply. "Great. You're going to ruin everything."

I braced myself for another insult. "What do you mean by that?"

Her white teeth gleamed in a smile as she leaned her ample chest against the side of the bar. "Davey in the back room is one of our best clients, and you look like his type. If you're any good, he's going to request you from now on, and then the rest of us will be left out in the cold."

Okay, Brian needed to get here *now*.

"Don't keep him waiting," Indigo cautioned as she turned on her stiletto and moved in the direction of the dressing room. "He won't tip as well if you do."

Stony nodded at Josie. "You can take the pole out here, Cin, while your friend entertains David."

Josie's face froze at his words. Self-assured Cinnamon seemed to have lost her spice.

"Uh, we prefer to work as a team," I said quickly. "You know, a package deal. Roger said we could stay together."

Stony scratched the top of his head thoughtfully. "He did? That's pretty unusual."

"Hey." My tone was sharp and surprised everyone at the bar, including myself. "We're not your ordinary strippers. Roger knows this and said we could make our own rules for the day. We've got a busy schedule, ya know? We're doing him a big favor by being here, and don't forget it."

Stony stared at me in amazement, and so did Josie. "Okay, okay," he said, holding up his hand in defense. "Hurry up back there and get changed." He turned to refill Wes's beer glass and shook his head in disbelief. "Jeez. Equal rights for strippers now. What's next?"

"We're not strippers. We're exotic dancers," I called out as Josie practically dragged me into dressing room A.

Once inside, she raised an eyebrow at me. "What the heck is wrong with you? You almost ruined everything."

"Gee, I don't know." Sarcasm dripped from my voice. "Maybe the thought of having to give a stranger a lap dance has something to do with it? Jos, I can't do this! It's disgusting! I can barely slow dance!"

She glanced at me in disbelief. "You've never even given Mike one?"

It was far too warm in here. "Okay, that's private information. Plus, what if David expects something—else?" I might drop dead of fright.

Josie stared at me like I was some type of moron. "He's a *man*, Sal. Of course he's going to want something else."

"It was a mistake to come here," I admitted. "I didn't know we'd end up—doing *this!* Isn't there some other way that we can keep David Webb here without having to take our clothes off?" I wasn't sure whether to throw up or run screaming out of the building.

Josie checked her watch and frowned. "Brian should be here soon. At least I hope so. Try not to panic."

Too late.

Indigo walked past us, and I was relieved that she was now wearing clothes. She had on a dark blue tweed coat and carried a large black leather Louis Vuitton bag. "Have fun," she told us. "There are some extra G-strings in the dressing table. Don't worry. They've been washed."

*Gross.* After she left, Josie and I examined the garments inside the table. The G-strings all looked incredibly tiny in size, but Josie and her size six figure could easily fit into one. *I* was a different story, though.

I gingerly picked up a red one that had blue and white stars glued on it. Maybe Indigo wore this one on the Fourth of July. "There's no way that I'm wearing this," I said, "even if it's been soaked in bleach. What is this—a stripper's bargain basement?"

Josie pointed a finger nervously at the adjoining door that was marked *Private. Customers and Dancers Inside.* She swallowed hard. "David Webb is in there, waiting for his lap dance. We can't afford to have him leave, Sal. This might be your only chance to nab him."

Bile rose in the back of my throat. Although I was usually comfortable with my weight, there were times when I became self-conscious, especially during bikini season. Mike always assured me that I looked gorgeous in everything, but I wasn't sure that I could carry this off. If I'd known we were going to chase some guy to an exotic dancer's club, and that I'd have to wear a G-string to entertain him, I would have done my homework first. At the very least, I would have talked to my mother. Maria Muccio was no stripper, but she'd once modeled for a lingerie magazine, and I had no doubt she could have provided me with a few pointers. Or at least advised me to run for the hills.

"Let's see if we can try this with clothes on first." I looked inside the dressing table again and found a short white skirt tucked away in the back of one of the drawers. It came to about midthigh on me and was sheer, covered with red, blue, and green feathers. Yeah, I'd heard that the ostrich look was in this year.

I pulled off my jeans and squeezed the skirt on over my underwear. It was a little snug, but I made it work. Then I proceeded to tie up the ends of the pink, V-neck T-shirt that I was wearing to show some bare skin. We'd just had these shirts made for the bakery. In blue lettering across my chest, the shirt read *Get a Free Fortune*. Good grief. What would David Webb think when he read my shirt? I didn't want to find out.

I watched in envy as Josie slipped on a pair of Daisy Duke–type jean shorts she'd found in the closet. They looked like a size zero to me and made her shapely legs even more fabulous. She tied up her T-shirt same as me and then glanced down at the rubber-soled black boots she was wearing. "These aren't going to cut it."

There was a shoe rack in the bottom of the closet that contained a few pairs of cheap stilettos—covered in glitter, of course. That seemed to be a requirement for everything at Bottoms Up. Josie winced in pain as she shoved her feet into a pair of red sandals. "These are at least a size too small for me."

I glanced down at my own knee-high, black leather boots with a low heel. "I'm leaving these on. This way I'm armed if I have to kick him in the face."

Josie looked impressed. "You go, girlfriend. That outfit is kind of cute on you. Different, but cute."

"Hey!" We both jumped at the sound of a deep male voice bellowing from the other side of the door. "Another gin and tonic, Stony. *Now.* And if I've got to wait any longer for my dancer, I'll take my business *and* money elsewhere."

## CHAPTER FIFTEEN

"I'll get the drink," Josie whispered. "You entertain him."

Panic rose inside me. "Wait—*what?* How am I supposed to entertain him?"

Josie rolled her eyes and gave me a slight push toward the door. "Go show him some of that special Muccio charm." She shoved a plastic bag with two fortune cookies into my hand. "Danny asked me to bring these home. Use them to distract him. It's all I've got, Sugar."

"Well, thanks a lot," I snapped as she ran out of the dressing room and back to the bar. *I can do this. No problem. Brian will be here any second.* With a deep breath, I opened the door to the private room. My mouth opened in surprise. I wasn't sure what I expected, but certainly not this.

The lighting in the room was dim, accompanied by the Barry White tune "Ecstasy" playing seductively in the background. It was as if I'd stepped back in time. David Webb was lying on a leopard-design couch, something that looked faintly reminiscent of the 1970s. From the stale smell in the room, it might have even been that old. David was watching a porn flick on the flat screen television mounted to the wall. On the opposite side of the room was a small wooden dance floor with another pole in the center of it. Gee, that was a surprise.

David set his drink down on the vomit green-colored coffee table and sat up when he heard me come in. His eyes scanned me up and down, and then a broad smile broke across his face. A smile that sent chills through me.

"Well, well. That's quite an interesting outfit," he said. "And who might you be, gorgeous?"

His voice was exactly as Mike had described the

gunman's—husky and deep. Even from a few feet away, I could smell cigarette smoke on him that mixed with the scent of Aqua Velva. Did men other than my father still wear that stuff?

David had on a zebra-print Speedo and nothing else. I cringed inwardly at the sight of him and desperately wished that I was on another planet. His upper arms and chest rippled with muscles, and I could imagine him crushing me with one single blow. Then I stared down at his wrist and froze.

There it was—the tattoo. A cobra with red eyes. Creepy and original. Bingo. I was convinced this was our guy.

David waved a hand in front of my face and grinned. "Checking out the merchandise already, huh? Come closer, sugar. What'd you say your name was?"

"Yes."

He stared at me blankly. "Yes, what?"

"Sugar. That's my name," I said in a feeble tone.

He patted his lap. "Well, come on over and let's get to know each other better, Sugar."

I glanced back at the door in a blind panic. Where the heck was Josie? How long did it take to get a drink in this dive? In desperation, I tried to laugh, but it came out sounding more like a wheezy cough. "Um, I thought maybe we could play a game first."

He stared down at my hand with the fortune cookies and grinned. "I like games. What kind of toys did you bring?'

"Fortune cookies." I tried to giggle seductively. "They're part of my act."

David looked at me like I'd been smoking something. "You're a little strange, but it doesn't matter. You're hot, and I happen to like a lady who's a bit different. Whips and chains get boring after a while."

*Dear Lord. Josie, did you get lost?*

David eyed the fortune cookies with mild curiosity. "Wow, what do you do with those? Is it painful?"

Heaven help me. I tried to avoid looking at his exposed skin and, instead, stared down at the floor. Mike was in great physical shape, thanks to constant running and weight lifting, but David had him beat by a mile. This guy was like a bear on steroids. He had muscles everywhere I looked—or tried not to look, that is.

"Um, I'm going to tell your fortune." My voice trembled as I stretched my hand forward to give him a cookie.

David didn't take it. His dark, calculating eyes were pinned on me, and I didn't like the expression I read in them. "You open it for me, sexy."

Having no choice, I cracked open the cookie and stared down at the message. Holy cow. Was this some sick joke? *You should have stayed home. This one is going to cost you.* What I really wanted to know—was the message for me or for David?

"What's it say?" he asked.

"Oh, *that*." I shoved the message into my boot and tried to giggle, but my nerves were getting the best of me. "It says that you're charming and all the ladies love you."

His dark eyes scanned me up and down again, lingering a bit too long on my chest. "Got that right. Damn, you're way better than saggy Indigo. What's your nightly rate?"

Did Josie forget me and decide to go home? "I doubt that you can afford me," I said lightly and walked across the room to pick up the remote for the television. "How about we watch a *Friends* rerun?"

"Whatever gets you in the mood, Sugar. I once had a dancer who liked to watch *Scooby-Doo* during her act. And no worries, I can *definitely* afford you."

"Oh, yeah?" I clicked through the channels, trying to gain some much-needed time. "What do you do for a living?"

"I build homes," he said in an arrogant tone.

"Really?" *You also steal and kill people.* "Do you mean modular ones?"

"No, not the manufactured kind. I've built a few in the area, and they were profitable, but it's time to move on and find a new location. I'm coming into a nice sum of money very soon. After it's safely tucked away in my pocket, I'll be taking off for a warmer climate. I hate Northeast weather."

That's why he was still in town. Had Trevor been keeping the money from his partners? If so, where was it now?

"Enough of the television," he said. "Put that remote down and come sit on my lap."

Having no choice, I whirled around to face him.

Although he still wore a smile and his tone was friendly, his dark eyes were ice cold. They seemed incapable of emotion, and I shivered. I'd seen eyes like that before—on killers.

"Here I am," Josie said breezily as she hurried into the room with a drink in one hand and a bowl of peanuts in the other. She placed the items down on the puke-colored coffee table and gave David a superior smile. "Hi there, handsome. I'm Cinnamon."

David looked her over without comment, his eyes lingering on her perfect, lithe legs in the tight short shorts, and then he dismissed her with a wave of his hand. "You're nice-looking, but I prefer brunettes. No offense, Cin."

Josie whispered in my ear. "It took forever for Stony to get off the phone and make the freaking drink. I was about ready to fix it myself."

David came up behind me, placing his hands on my waist while I was pretending to watch television, and I tried not to stiffen. "Dance for Daddy, Sugar."

I locked eyes with Josie, and the panic in mine must have mirrored her own. Josie knew that I had two left feet. Mike always teased me about stepping on his toes when we slow danced. This was not going to end well.

Josie cleared her throat nervously. "Hey, hot stuff," she said to David. "We're having a special deal today. Two dancers for the price of one."

He frowned at her. "You can leave now, Cin. Tell Roger thanks, but no thanks. Sugar here's exactly my type. We're going to have fun tonight. Just don't tell the girlfriend," he laughed.

My mouth dropped open. "You have a girlfriend?"

He shrugged. "Yeah. So what? Hey, a man has needs. One woman can't take care of all this." He flexed the muscles in his arm.

"Boy, that's the truth," Josie mumbled.

David pulled a fifty-dollar bill out of his wallet. "My girl is quite outspoken. She loves it when I call her boss. I'm crazy about her, but every guy needs a little variety now and then." He waved the bill at me. "Now, I said to dance. Cin, I think there's a pole in the bar with your name on it."

"Where the heck is Brian?" I whispered to Josie. Maybe

he thought I was like the boy who cried wolf one too many times and had decided to let me deal with this on my own. If that was the case, stick a fork in me because I was done.

I did some simple moves with my feet and jiggled my hips back and forth while David burst out laughing. "Okay, stop with the jokes, Sugar, and lose the outfit."

"Oh, but she's just getting warmed up," Josie said. "The best part is yet to come."

"That's right." I attempted a spin, and my left boot caught the leg of the coffee table. With a gasp, I tripped and went sprawling across the floor. Josie started toward me, but David beat her to it. He reached down and lifted me from the floor with one hand.

"Get lost, Cin." His former, lighthearted tone was now tinged with irritation. His hand released mine and went around my waist, pulling me tightly against him. Then he leaned down and kissed my neck. "I've never seen such a clumsy dancer before. Something tells me that your talents must lie elsewhere."

His hand went toward my chest, and my instinctive reaction was to shriek and smack it away. My engagement ring caught his lip, and blood immediately began to gush from it. David let out a groan and brought a hand to his mouth.

"Ow! What the hell, Sugar!" A string of four-letter swear words popped out from between his blood-covered lips as he fell heavily back onto the couch. He grabbed a cocktail napkin and brought it to his mouth then lunged forward, his eyes dark and dangerous as they settled on me. He grabbed me tightly around the wrist, and I yelped in pain. "You're going to pay for that, you little tease."

In desperation, I fought to free myself as he shoved me to the floor and wrenched my arm behind my back. My voice was muffled as he pushed my face into the thick, foul-smelling carpeting. I struggled, but it was to no avail—the man was too strong for me. Josie let out a bloodcurdling yell like Tarzan, and David responded with an *oof,* releasing his hold on me. I rose from the floor in time to see David throw Josie off his back. Someone pounded on the door, and we all froze in response.

"Police. We're coming in." The voice sounded like it belonged to Adam.

David looked from me to Josie and muttered an expletive under his breath. "This was a setup." Without saying anything further, he picked up a chair and hurled it at the window. The glass shattered into a hundred pieces as he quickly grabbed a blanket off the couch and hoisted his almost naked body through the window frame. Josie and I each caught him around a bare, hairy leg.

"Get in here!" Josie screeched at Adam.

"You must have locked it when you came in," I said to her as we struggled. There was no time to unlock the door while we both tried to avoid being kicked in the face by gorilla man.

A loud thud sounded behind us, and the door flew open. Brian and Adam both entered the room with their guns drawn. "Freeze!" Adam said.

"He has the same tattoo on his wrist that Mike described—the cobra." I panted, still breathing heavy from my exertion.

Brian reached forward and, with one swift movement, jerked David out of the window and onto the floor. Before David could even attempt to move, Brian had cuffed his hands behind his back and Adam had started to read him his rights.

"What the hell's going on here? This club is legit. I pay for my drinks and the entertainment. Why are you arresting me?"

"Anything you say can and *will* be held against you." Adam put special emphasis on the word.

David ignored him and glowered at Josie and me. "These two should be arrested for impersonating strippers. Sugar here can't even dance without falling over."

Brian's mouth twitched slightly at the corners as he pulled David to his feet. "We're arresting you for armed robbery at the Colwestern Mini-Mart on March 23rd and the murder of Trevor Parks."

David cursed angrily under his breath. "I didn't shoot him. I didn't kill anyone. Honest."

His words stopped me cold. I remembered Mike saying that the shorter guy had been the one to shoot Trevor. I crouched next to him on the floor. "Did you shoot my husband?" I had to see his face as I asked the question.

"Sally." Brian held up a hand and gestured for me to move away. "Don't worry. We'll take it from here."

I continued to stare at David. Eyes that had been ogling me only minutes before now avoided me like the plague. "Answer me," I hissed.

"Come on, sweetheart." Josie wrapped an arm around me. "Brian will take care of this lowlife."

"I said I didn't kill anyone." David wouldn't look at me.

"Weren't you listening?" Adam asked sharply. "I just read you your rights." Without another word he lifted David to his feet and shoved him toward the main room of the bar.

Josie pointed at David's clothes on the couch. "He might get cold without those, Adam."

Adam draped the jacket around David's shoulders and picked up the rest of his clothes. A crowd of curious onlookers, Stony included, were elbowing each other at the bar for a peek into the private room.

"I'll put him in the car," Adam called over his shoulder to Brian. "Will you be long?"

Brian shook his head. "Give me a minute." He looked at me and then seemed to really see me for the very first time—or at least my outfit. His eyes narrowed as he took in the short, sheer skirt and my now cropped T-shirt then jerked his head up to meet my gaze. His cheeks were tinged a bright red. "What the hell have you got on?" he asked, sounding like my father.

The words made me even more self-conscious. In desperation, I reached for the leopard-striped throw blanket on the back of the matching couch and wrapped it around me before I could think twice about it. Maybe some women could carry this outfit off, like my mother, but I wasn't one of them.

Josie seemed to be enjoying this. "David Webb liked Sal," she told Brian. "He was dying for a lap dance."

"If you breathe a word of this to Mike, you're dead," I warned.

"At least we didn't have to wear the used G-strings," Josie said thoughtfully.

Brian looked at her like she had corn growing out of her ears, and then his eyes lowered to the short shorts she had on. He cleared his throat and stared at the television screen. Another mistake. A new porn flick had just come on. He quickly found the remote and, thankfully, shut it off. "I'm not sure how you ladies managed to get yourself into this mess, but then again, nothing surprises me where either of you are concerned."

"Aw, Brian," Josie teased. "What a lovely thing to say."

A muscle ticked in Brian's jaw. "Didn't you stop to think when you followed that guy in here that it might lead to something you weren't prepared to deal with? You both happen to be very attractive, and this is an entertainment venue—sort of. Women dance topless on the stage out there. Where did you think you were going—to a bake sale?"

Josie started to laugh hysterically while I nudged her in the side. Brian was still the law, and we were probably only one step away from being placed in handcuffs ourselves.

"We got a lead from Laura Pusatere—the woman Trevor helped build the house for," I explained. "She told me that a man named David Webb sold them the house and that he had mentioned another one he was building on Fairlawn Avenue."

"Sal and I drove over, and we saw a man who fit David's description showing a house—a for sale by owner," Josie continued. "When he got into his car, we decided to follow him. That's when I called you. We certainly didn't know he was coming *here*, Brian."

"You should have left it up to the police," Brian said.

I bit into my lower lip, trying to control my temper. "But you didn't even act like it was an emergency on the phone. And I was not going to risk losing this guy. I think I have an idea why he or his partner killed Trevor. Trevor must have been sitting on some money, and David's not leaving town until he gets his share."

"But why kill the guy if you don't even know where the money is?" Josie asked.

Brian broke in. "Well, he won't be setting foot in here again for a long time. If those fingerprints we lifted from the mini-mart match his, he's going to be spending a lot of quality years in a jail cell."

# CHAPTER SIXTEEN

---

Since Josie and I were not allowed to be present while the police questioned David, I dropped her off at her house. Brian had promised to call me tonight and relay everything that happened, if I promised not to show up at the police station. Brian would not break the rules, even for me, and I certainly didn't expect him to. It was still sad to think about his leaving town, but if I asked him to reconsider, he might interpret it the wrong way.

When I arrived home, Grandma Rosa was putting supper on the table. The house smelled wonderful. She'd fixed a marvelous garden salad with balsamic dressing, a large platter of antipasto, homemade bread, pasta fagioli, and tiramisu for dessert.

Grandma Rosa rolled her eyes at me as I pecked her on the cheek. "Your husband is in the spare bedroom. He said he is doing some paperwork."

Uh-oh. I knew what he was really doing. With apprehension, I opened the door and peeked in. He was sitting at the desk, his ledger in front of him along with a pile of receipts. He was wearing jeans and nothing else. He even made an arm sling look sexy. His dark blue eyes bore into mine and didn't look happy. "I was wondering where you went," he said.

This wasn't the best time to tell him that I'd been temporarily employed at Bottoms Up for the afternoon and came close to being attacked by the Hulk himself. I'd save it for another time—maybe. I wrapped an arm around him and ran my fingers through his dark, unruly hair. "Sweetheart, you shouldn't be out of bed."

"That is what I told him," Grandma Rosa said from behind me. "He is a stubborn one. Dinner is ready when you two get done talking. Unless Mike would like to have his in bed."

He shook his head. "No thanks, Rosa. I can't take this lying down bit anymore."

Eight weeks of no work. I blew out a sigh. He was going to go crazy and probably drive me nuts in the process as well.

After Grandma Rosa had returned to the kitchen, Mike looked up at me, his jaw set in a determined lock. "I searched through all my records. From what I can figure, my so-called *friend* Trevor ripped us off for about fifty grand, including the money I got paid for the renovation job. This is going to hurt us big-time, Sal."

It was worse than I'd imagined, but I tried not to show my concern and pecked him softly on the lips. "Don't beat yourself up over this. It could have happened to anyone."

Mike banged his good hand down on the top of the desk with such force it made me jump. "I trusted that SOB," Mike said between gritted teeth. "There are very few people in this world I trust and look what it got me. Look what it's done for both of us."

"But it's not your fault," I protested.

He shook his head in disgust. "The way I figure—it must have all started when I was so consumed with getting that damned foundation done for the mansion before the first snowfall back in December. Remember?"

I nodded, recalling how on Christmas Eve he'd gotten home later than usual. I'd planned a romantic dinner for us with candles and hoped we'd enjoy a roaring fire, open our gifts, and spend the rest of the night in each other's arms. Mike had fallen asleep on the couch before any of that could take place.

"You were working around the clock. You can't keep track of everything." I'd offered to help him with the paperwork back then, but he'd assured me he was fine. Mike knew I had a lot going on as well, since Christmas was always a busy time for the bakery.

Mike closed his eyes. "I was stupid. I needed someone to rely on and wanted it to be Trevor. He arranged for deliveries to the sites and ordered parts for his personal use. Now that I look back, I remember scanning one invoice and thinking there was too much sheetrock. Then I got distracted with something else and forgot about it." He clenched his teeth in anger. "That jerk was padding my jobs."

My brow wrinkled. "I don't understand."

"He needed five pieces of sheetrock for that job," Mike explained. "I asked him about it, and he said it was a misprint—five, not fifty pieces. But I see now that I was charged for the fifty. He was helping himself to the extra and using it for his home sale projects with his buddy." He crumpled the sheet into a ball and threw it across the room. "Damn it. I should have been more careful."

It broke my heart to see him blame himself, but there was nothing I could do. My phone pinged from my back jeans pocket. I drew it out and glanced at the screen then sucked in a deep breath.

"More good news?" Mike asked.

"Actually, yes. The guy who shot you—his name is David Webb—was picked up this afternoon by the police. Brian texted me and said that they found a gun in his glove compartment. It matches the one used at the market."

"The guy with the cobra tattoo? Muscular build? How did they find him?" He stared up at me with suspicion etched into his face. My own must have been readable because he sighed. "You had something to do with it, didn't you?"

"Sort of." There was no way I was going to tell him about David Webb and his attempts to manhandle me. Even with one good arm, he'd be out of the chair and down to the police station in minutes. "Josie and I tailed him from another house that he's trying to sell."

"You mean another house that our money paid for," Mike said bitterly. "What about the little guy who killed Trevor? The one with the squeaky voice?"

"We don't know who or where he is yet. Hopefully David will make a full confession to Brian."

Mike slumped forward heavily in the chair. "I was stupid, Sal. So stupid. You married an idiot."

"Stop it!" I said angrily. "You're not stupid. You're hardworking, kind, and a beautiful man. I won't have you doing this to yourself. Trevor took advantage of us, and there were others too. He even stole money from his own sister."

"That son of a—" Mike stopped when he saw my grandmother standing in the doorway.

"Enough of this," she said sharply. "Dinner is getting cold. You need to get your strength back, and Sally must eat too. Things will work out, so do not spend time worrying. There is no sense in crying over spilled coffee."

A slow smile spread across Mike's face. "I think you mean milk, Rosa."

"That is good too. Now come."

With a sigh, Mike got out of the chair and stuck his left arm into the sleeve of a gray flannel shirt. I was ready to support him, but he didn't need my help. He wrapped his arm around my shoulders, and we made our way to the dinner table. My stomach rumbled when I looked at all the food. It was good to have an appetite again, and Grandma Rosa was right. Things would get better soon—I was confident of that.

"*Cara mia*," my grandmother said after we'd all sat down. "While you were out this afternoon, that crazy television anchor came by and asked for you. He is the one who interviewed your father, remember? The man named Jerry Moron."

I almost choked on a piece of bread. "His name is Jerry Maroon, Grandma."

"Whatever. He wanted to know if Mike would be up to an interview tomorrow morning. He left his card but said you had one already. He said to call him anytime and that he would only need about an hour's notice."

"I'll bet he does," Mike muttered. "All those guys care about is building the ratings for their shows."

I placed my hand on top of his. "We might be able to work this to our advantage."

Grandma Rosa poured some espresso into a demitasse cup. She offered us one, but we both shook our heads. The coffee was strong—stronger than what I usually drank. "He said that he could get a cameraman and do the interview live in your living room. It would be like the one he did for your papa. Nutsy cookie," she mumbled.

Mike laughed. "Who? Jerry or Domenic?"

"Both," she muttered.

"Oh, man." I put a hand to my mouth. "I forgot to watch Dad's interview. He's going to be upset."

"Do not worry," Grandma Rosa assured me. "He had it recorded and plans to show it at the book signing. When are you going to have Mike's birthday dinner?"

"I thought we could do it Sunday night, a day after the signing. As long as it works for everyone."

Mike stared down into his half-eaten bowl of soup. "I'm really not in the mood for a party, Sal."

I touched his hand. "It's not only for you. I think I need a little pick-me-up too."

He looked up, and the sorrow in his eyes saddened me. "I'm sorry, baby. As usual, I was only thinking about myself."

"You're not," I protested. "I thought it might help lighten the mood a bit."

"I will make the dinner this time," Grandma Rosa announced. "*Cara mia*, you need to get some rest. Both of you are exhausted."

She was right. We were tired—Mike from pain and medication and me from the blows that life had been dealing us.

"Okay, fine, maybe you're right," Mike conceded. "With any luck, the other guy will be in custody by then too."

The doorbell rang, and I held up a hand to Grandma Rosa. "I'll get it."

Spike trotted over to the front door with me. I glanced through the small window and saw Brian standing there.

"Come on in." I held the door open wide. "Would you like to join us for dinner?"

"No thanks. I've already eaten." He shut the door behind him and reached down to pet Spike. "I was going to text you again, but since I was nearby, I figured it would be just as easy to stop by and talk to Mike as well."

Mike stood, and Brian gestured for him to sit back down. "Don't get up on my account. How are you feeling?"

"I'd feel a lot better if you told me both of those two scumbags were now in custody." Mike's eyes searched his face for confirmation.

Brian sat in the one empty chair opposite me. "I wish it was that simple. First off, David Webb's real name is Benjamin Silvers, and he's originally from Virginia."

Mike nodded at me. "That's the guy who gave Trevor a reference. All part of the setup, I guess."

"Did Trevor actually work for him?" I asked.

"Not quite," Brian said smoothly. "We ran a check on Benjamin and found he's wanted in Virginia for embezzlement and theft. It seems that he's also quite the computer hacker. He stole the identity of a David Webb from Saratoga, New York. The real David Webb is a licensed real estate attorney."

"That was certainly convenient for their so-called business," I muttered.

"The guy did his homework," Brian agreed. "This way, when he sold a house, he could offer proof that he was also an attorney if anyone asked to see his credentials. From the sound of things, David was only dealing with buyers who brought cash to the table so that there was no need to involve a bank. The inspections all checked out since the construction was good, the buyers got a discount, and he gave the agents a larger commission than usual. Plus, he had the certificate of occupancy and building permit, which is all the buyers and agent cared about besides the inspections."

I was confused. "How did Trevor get ahold of the money then, if it was all going to David?"

"Apparently David, I mean Benjamin, wasn't as clever as we thought. For the last couple of homes, Trevor went with him to close the deals and collected the money, saying he was investing most of it in the stock market for them. After a while David finally got suspicious, and when he confronted Trevor, his buddy told him it was every man for himself."

"Where's the money then? Tina told me she can't even pay her rent," I pointed out.

Brian shrugged. "It could be a front. A lot of times people won't fix up their house or say they're broke for this very reason. For all we know, the cash might be in their apartment and she was involved too."

"What about the other gunmen? Did this joker Benjamin give him up?" Mike asked.

Brian shook his head. "He wouldn't say much until his lawyer arrived, but he did keep repeating that he hadn't killed anyone. You know, Sally, the same thing he was saying at the strip club."

My stomach constricted. *Great. Thanks for that, Brian.*

Mike gripped the table tightly with his good hand. "What strip club?"

"I told you that we followed David," I said uneasily. "Turns out, that's where he went—ah, to Bottoms Up."

Mike's blue eyes resembled steel as he glared at Brian. "Did you use my wife as some kind of bait for that freak?"

"It wasn't anything like that," I protested. "Josie and I had a drink and talked with him until the cops arrived." Okay, so I'd conveniently skipped over a few parts, but were they necessary to bring up now?

Brian glanced from me to Mike, and his face colored slightly. Thankfully he didn't contradict my story. "After Benjamin and his attorney met in private and he learned we'd discovered the gun in his car, he agreed to talk to me. He told me select things, though—about how he'd first met Trevor, and admitted that his gun went off accidentally when Mike jumped forward." He turned his attention back to Mike. "He claims he didn't mean to shoot you, and a couple of eye witnesses have concurred with this. However, he wouldn't tell me anything about the other gunman."

"Why is he protecting this guy?" I asked angrily. "Do you think it's a relative? Maybe his brother? A good friend?"

"He's probably holding out for a deal," Brian remarked. "It's already been hinted at."

"Figures." This discussion was starting to make my blood boil. "And he's going to get one, isn't he?"

"That's not up to me," Brian said honestly. "But yes, there's a chance he may get what he wants if he gives us information on his partner—the person who killed Trevor Parks."

"Does the media know that this David, I mean Benjamin—whatever the hell his name is," Mike said with sarcasm, "is in custody?"

Brian shook his head. "We're keeping it quiet for now, in hopes he might lead us to the other gunman. We've got an officer stationed at Benjamin's home in Colgate in case he shows up there."

"David, err, Benjamin mentioned a girlfriend to me," I said suddenly.

Brian raised an eyebrow. "He didn't say anything about a lady friend. Does she live with him?"

I shrugged. "No idea. Their relationship seemed kind of casual." If this woman had known what Benjamin had been doing earlier today, she would have choked the life out of him. It sickened me to realize this guy would serve less time if he helped the police, but sadly, that was the way things worked in our world. "He must have told you something else. Did he say anything about the other gunman? How did he and Trevor meet?"

"Apparently Benjamin and Trevor met about a year ago when they worked at a large construction company in Virginia together," Brian said.

"Roberts Construction?" I asked. "That's the name his ex-wife, Erica, gave me, but I never called the owner."

Brian nodded. "That's right. From what Benjamin says, the owner wasn't aware at first that Trevor had ripped him off. He left before they caught on. Trevor worked in purchasing for a while and began doing the same thing he did to Mike, stealing materials. One night, Benjamin returned to a job site when he realized he'd forgotten something. He spotted Trevor smuggling an order into his car that had been left there earlier. Trevor offered to cut him in for his silence. Thus the start of a true friendship was born."

We all did a universal eye roll at this remark.

"When Trevor moved here after his divorce, Benjamin decided to come along too and see what deals they could find. Benjamin knew all about the scheme to steal from your business, Mike, and apparently you weren't the first one Trevor pulled this on."

"Gee, that makes me feel better," Mike said bitterly.

Brian went on. "Like I said before, when he found out Trevor was freezing him out, he refused to go away. Benjamin took to following Trevor around and told him if he didn't get his share, he'd make trouble. Finally, Trevor agreed to meet him outside a local restaurant with some cash."

"That must have been when Mrs. Gavelli spotted him," I said excitedly.

"Benjamin said that Trevor handed him an envelope full of money, but most of it turned out to be dollar bills," Brian explained. "Trevor told him that he was on his own from now on, and Benjamin was furious. What did Trevor care if Benjamin turned him in for stealing from Roberts Construction, especially since Benjamin was guilty of it too. Well, Benjamin wasn't going to stand for being cheated and told his anonymous friend—aka the other gunman—about it. His friend decided that they should start threatening Trevor."

"The other gunman—he was in on it from the beginning?" Mike asked.

"According to Benjamin, no," Brian said. "The other gunman offered to help when Benjamin told him what Trevor had done."

This seemed strange to me. Why would this other person go the extra mile for Benjamin and put themselves at risk if they weren't involved in the larceny?

"They both decided to keep Trevor in their sights," Brian continued. "I guess they thought he'd lead them to the money eventually. The money that Benjamin says belongs to him. What's strange is that he knew it wasn't in Trevor's bank account. Why Trevor would share that information with Benjamin, I have no idea."

Something here didn't fit, but I couldn't put my finger on what it was.

"They followed Mike and Trevor to the mini-mart that night and decided to rough them up when they came back outside. They put on ski masks in case anyone recognized them. But Benjamin's friend got antsy and ran inside the market. He said that he had no choice but to follow."

"So Trevor was killed for the money he was keeping. Some of which was *our* money," Mike said tightly. "But why kill him until you knew where it was? That doesn't make any sense."

"Because it wasn't only about the money," I said thoughtfully.

Both men and Grandma Rosa looked over at me.

"I think there's more to this," I explained. "Benjamin isn't telling you everything, Brian. These guys wanted Trevor out of the way for some other reason too. It feels like revenge to me."

Brian looked impressed. "Interesting theory, Sally. Keep it up, and you may put me out of a job."

Mike picked up my hand and kissed it. "Way to go, Betsy Drew. You always come through."

"Nancy Drew," Grandma Rosa corrected him.

We all smiled at this one. My grandmother's subtle way of getting even with us for correcting her over the years.

"I could be wrong." But I didn't think I was. Who was this other guy Benjamin had taken up with? Was it someone connected to Trevor—a friend or relative? Did Tina or Erica know, or were they involved? What about Trevor's brother, Curtis, who hated the sight of him? Morgan claimed to love her brother, but he had stolen money from her too. Had she hired someone to get revenge?

Mike blew out a sigh. "We're not going to get our money back, are we?"

Brian looked grim. "I don't know, Mike. Try to think positive, okay? If we can get Benjamin to talk to us about this other guy, maybe it will all come together."

Sure, money wasn't everything, but Mike and I worked hard for what we had. The most important thing was that my husband was alive, and I hadn't lost sight of that fact. This was our livelihood, though. We didn't deserve to be going through this, and the sad part was that others had suffered as well. It needed to stop—and now.

"I'm planning to call Jerry Maroon tonight and go ahead with the television interview for tomorrow as planned." I turned to Mike. "If it's okay with you, babe."

Mike nodded. "Yeah, I'll talk to him. But he'd better understand I'm not doing this for sympathy or for people to send me donations." He sighed heavily "I realize we may never get our money back. It is what it is. But at least I'll have the satisfaction of knowing they won't be able to do this to someone else."

Grandma Rosa, who had been silently observing the conversation up until now, nodded her approval. "You are a sensible man. You and Sally will come through just fine." She smiled encouragingly at me. "Better things are coming your way."

"There's a good chance the other gunman might see the interview, right?" I asked Brian.

He nodded. "Definitely. When you're a criminal on the run, you always want to get some idea of what people are saying about you."

"Then it's settled. It would be great if Jerry can run the interview twice tomorrow." I paused for a moment. "The media won't find out that Benjamin is in custody, right?"

Brian narrowed his eyes. "Sally, what have you got up your sleeve?"

"I'm not sure yet," I confessed. "But I'll come up with something, don't worry."

"There's no doubt in my mind." Wearily, Brian rose to his feet. "If we find anything else out about Benjamin, I'll be in touch. Please let me know what time the interview is scheduled for because I'd like to be here."

A studio audience. How nice. "Will do," I said as Grandma Rosa shut the front door behind him.

Mike stirred the spoon idly around in his soup bowl. "Are you going into the bakery tomorrow?"

"Yes, at least for the morning. I'm hoping that Jerry can fit us in close to noon, and I'll run home for an extended lunch. Plus, I don't want to keep asking Gianna. She's due any day, and it's not good for her to be on her feet so much."

He merely nodded and kept stirring with the spoon but made no attempt to eat more. This bothered me since pasta fagioli was his favorite. I'd seen him polish off three bowls in one sitting before. I reached for the bowl. "Want me to warm it up for you?"

Mike shook his head. "Thanks, princess, but my appetite's gone." He looked up at my grandmother, who had come back to clear the table. "I'm sorry, Rosa. You went to a lot of trouble on my account."

"Bah." She patted him on his good shoulder. "It is fine, my dear boy. You go rest. I shall make you a big breakfast tomorrow morning. You will need your strength for the interview."

My phone pinged with a text from Josie. "Oh, this is great!" I looked up at Grandma Rosa excitedly. "I'll have to leave early tomorrow morning. We got an order for 200 cookies for a party tomorrow night. Boy, we can sure use that dough now."

I laughed out loud, pleased with my attempt at a pun, but it was met with ominous silence. Mike got to his feet and kissed me, then walked into our bedroom, shutting the door quietly behind him. Worried, I dropped the dishes in the sink and started to follow him.

Grandma Rosa reached out and placed a hand on my arm. "Let him be, *cara mia*. Sometimes a man needs to be alone with his thoughts."

# CHAPTER SEVENTEEN

It was wonderful to be back at work the next morning. Even though it had only been a few days, I'd missed the scents in my bakery and working side by side with my best friend. It was good to know that some things were still within my control.

The smell of chocolate wafted through the air to greet me. Josie had made chocolate brownie cookies—a new recipe she'd just created that could satisfy anyone's chocoholic craving for a week. Her raspberry cheesecake cookies practically melted in my mouth. My stomach rumbled, and I ate two of each kind, still warm from the oven, when I thought Josie's back was turned.

"Good to see you eating cookies again." Josie grinned as she placed messages in a tray of fortune cookies and quickly folded the corners around them. "And I'm so happy Mike is doing better. Did he mind your coming in today?"

"No. Honestly, I think it's good for both of us. My hovering is starting to make him a little crazy. Plus, he keeps beating himself up over what Trevor did. He's angry at the world right now. It's not fair, Jos. He's worked so hard his entire life." My voice trembled. "Mike didn't deserve this." No one did.

She nodded soberly. "I know, Sal. There are a lot of things in this life that aren't fair. But as your grandmother would say, don't cry over spilled eggs."

"She says coffee, but hey, whatever. Grandma is always original."

Josie shook multicolored sprinkles over the tray of vanilla cookies she'd finished baking. I'd given her my recipe for the ones I'd created in honor of Mike's birthday, and Josie had loved it. She was convinced they'd be a big hit in the shop, too.

"Was Mike still sleeping when you left this morning?" she asked.

"No. He and my grandmother were playing Go Fish." I wiped my hands on my apron. "And I think he was trying to cheat."

We both laughed. "See? Things are looking up already," Josie said. "I'm convinced the two of you can make it through anything. Look at what you've overcome already."

Her words filled me with hope. "Thanks, Jos. I needed to hear that."

Josie added butter and confectioners' sugar to the mixer for her buttercream frosting. "When does Mike start physical therapy?"

"Next week." After Mike had gone to bed last night, I'd taken the plunge and applied for a home equity loan online. We'd been approved, so that was good news, but it still hurt that we'd had to resort to this. Sadly, there were no other choices for us right now.

"On to your favorite topic," I said. "The book signing for Dad on Saturday—do you think it would be okay to charge for the cookies?"

"The famous coffin cookies? Hell yes, we're charging. By the way, we're already getting orders. How word got out about these things, I don't know. It's going to take an entire day for me to make them." She studied me carefully. "It's none of my business, but how bad are things financially? In the past, you would have given the cookies away."

I blew out a sigh. "True, but I can't—not this time anyway. Besides, it's not fair to you. You're doing all the work, so I want you to take a share of the profits as well."

Josie wiped her hands on a dishtowel. "Sal, you've always done so much for me and the kids—bringing them toys, paying for my trip to Florida for the bakeoff. You even lent Rob and me money when I was arrested last year for Kelly's murder. Please let me do this for you. Charge whatever you want for the cookies, but I'm not taking a red cent."

A lump grew in my throat. "But it's not right," I managed to choke out before I dissolved into tears.

Josie put her arms around me and patted my back until I'd composed myself. She handed me a napkin to wipe my eyes, and I noticed that hers were moist as well. It was when you were down and out that you knew who your true friends were. Josie always came through for me. She'd even saved my life a few months back when I'd been locked in a freezer.

After giving me an encouraging smile, she went over to the ovens and removed a tray of fortune cookies. "I know that I complain about your dad and his weirdness, but I still enjoy making the cookies. Who knows, maybe these little coffins will put me on the map and make us famous someday."

I laughed and glanced at my watch. It was already past ten, and we'd only had two customers so far. Yes, I hated slow days like this, but on the bright side, it had allowed us to finish up the cookie order, which was good since I had to leave soon.

The bells on the front door jingled away. Hooray for more customers.

"Be with you in a second," Josie yelled into the storeroom.

"That's okay, honey. It's only us," a female voice giggled in return.

Josie and I exchanged glances. The voice belonged to my mother, and the "us" most likely meant that my father was with her. Heaving a sigh, I lifted two trays of jelly cookies from the oven and put them on the rack to cool. Then I followed Josie out to the storefront.

My father and mother were talking in low, hushed voices. When they saw us, they pointed at two cardboard boxes sitting on top of one of my white tables by the window. Books. My father's book to be exact. Yes, it had started already.

I cringed inwardly but tried to put on a brave face. "You're here a little early, aren't you? The signing isn't until Saturday."

My mother gave me a kiss. "Hello, darling. Hi, Josie. Daddy's trying to figure out if there's a way we can fit more tables in here. We're expecting quite a crowd, you know."

"I thought it was going to be like an open house," I said. "People coming in from eleven to three o'clock. Staggered, so to speak."

My father acted like he hadn't heard me. "The media will be here about noon. I expect a line down and around the block, so make sure coffee and cookies are ready to go, Sal."

My mother giggled again and removed her coat. She was wearing a tiny black satin dress with spaghetti straps. "We thought we might do a feature on stylish mourning clothes," she said. "I'll be wearing this dress. It's to let people know that, even though death is a somber event, you can still be stylish. Your father's thinking about featuring funeral wear on his blog soon."

Why did I feel like this book signing was going to turn into a three-ring circus? "Um, I don't know if that's a good idea," I said carefully. "People might be offended by someone coming to their loved one's funeral in such an—uh, outfit." For lack of better words. To me, it had barely more cloth than the bikinis she loved to wear in the summer.

My father prattled on. "Sal, we can use the upstairs apartment, right? I've rented some tables, and they'll be delivered this afternoon. Your mother will entertain people upstairs while my publicist and I sign books down here."

"You have a publicist?" Josie looked at me and mouthed *how?*

I merely shrugged. I'd been so involved with Mike and tracking Trevor's friends and family as of late that I had no idea what else my father had planned.

Dad puffed out his chest. "Yep. He thinks we'll sell a few hundred. The ranking on Amazon is already going up. I broke a million yesterday."

"A million copies?" Josie gasped.

"Nah. My book was sitting in the one millionth spot. But it will be in the top ten by next week," he said with confidence. "Mark my words."

Oh brother. "Dad, are you expecting people to stay around all day? That means more work for Josie and me. I can't ask Josie to do that, and—"

"But I'd insist on paying her." Dad whistled cheerfully as he walked behind the display case and started to reach for a fortune cookie in the case.

Josie rushed forward and grabbed a piece of wax paper. "I'll get it for you, Domenic. And it's okay, Sal. I could use the dough." She gave me a wry smile. "Another pun."

Dad looked at me thoughtfully. "I spoke to Jerry Maroon this morning. He said that he's coming to your house for a noon interview. Want me to coach you a little first?"

That was all Mike and I needed. "No thanks, Dad. I think we have it under control."

My mother cleared her throat. "Honey, it's past ten. Why don't you go ahead and leave now? Daddy and I can stay here and help Josie."

"Lucky me," Josie muttered under her breath. She gave me a little nudge. "If your mom waits on customers, I can work on the coffin cookies."

Dad walked into the back room, sniffing the air. "Hey, I smell them! Where are those babies? I can't wait to see how they turned out."

Josie clapped her hands at him. "Domenic, the first round is in the cooler, and I still need to frost them. Why don't you stay out front with Maria and let me handle the baking part, please?"

"Sure thing," my father said. "Jerry said he'd stop over later. He thinks they could do a future segment about your shop, Sal. You know, title it The Un-Fortune-ate Bakery. Get it?"

Gee, everyone was full of puns today. "Sure, Dad." I glanced at Josie with apprehension. "Are you sure you don't want me to stay? I've got some time."

She pointed at the door. "Go now, before I change my mind. You're coming back this afternoon, right?"

"Yes, Jerry said we should be through by one o'clock."

"Good." She reached for a pair of plastic gloves and put them on. "I don't think I'll have choked your father by then. *Maybe*."

\* \* \*

It felt like I'd been railroaded out of my bakery, even though I knew Josie and my parents meant well. I hoped the signing wouldn't turn out to be a disaster, but it was out of my hands. At least it would be a distraction from real life. I was so looking forward to Mike's belated birthday dinner on Sunday.

There was close to an hour to kill before Jerry needed me at the house. I should go home to my husband, but he was in Grandma Rosa's capable hands. The best thing I could do for him and for myself was to find the person who had killed Trevor, which would hopefully lead us to the money he'd ripped off from us.

In deep thought, I sipped the orange juice I'd bought from the bagel shop across the street from my bakery. Hopefully the vitamin C would kick in soon because I was dragging today. What should I do? Who else was left to pay a visit to?

I started the engine, and my car moved down the street, but I was unsure where it was headed. Time to review what I knew so far. One of the gunmen was in custody. He had refused to give up the identity of the other gunman. Benjamin Silver, or Mr. Lap Dance as I referred to him in my mind, had known Trevor but insisted he hadn't meant to kill anyone. Mike himself had said that the shorter guy had done the deed. Trevor's shooting felt—no, it *was* personal. Was the man connected to Trevor's family? Intuition told me that a relative must be involved. But who and why?

Brian said that no one knew David Webb was in custody—yet. The arraignment wasn't scheduled until tomorrow. That should give us enough time to bait the other gunman. Perhaps talking with both Erica and Tina again would prove to be useful. What if the television interview backfired? Perhaps I should go see Morgan as well. Curtis was undoubtedly back in Virginia by now.

Since Erica's house was closer, I headed there first. As I drove down her street, I noticed that her truck wasn't in the driveway. When I knocked on the door, the only response I received was Donny's incessant barking. With a sigh, I got back into the car and checked my watch—10:45. Jerry wanted me at the house by 11:30 if I was to be featured in the interview as well. He planned for it to go live at noon. With no time to waste, I started the car and zoomed over to Tully.

The station wagon was gone from the front of the duplex, and in its place was a black SUV with a Virginia license plate. My heart gave a little jolt. Why was Curtis here? Was he bullying his brother's fiancée? What a creep. Curtis might think Tina knew where the money was. How far would he go to get his hands on it? I prayed he wouldn't harm her or the baby she was carrying.

I drove around the block and parked farther up the street this time, behind a large white van that partially blocked my car. I moved over to the passenger side and waited, hoping someone would emerge from the house soon.

After a few minutes, Curtis appeared on the porch, looking suave and professional in a black suede overcoat and matching dress shoes. Tina was behind him. He looked sharply to his right, then to the left while I crouched lower in the seat.

Satisfied, he turned back around to face Tina, and she placed her arms around his neck. Their lips met in a wild, passionate kiss.

# CHAPTER EIGHTEEN

"Are you sure about this, Sally?" Brian asked.

I raised an eyebrow at him. "Brian, I might be suffering from a lack of sleep, but I know what I saw. It was definitely Curtis kissing Tina. Not a brotherly type kiss, either. Mark my words, they're having an affair."

Mike shook his head in disbelief. We were seated on the couch in our living room while Brian sat across from us in the armchair. Jerry Maroon was standing by the fireplace, talking quietly with the cameraman. Grandma Rosa was sitting at the kitchen table, crocheting. She was quiet and reserved, but I knew those large brown eyes of hers missed nothing.

After I'd left Tina's—still in shock—I'd called Brian. He'd wanted to come for the interview anyway. It made me a bit nervous to have him there, in case I slipped up and said something on the air that I shouldn't.

Jerry seemed surprised by Brian's presence but to his credit said nothing. Maybe he was planning to take notes for a future interview with a police officer. *Officer Jenkins, why are you so involved in Mrs. Donovan's personal life? Don't you realize she's a disaster waiting to happen?*

I forced the thoughts out of my head and tried to pay attention to what Brian was saying.

"There aren't grounds to arrest either one of them yet," Brian remarked. "Even if they are having an affair, it doesn't mean they killed Trevor."

"What if you talked to David—I mean Benjamin—about this?" I asked. "If he thinks we know that Curtis and Tina are working together, maybe he'd be willing to give them up. What would he have to lose at this point?"

"It's possible. We can schedule another talk with him when his lawyer is present. If we hadn't gotten Benjamin's fingerprints from the market and the tattoo hadn't been so unique, there wouldn't be enough grounds to arrest him. Don't expect too much though. He's waiting for us to offer him a deal first."

"Maybe Benjamin was having an affair with Tina as well," Mike suggested. "That might explain why he doesn't give her up to the police. Maybe he'll expose Curtis if he realizes we know about the affair."

Brian made a note on the pad in front of him. "By the way, I forgot to tell you earlier that Tina called 9-1-1 yesterday morning to report her apartment had been broken into while she was at the grocery store. Nothing was taken, but drawers were dumped out and the place had been left in a mess."

"Was she telling the truth?" I asked.

He shrugged. "Hard to say. I wasn't available at the time, but a couple of my co-workers went over to make out the report. The place was trashed, but yeah, she could have done it herself. If not, then someone may have been there looking for something."

"Like the money Trevor was keeping from his partners." Where had he hidden it? And who else had been in on the larceny with him?

Jerry came over and looked expectantly at Brian, who eased himself out of the chair. "Thanks, Officer. Now, if you'll go join Granny in the kitchen, we can get this show underway." He sat down in the chair and crossed his left leg over his right. "Mike and Sally, just act natural. We're going with a plea for the gunman to give himself up, right?"

Jerry didn't know that I had a different plan in the works. When everyone else found out—especially Brian—this might turn into National Choke Sally Day. "Sounds good." I reached for Mike's hand. "Are you feeling up to this, sweetheart?"

He nodded. "Sal, I want this person caught. Even if we can't get our money back, I don't want it to happen to someone else."

"I feel the same way."

Jerry straightened the mic on his collar. "Okay, guys, try to talk directly into the mic. Don't cover it with your hand, okay?" He looked over at the cameraman. "What's the good word, Stew?"

Stew adjusted the lens and nodded. "We're going in ten seconds."

Jerry looked into the camera lens, waited for the signal from Stew, and smiled so wide that his face must have hurt. "Good afternoon, Buffalo. Jerry Maroon here with a special interview coming to you straight from the home of Michael and Sally Donovan in Colwestern. Michael was the shooting victim of a robbery at the local mini-mart the other evening—wasn't it your birthday too, Michael? What a stroke of bad luck."

A muscle ticked in Mike's jaw. He hated to be the center of attention and the possible object of pity. "Yes. And Mike is just fine, thanks."

Jerry seemed taken back but quickly recovered. "Tell us what you remember from the robbery. The pain when the bullet hit you, the agony and uncertainty of not knowing if you'd ever see your lovely wife again. Were you conscious at all?"

A slow anger was building in the bottom of my stomach, and Mike stiffened against me. If Jerry didn't stop soon, Mike might break the camera over his head. Jerry had not given us any indication he planned to take the interview in this direction. Our sole intention was to set a trap for the other gunman, and he knew it.

"Yes, I was conscious." Mike pursed his lips together. "And yes, I was afraid I might never see my wife again, but that's not the point right now. We want to find the guy—"

"The other man who was with you," Jerry interrupted. "He was your business partner, correct?"

Uh-oh. Jerry was stepping into dangerous territory. "He worked for me," Mike said cautiously. "I was giving him a lift home."

Jerry clucked his tongue like a chicken. "So sad to hear about Trevor Park's death. Such a tragedy. He was stealing money from your company, right?"

"I don't see what that has to do with anything, Jerry," Mike went on, gripping my hand so tightly that I almost yelped in pain. "We're here today because we want to get the man responsible for—"

"Yes, it's true," I cut in. "We believe the gunmen were in on the larceny with Trevor. Trevor was keeping secrets and money from them, and we believe they killed him deliberately."

From across the room, I spotted Brian's mouth drop and his face turn crimson. I was half expecting him to run across the room with his gun pointed at me.

Jerry's full attention was focused on me now, and his emerald eyes shone like a cat's. "Please go on, Mrs. Donovan."

Mike covered my hand with his as I continued. "Trevor was cheating his partners. He had money hidden away, and they were looking for it."

"How do you know this?" Jerry asked. "Is one of them in custody?"

Damn this guy. "No," I lied. "Trevor told Mike all about it the same evening he was killed. He was nervous and upset, so Mike asked him what was wrong, and he spilled all the details. We believe that he knew these guys were planning to kill him."

"Sal," Mike whispered in alarm.

"How interesting." Jerry leaned forward in obvious excitement. "Did Mr. Parks tell you where the money was hidden, Mike?"

I silently prayed that my husband would go along with it. This was our only hope if the other gunman was watching.

"Yes," Mike said. "He did tell me, and now that I'm home from the hospital, I'll be informing the police soon."

The cameraman caught Jerry's eye and pointed at his watch. Jerry clearly wanted more information, but it looked like he was out of luck and time. "Thank you both for joining me today," he said. "Please keep us updated on your health." His eyes widened as he stared into the camera. "Back to you, Joyce."

"That's a wrap," Stew said. "We're off the air."

Mike released my hand, rose to his feet, and crossed over to Jerry. His face was pinched tight with anger as he pointed a finger into Jerry's chest. "What the hell was that about? You were supposed to help us set a trap for this guy, not point out what a pitiful idiot I was to everyone."

Brian came forward and put a hand on Mike's shoulder. "Ease up, Mike."

Jerry looked from Mike to Brian, and a slow grin spread across his face. "Well, son, if you can't take the heat, I suggest you stay off the television." He glanced slyly over at me. "Seems you would have learned from the spectacle your wife has made of herself on the boob tube. Let's see…a food fight on Donna Dooley's show is the first thing that comes to mind. And then there was that classic episode of *Cookie Crusades* when—"

Mike swore and pointed at Stew. "Take your friend and get the hell out of my house before I do something I'll regret later."

Jerry roared with laughter. "Right. Like you could do anything to me in your condition. And I doubt you need a lawsuit since you're already broke."

I inserted myself between Mike and Jerry. "Don't underestimate my husband. Then again, he'd never stoop to your level, so you're safe."

"Ooh," Jerry mocked me. "That's good because I was really scared."

Anger flickered inside me like a flame. "That was a rotten thing you did. I didn't see my father's interview but can only hope that you didn't humiliate him the same way."

Jerry roared with laughter as he shrugged into his coat. "No worries there, honey. Your father does that all by himself. I feel sorry for you, Mrs. Donovan."

My anger threatened to boil over as I thrust a finger toward his face, the same way Mrs. Gavelli always did to me. "Don't you dare feel sorry for *me*. You're the one I'm sorry for. You enjoy degrading people. You think this makes you a big important man, but it's the opposite. As for my father, he may be a little different, but he's ten times the man you are. You could learn a lesson from him. At least he treats people with respect. Now, I believe my husband told you to leave our house."

The room had grown eerily silent. Jerry's eyes were cold as they stared into mine. "Sure thing, honey. I think we're done here."

Stew had already packed up his equipment, and after giving us a curt nod, he left. Jerry glanced over at Brian and then at my grandmother, who was still seated at the kitchen table crocheting. She wasn't even looking at us, but I knew she hadn't missed a single word or action.

Jerry's eyes brightened again. "Hey, maybe you can give your dad a message for me. Something's come up, so unfortunately, I won't be able to get a crew over to that fabulous book signing tomorrow. So sorry to miss the earth-shattering event. Please give him my profound apologies."

"Jerk," I spat out and slammed the door after him.

Mike planted an affectionate kiss on top of my head. "You did great, princess. I'm so proud of you. Wow, what a fireball I married! I hate it when people like him think they can treat others like garbage."

My grandmother cleared her throat, and we all looked over at her expectantly. "I am proud too, *cara mia*. It must have been difficult not to want to slap the head off Mr. Moron."

We all laughed.

Brian folded his arms over his chest and gave me a shrewd look. "I hate to be the one to burst your bubble here, Sally, but do you realize what you've done? If the other gunman was watching, you and Mike have just put yourselves in grave danger."

Mike put his arm around my shoulders, and I snuggled against him. "If he takes the bait, we'll be ready for him. Grandma, maybe you should go back home."

"Bah," she snorted. "I am fine. Do not worry about me."

"You guys are going to need police protection," Brian remarked.

Mike frowned. "We'll be fine on our own. If we see anything suspicious, we'll call for help."

Brian sighed as he ran a hand through his thick blond hair. "No. Sally tried something like this before, remember? And it almost got her killed." He glanced out our front window. "Maroon is re-running the interview at six o'clock tonight, right? Most people watch the news during their dinner hour after work. We'll get a car over shortly afterward to keep an eye on your house. I'd say sooner, but we don't have any spare officers available this afternoon. You should be okay till then." He looked over at my grandmother. "Is that your Buick on the side of the road, Mrs. Belgacci?"

Grandma Rosa glanced up from her crocheting. She was finishing up a white sweater and matching hat for Gianna's baby. Gianna had asked for it, wanting to bring the baby home from the hospital in something special, and my grandmother had been happy to oblige. "Yes," she said. "I can move it across the street if it will be in your way."

Brian scratched his head thoughtfully. "Perhaps down the street a bit. It may look better if the gunman thinks no one else is here." He turned to Mike. "Your truck is in the garage?"

Mike nodded. "Yeah, Johnny drove it home for me after the robbery the other night. I haven't been in it since." He heaved a long sigh. "I've got to clean out my toolbox on the back... That thing has been a mess for months. At least it will keep me busy for an afternoon. Especially since I won't be good for anything else for a while."

I kissed him on the cheek. "Stop talking like that." I noticed that Brian's face turned red as he watched us. Jeepers, did I have to feel guilty about kissing my husband now too?

"There's a gun stashed away in the bottom drawer of our dresser," Mike volunteered. "I can still manage it left handed if needed."

Brian rolled his eyes. "Yeah, I remember about your gun. You took it with you when you left town after Colin was killed. By the way, that didn't make you look very good."

Mike ignored his comment. "It's licensed, and that's all that matters."

Brian heaved a sigh. "Okay, let's hope it's not needed. We'll have someone out here later tonight. To make sure I have all my facts straight, we're looking for a guy about Sally's height with a possible squeaky voice?"

"And an axe to grind," Mike put in.

"Curtis is too tall to be the gunman," I said. "But if he's having an affair with Tina, I think he must be involved." Another idea struck me. "Trevor's ex-wife, Erica, might know something. Maybe I should talk to her again. She's close to Trevor's sister, Morgan, and doesn't like Tina. She said that Trevor was involved with Tina while he was still married to her, although Tina denied it."

Brian rubbed the back of his neck. "No harm in checking it out, I guess. Are you going to stop and see her?"

"I don't have time right now. I need to get back to the bakery and help Josie, but I'll call her from there."

"Please be careful," he said. "Remember, we'll be watching the house tonight. I want to nail this guy as much as you two do."

## CHAPTER NINETEEN

When I arrived back at the bakery, I was both surprised and delighted to see several customers waiting in line. Maybe things were finally looking up.

Josie glanced up in relief from behind the display case. "Thank goodness," she said. "I was about to call Mickey and see if he could stop in for a couple of hours to help."

I ran into the back room, washed my hands, and then waited on the next customer in line. It was none other than Mrs. Gavelli's stud, Ronald Feathers. "Hello, Mr. Feathers. What will it be? The usual? Two jelly cookies to go?"

He shook his head. "No, cutie. I want to try some of those special coffin cookies I keep hearing about."

"Heaven help us." Josie rolled her eyes toward the ceiling.

"How does everyone know about these already?" I asked her in a low tone. "They were supposed to be kept under wraps until tomorrow."

Josie looked sheepish. "Sorry, Sal. I put some in the case because people have been asking for them. It saves me running into the back room every two minutes."

"Didn't you read your father's blog this morning, honey?" Mrs. Jackson addressed me. She was a sixty-something woman who wore her grayish hair in the outdated beehive style. "He talked about the cookies in his post."

That explained everything. My father couldn't keep a secret if his life depended on it. Sighing, I glanced into the case at the aforementioned cookies. They did look good, but then again, so did everything that Josie made. Josie had used the recipe for the fudgy delight cookies—a standard sugar cookie recipe with the addition of fudge. She'd shaped and cut the dough to fit the coffin cookie cutters she'd bought online. I still couldn't believe that there was such a thing. After she assembled them, the cookies and lid were covered in chocolate fudge frosting. She'd even created a display of white flowers in the shape of a cross on the lid. Their similarity to a real coffin was so lifelike that it was creepy. Still, Josie had done a terrific job.

Because of the extra labor involved with making each cookie, we had decided to charge a higher price than usual. I was all for selling some today—we couldn't afford to turn away business at this point. "Can we spare some extras for the customers?" I asked.

Josie nodded. "I've got batter in the fridge for a thousand. I'll be here all night, but that's okay." She whispered in my ear, "I hate to say this, but they might become our biggest seller yet. Even more popular than the fortune cookies."

It was a disturbing thought. Given everything that had been happening in my life lately, though, we needed the extra money they were bringing in. I placed two in a box for Mr. Feathers, accepted his handful of quarters, and then waited on Mrs. Jackson.

"I'll take a dozen of those death bed cookies," she piped up cheerfully. "And I can't wait to see the clothes your mother's going to model during the fashion show portion of the book signing."

I sucked in a deep breath but managed a small smile for her. The so-called book signing was turning into a freak show. Hopefully my father was not planning on bringing the coffin that he kept in his living room. I'd be forced to put my foot down then.

The rest of the afternoon passed quickly. When the crowd started to thin out at about three thirty, we decided to shut the doors early to work on the cookies. With Josie's instructions, I helped assemble them but left the decorating part to her. When I glanced up at the clock again, I saw that it was almost five. I'd forgotten about calling Erica and reached for my phone. She answered on the first ring.

It took a minute for her to remember who I was. "Oh, right. Sally—the one whose husband got shot along with Trevor.

I saw you on the news during my lunch break today. Was that taped at your house?"

"Yes, it was live." I didn't plan on watching the interview myself. My television experiences never went well. "Erica, I'm wondering if I can ask you something. It's extremely personal."

There was silence on the other end. "Hmm. I'm guessing it has something to do with Trevor and that cheap tramp he knocked up."

"You know that Tina's pregnant?"

"Sure, I know. Morgan told me after Trevor confided in her. He was real upset about it too."

"How come you never had any children?" Oh, shoot. Me and my big mouth. "I'm sorry, another personal question. Please forgive me. That's none of my business."

A dog whined in the background as Erica spoke. Good old Donny, no doubt. "Oh, that's all right," she said. "We talked about kids a few times, but I never wanted them. Trevor didn't seem to care either way. He said that I was the boss and the decision was up to me. To find out that bimbo was knocked up must have felt like someone threw cold water over his head. She definitely trapped him." As she chatted, the barking in the background grew louder and more incessant. "Donny, shush!"

I exhaled sharply. "There's more. Your assumption about Curtis and Tina carrying on seems to be correct."

Donny continued his yapping. "Are you serious?" Erica asked loudly to be heard over the dog. "How did you find out?"

"Unfortunately, yes. I saw them together in an embrace." Donny's barking was giving me a headache. I loved dogs, especially my own, but this little dude was trying my patience.

Erica shouted into the phone. "I didn't know. But yeah— it would make sense. Maybe the two of them were planning to do away with Trevor so that they could be together. Maybe it's not even Trevor's baby."

The same thought had occurred to me as well, but I refrained from further comment. Mercifully, Donny's barking subsided. I had the feeling that Erica was trying to pump me for more information, but I didn't trust her. I couldn't afford to trust any of Trevor's friends and relatives, having learned the hard way before. "Well, I have a feeling everything will be fine soon."

"Yeah, that was obvious from your interview. I'm very happy to hear it. Hey, what time is your bakery open until? I'm having a craving for those awesome raspberry cheesecake cookies you guys make. It would give us the opportunity to talk some more."

"I'm sorry, but we're already closed for the night and I'm leaving for home shortly. We reopen tomorrow morning at nine if you'd like to stop by then."

"Bummer. Okay, tomorrow morning sounds good." She hesitated for a second. "Listen, I have some more information about Trevor—stuff that no one else knows, not even Morgan or Curtis. It might help you to track down the other gunman."

I gripped the phone tightly between my sweaty hands. Did Erica know where the money was? Maybe I should meet her tonight. No, I needed a breather, and I wanted to be with Mike. "Okay. I'll make sure I'm here first thing in the morning."

The barking began again. "No problem," Erica said to me and then addressed the dog. "Damn it, Donny. I swear if you don't stop that barking, you get no treats tonight. It is a shoe you are barking at. A *shoe*. Not another dog."

I rolled my eyes as I listened. Donny sounded like a smart one. There was a loud crash, and Erica let out a small squeak.

"Are you okay?" I asked.

She sighed into the phone. "Yeah. That dopey dog knocked some dishes off the dining room table. He was on the chair and reached up to—oh, I need to go before he gets glass in his paw. I'll see you tomorrow morning." She clicked off without another word.

I shrugged into my coat, overwhelmed with guilt as I watched Josie getting out more batter for the cookies. "Maybe I should stay. This isn't right. Grandma's with Mike, and neither one of them will mind."

She waved a hand at me. "Sal, have you seen the bags under your eyes? Go home, have a nice dinner cooked à la Grandma, then cuddle up with your man for the night. If you feel inclined to come in early, that would be great, but no worries. You look like you're about ready to drop."

"I've been having a tough time sleeping lately," I admitted. "Oh, and don't forget, I'm holding the birthday dinner for Mike on Sunday. I hope you can make it."

She raised an eyebrow. "Are you really feeling up to cooking an entire meal for your family?"

"That was the initial plan, but Grandma Rosa offered to do it. This time, I wasn't too proud to take her up on it either."

"That woman is a godsend," Josie declared. "I'd give my right arm for a grandmother like her. For what it's worth, I think that's a good idea. I know you want to prove you can do it all on your own, but that book signing is going to wear us both out."

"The book signing is on Saturday, the day before."

She shook her head. "Doesn't matter. We'll be tired out for the entire weekend. I can only imagine what your parents have up their sleeves."

I cringed inwardly, thinking about my mother parading around in sequined, revealing black minidresses while my father signed books and popped coffin cookies into his mouth, dribbling frosting and crumbs everywhere. "Yeah, you're right. I love them dearly, but they are exhausting to be around."

"How did your conversation with Erica go?"

I shoved my phone into my purse and paused a minute before answering. "Fine. She wants to stop over tomorrow morning to tell me a few things about Trevor. I wonder if I should have Brian come by as well."

Josie cocked her head to the side and studied me. "What's bothering you? Do you think she's lying?"

"I don't know. That entire family is a bunch of liars. I don't know who or what to believe, but I'm convinced one of them was in on Trevor's murder. Erica's dog kept barking in the background, and I feel like I missed something that she said. Maybe it will come to me on the drive home."

Josie started to assemble another cookie. "Dogs are too much work. The kids keep pestering me for one, but who do you think would be cleaning up after it? Not them, that's for sure."

"You could use a watchdog when Rob works nights," I remarked.

She snorted. "No one in their right mind would come near my house. My boys are scary enough by themselves."

Fair enough. I'd babysat her kids and knew she spoke the truth. "All right, I'd better take off. Thanks for everything."

She winked at me. "That's what friends are for, hon."

On the drive home, I was once again reminded of how lucky I was. The air outside was chilly and damp, but thoughts of my family and friends warmed me. We couldn't change what had happened in the past, but there was still the future to look ahead to.

My phone buzzed, and I activated the hands free on my steering wheel. "Hello?"

"Princess," Mike said. "Where are you?"

"Only minutes away. Is everything okay?"

"All is good. Your mother said she texted you, but maybe you didn't see it yet. Gianna's gone into labor."

I gripped the steering wheel tightly between my hands. "Oh my God! I need to get to the hospital!" Sleep and dinner would have to wait. "Has Grandma left yet? Did she fix dinner for you? Did Brian leave a car outside?"

"Slow down," he laughed. "I haven't heard from Brian, and no, I don't see a car outside, but remember he said after six o'clock. It's only five thirty. Your grandmother just left, and yes, she fed me. She thinks it will be a while before Gianna delivers. She said the contractions are still a few minutes apart and the first baby usually doesn't come that quickly. But the doctor told Johnny to bring Gianna in anyway."

"Well, I want to be with her. Okay, I'll grab something to eat quick, give my man a kiss, and then be on my way out. Do you want to come with me?"

"I'm kind of tired, so I think I'll stay here," he said. "Your grandmother started to change my bandage for me. I told her I'd finish it, but I could use a hand when you get in. Oh, and don't take any chances. Park in the garage."

"Okay, see you in a minute."

As I pulled into our driveway, I thought about Gianna and her baby and the baby that Trevor would never know. If it even *was* his baby. What information did Erica have for me? I tried to recall what she'd said and replayed the conversation in my mind. Babies. It was all about babies these days. Gianna's, Trevor's. Erica said she hadn't wanted kids. Trevor said the decision was hers because she was the boss. Who else had said something like that recently? Donny's barking had driven me crazy. I didn't know how Erica could stand it. Then she'd shrieked—no, wait. That wasn't right. She'd squeaked, like the gunman who'd killed Trevor.

That was it. David—Benjamin had told me that his girlfriend liked to be called "boss." An icicle formed between my shoulder blades. Could it be... Oh my God. What if Erica had been the other gunman? She was my height. The other robber hadn't spoken a word, but Trevor had known this person. Had anyone else thought that the gunman could in fact have been a gunwoman?

Despite what Tina had told me, Trevor had been cheating on Erica while they were still married. Of course, Erica hated them. How could she not? Erica must have been the one who'd broken into Trevor's apartment looking for the money. She was having an affair with David—Benjamin, which explained why he wouldn't reveal his accomplice. Erica had told me that she had a new man in her life and that this time it might be the real thing. What a pair.

I'd call Brian as soon as I got inside. Impatiently I pressed the button on the remote clipped to my visor, but the garage door wouldn't open. Oh no. I hoped that wasn't broken too. There was no extra money available for repairs like this now. I got out of the car and tugged at the handle on the bottom of the door. Then I noticed there was something wedged into the side of the door. A piece of cardboard. Where had that come from? As I pulled it out, a step sounded behind me. I whirled around but wasn't fast enough.

Something heavy and painful crashed down on my skull. Stars appeared before my eyes as I staggered to my knees in the driveway. A swift kick to my chest followed, and I was flat on my back on the cold, hard gravel. The pain was excruciating as I gasped for air, but I did manage to open my eyes briefly and stare at the figure above me.

Erica leaned over me, a cruel smile displayed on her face. She held a length of rope in one hand and a gun in the other. I continued to lie there, unable to move and fighting the darkness that had started to descend upon me.

She placed a piece of electrical tape across my mouth. "Found this in your hubby's tool box. The perfect solution. Now I don't have to hear your irritating voice anymore." She lifted the garage door and then proceeded to drag my body across the cement floor. "Let's go inside. I'd like to get to know that good-looking husband of yours a little better."

## CHAPTER TWENTY

"You're not going to get away with this." Mike's voice drifted somewhere above me. "And you'd better pray that my wife wakes up soon."

My head was throbbing with pain as I struggled to open my eyes. At first I couldn't remember what had happened, but I knew that I'd blacked out for at least a few minutes. The light hurt my eyes, but I couldn't shield them since my hands were tied behind my back. Spike was sniffing at my hair. He seemed satisfied that I was okay, because he trotted across the floor and into our bedroom, probably in search of a cozy place to nap.

I was lying on my back on the carpeted floor in front of the couch, with a full view of the kitchen and living room area. Mike was seated at our round oak dining room table. I could see that his legs and left arm were tied with rope to the chair. His right arm was free but useless in the sling. When he spotted me looking at him, his eyes softened with apparent relief.

Erica was busy rummaging through our kitchen cabinets and drawers, dumping contents onto the floor as she went along. No doubt she was looking for the money Trevor supposedly had. My insides went cold as I watched her. What would she do to us when she didn't find it? But I already knew the answer. Erica had killed her ex-husband in cold blood, and she wouldn't hesitate to get rid of us too.

Erica slammed one of the drawers shut and came to stand beside Mike's chair, looking down at him like he was lunch. She glanced in my direction and laughed as she watched me struggling with the ropes around my wrists. With her gaze pinned on me, she ran her hands freely through Mike's curly hair. Rage burned inside me like an inferno. *Who does she think she is?* The more I struggled with the rope, the more it cut into my flesh. Defeated, I finally lay still. It was useless. All I could do was lie here and watch as that woman put her hands all over my husband.

"I'm glad I didn't take that tape off your wife's mouth," Erica said as she ran a finger down Mike's chest. "I bet you could still show me a good time, even with one arm, huh, hot stuff?" She looked over at me again, and I shot her a death glare in return. "I'm sure Sally wouldn't mind if we got to know each other." She undid two of the buttons on his shirt and ran a hand over his bare chest while looking at me, clearly enjoying my silent rage.

"Take your hands off me," Mike said quietly. "I already told you we don't have the money."

She cocked an eyebrow at him. "I saw the interview on television. You said you knew things."

"That was just a ruse to attract the other gunman—excuse me—*gunwoman's* attention."

Erica made a face "Well, if that's true, you're stupider than I thought. Because that would mean I have no choice but to kill you both. As you may already know, killing people doesn't bother me." Erica laughed. "Trevor always used to tell me I had no conscience. Guess he was right."

A chill swept through me as I watched her pick up the gun and cross the room. She stood over me, pointing the gun at my head. "Now, Mikey, tell your wife you love her one last time before I pull the trigger."

"Don't do this!" Mike yelled as he struggled with the rope. He stared at me helplessly, then back at her, and I had a sense of what was coming. "Hey, what's the rush there, beautiful? You're right—maybe we *should* get to know each other a little better. But let Sally go first. She's not involved in this."

Erica whipped her head around in surprise and walked back in his direction. "Are you kidding me? Your nosy little wife came to my house with her bakery sidekick asking questions about Trevor. She also quizzed his brother and sister, not to mention that tramp he was shacked up with. The police have Benjamin in custody, don't they?"

"How do you know?" Mike asked.

"We were supposed to meet up earlier today, and he never showed. That's very unlike him without calling first. I want my money. I deserve it for putting up with Trevor, his lies, and the humiliation for eight long years."

"Were you and David—I mean Benjamin—having an affair?" Mike asked.

She ran a finger down his cheek. "Yeah, but there's no reason for you to worry, gorgeous. We started carrying on when Trevor and I lived in Virginia. He was only a casual roll in the hay. Stupid me—I thought he had money at first. Trevor brought Benjamin home for a beer one night, and it was obvious he wanted me. He was into me, I was into money, so we started to hook up. I knew Trevor was cheating on me, so this was my way of getting back at him."

I couldn't keep track anymore. Tina was fooling around with Trevor's brother, Curtis. Trevor had been fooling around on Erica with Tina while Erica had been fooling around with David. My brain hurt, and I wasn't sure if it was from the blow of the gun or trying to figure this mess out. Did any of these people have morals?

Erica sat down on Mike's lap. He looked over at me anxiously and then, having no choice, kissed her on the cheek. Nausea built in my stomach. I knew why he was doing this, but it still didn't make it any easier for me to watch.

It seemed to be working, though. She grabbed Mike's face between her hands and kissed him long and hard on the mouth. To his credit, he didn't flinch, while bile rose in the back of my throat.

"My, something tells me you're going to be more fun than both Benjamin *and* Trevor," she purred seductively.

Mike kissed her again. "Let my wife go, and you can take me with you."

She drew back and studied him. "Sorry, no can do. Still, that doesn't mean we can't have a good time while she watches."

This might be worse than having a gun held to my head.

Mike cleared his throat, his eyes fixed on me. "First, tell me what else happened. You and Benjamin followed Trevor to Colwestern?"

Erica tapped Mike's chin and redirected his gaze back to her. "That lousy creep kept me in the dark about everything. He never even told me anything about his house-building racket. I had to learn it all from Benjamin. Then Trevor told me he'd met someone. Bull. He'd been wanting out of our marriage for a while, and Tina was the excuse he needed. Benjamin's the one who told me all about the embezzling. The only reason he even knew is because he caught Trevor stealing supplies. He had no choice but to cut Benjamin in."

"Then you decided to move here to keep an eye on him?" Mike asked.

"Trevor thought that I did it just to make his life miserable, but I wanted what was rightfully mine. Benjamin knew Trevor was lying about the money he was making from the start. They were supposed to go fifty-fifty on every deal. Trevor stole the materials from saps like you while Benjamin acted the part of house builder and real estate agent. When he went to Trevor demanding the rest of his money, Trevor gave him a small payment and then told him to get lost."

She leaned over to kiss Mike's neck. "What did Trevor care if Benjamin went to the police, because Benjamin was guilty too. We knew it was only a matter of time before he moved on to another town and another schmuck like you. No offense, honey." Her lips traveled down Mike's chest. "When someone's as good-looking as you, they don't need a brain."

Even from across the room, I spied the veins bulging in Mike's neck. If I ever got these ropes off, I was going to lunge for her throat.

"By our calculations, he was holding on to close to a hundred grand, which he'd gotten from you and some other loser he worked for after he left Roberts Construction. Benjamin and I had both had enough of his deceit."

"You killed him—over a lousy fifty grand apiece?" Mike's voice was incredulous.

Erica tossed her head. "It wasn't just about the money. Revenge was important to me too." She moved his open shirt aside and ran both hands freely over his chest. "You almost ruined everything when you stepped forward, handsome. Benjamin wasn't planning on shooting anyone. He thought we were only going to scare Trevor into telling us where the money was. What a dope."

"How did you expect to find the money if you killed him?" Mike asked. I had to admit he was doing a great job with his questioning. If we ever got out of this mess, Josie and I might have to expand our crime-stopping business.

"I already told you," she said angrily. "It wasn't just about the money for me. It was more about making him pay—for the humiliation, for what he'd done to me. I figured I'd find the dough eventually. I thought he'd stashed it somewhere in his apartment. I used my set of picks to break in there the other day when that bimbo Tina wasn't home. I thought for sure he'd hidden it there, but nothing. The best part? She was fooling around on Trevor too. With his own brother! I was hoping someone had seen them together and reported it to the police." She glanced at me triumphantly then rubbed her body against Mike's. "Your wife took care of that."

I didn't know how much more of the Erica show I could bear to watch.

"When I saw your interview today," she continued, "I figured I was going in the wrong direction. I didn't know why the hell Trevor would confide in you, but hey, he wasn't as smart as he thought he was. Now hand over the dough."

"I told you we don't have it." Mike said tersely.

Erica pointed the gun in my direction. "Well, you'd better find it quick or Little Miss Baker dies."

"Hey." Mike kissed her on the lips. "There's no need for that. We were just starting to have fun. But I can't do much while I'm tied to this chair."

How I prayed that she'd take the bait. I'd never felt so useless before in my life as I stared at the clock on the wall. Only 15 minutes had passed since I'd come to. How was that even possible? And where was our police protection? The news hadn't finished airing yet, and Brian had not said for sure when the patrol car might arrive. We were doomed. This woman was going to kill me, have her way with my husband, and then most likely kill him too. We needed a miracle.

Erica laughed like a hyena. "As much as I'd like to, I can't untie you, studly. Don't worry. We'll figure something out."

Mike gave a low chuckle. "I'm not a magician, honey. One arm is tied, and I can't use the other. Let's take off in your car and leave Sally here. No one's going to find her until at least tomorrow, and you and I could be out of the country by then."

She sighed audibly as he kissed her again. His charm was working. "Okay, I'm only untying your arm for now. I'll help you along. What shall we do first? Or would you like a lap dance?"

"Sure," Mike said unconvincingly, and I thought I might throw up. Where was Erica yesterday? Maybe she could have given me some pointers.

After she'd untied his arm, a flash of light flashed across our front living room window.

Erica whipped her head around. "Did you see something?"

Mike took that split second to knock the gun from her hand. Erica shrieked and scratched at his face with her long, jagged nails. He lifted her with his left arm and threw her onto the floor. She was reaching for the gun when the front door burst open and Brian and Adam appeared.

"Drop the weapon," Brian ordered.

Erica started to cry as she set the gun on the floor in front of her. "I was only protecting myself. He tried to attack me."

Without a word, Adam moved forward and grabbed the gun off the ground. He removed a pair of handcuffs from his belt and forced Erica onto her stomach, much in the same manner he'd cuffed her boyfriend yesterday. She cursed angrily under her breath as he started to read her rights.

Brian hurried over to untie me then tore the tape gently from my mouth. "Are you okay?"

I nodded weakly as he helped me to my feet. The room spun a couple of times, and I sat down on the couch. Brian crossed over to Mike and untied his legs from the chair. He was at my side in an instant, pulling me against his chest.

"God, princess." His voice trembled. "I was so scared she was going to kill you."

"We're safe now." I smiled up at Brian as Adam led Erica out the front door. "Thank goodness you guys showed up when you did."

Brian pointed at the doorway, where my grandmother was standing. "Don't thank me. Thank your grandmother."

Grandma Rosa came over to us. We both stood and wrapped our arms around her.

"How did you know we were in trouble?" Was it that psychic ability of hers again? "I thought you'd gone to the hospital."

She pointed toward the kitchen. "See that small white box on the table? I was halfway to the hospital when I remembered the sweater for Gianna's baby. I decided to turn around and come back because I knew your sister would ask for it right away and I did not want her to have a horse when she found out I had forgotten it."

Mike grinned at her. "That's *cow*, Rosa."

Grandma Rosa shrugged. "Whatever. I saw Sally's car in the driveway and did not know when she was planning on leaving for the hospital. Brian said to park my car further down the street and that is what I did. When I walked up the driveway, I saw the shadow of someone in the living room. A person with a gun in their hands. Then I knew that Trevor's killer was here, so I got back into my car and dialed Brian's number."

I blew out a long breath and hugged her close. "Grandma, you saved our lives. She was going to kill us both."

Mike closed his eyes for a moment. "Sorry you had to see that, baby. If I'd had to kiss Erica one more time, I was going to be sick for sure."

Brian raised an eyebrow. "What exactly happened here?"

"Nothing," I said. "Erica was attracted to Mike, so he played along in hopes it could work to our advantage. He got her to untie his arm and managed to knock the gun from her hand."

"Nice going," Brian said and grinned at me. "Guess you can't take credit for apprehending the criminal this time, huh?"

I put my hands on my hips. "Well, excuse me. It's a little hard to do when you're tied up and your mouth is taped shut."

"Let her be." Grandma Rosa patted my cheek. "Sally is a good detective. She and Josie should have their own crime-stopping business."

"You mean like Holmes and Watson?" Mike joked while I chuckled at the irony of her words.

She shook her head. "No, I was thinking about that television show I like to watch with the two women detectives. You know, the old reruns—*Cagney & Stacey*."

I laughed. "*Lacey*, Grandma."

She nodded. "I like that too."

# CHAPTER TWENTY-ONE

"Gianna and the baby are coming home tomorrow. Did I tell you that he weighs over nine pounds?" There was immense pride in my voice, as if the baby was my own. "He's absolutely gorgeous."

Mike chuckled into the phone. "Yeah, only about fifty times already. Hey, I know it's not possible since Gianna was two weeks early, but she couldn't have planned this any better. She has a legitimate excuse for missing your father's book signing today."

I had to laugh—Mike was right. Gianna had been dreading the book signing even more than childbirth. I peered out from the back room at the crowd in my storefront. The place was mobbed. Josie and Grandma Rosa were both at the counter serving up goodies to customers. Mickey, our driver, was going around to tables with a carafe of coffee in his hands. The line of people at the counter had been steady all day long—truly a blessed thing to see. Customers were buying other things besides the coffin cookies, which had already sold out. Although I hated to admit it, the book signing for *How to Plan and Enjoy Your Funeral* had been fantastic for my business.

Mike had begged off from the event, claiming his arm hurt. "Are you feeling better now?" I teased as I removed more fortune cookies from the oven. "Or were you following Gianna's lead?"

"Hey," he protested. "I'm still technically an invalid, remember?"

"Poor baby," I crooned into the phone as I placed messages inside the cookies and rolled the sides of the dough up around them. We'll have to get you all better when I get home."

His voice turned low and sexy. "I like the sound of that. When *will* you be home?"

"The signing finishes in a little while." I glanced at the clock. It was almost three. "Then Josie and I will clean up and close the bakery. So, say about four? We can have an early dinner, but then I want to go back to the hospital to see the baby again. And you need to meet your nephew too."

"Okay, but then the rest of the evening belongs to us. I'd say we deserve it after everything we've been through this week."

"We definitely do. Tomorrow night we're going to celebrate with the rest of the family. Gianna is planning to come by for your dinner—at least for a little while."

"So soon?" he asked in amazement. "It will be their first day home with the baby."

I adjusted the phone between my ear and shoulder. "Gianna knows it means a lot to me. It was her decision, but she wants to come."

"Does this kid have a name yet?" Mike wanted to know.

"I guess we'll find out tomorrow night at your dinner. Mrs. Gavelli is coming too." I wasn't crazy about that part, but she'd offered to make her chocolate cheesecake, and I knew how much she was already in love with her great-grandson. "Last night when I stopped in Gianna's room after getting my head checked, she was there too. She kept insisting that they call the baby Alessandro after her husband."

"Alessandro Gavelli. That's quite a mouthful for anyone, let alone a new baby. Well, I'll be in the garage when you get home, cleaning out my toolbox. I'm going crazy sitting in this house."

I whisked another tray of cookies into the oven. "Don't overdo it, okay? I swear, you are the worst invalid in the world."

"Well, when you get here, I can think of some other fun things for us to do," he teased.

My heart overflowed with happiness. "I'm going to hold you to that. Love you."

"Love you too, princess."

My father stood in the doorway of the back room, jelly cookie in hand. "Hey, Sal, guess what? We're officially out of books. All five hundred of them sold."

"That's amazing, Dad." Also kind of scary, but I didn't add that part out loud.

"Hmm." He popped the cookie whole into his mouth. "Your mother wants me to start featuring some funeral fashions on the blog. She's getting a lot of interest from the crowd upstairs."

Good grief. There was no end to my parents' madness. One of their farfetched ideas always led to something else. I glanced into the storefront again. Josie and Grandma Rosa were still waiting on customers, but the line was growing smaller. People were leaving with autographed copies of books under their arms.

"Yep, real successful. Gonna have to do this again soon, Sal." He pointed a finger at Brian, who was approaching us with Ally at his side. "I sold the last one to your cop friend and his lady here a minute ago."

Brian held up the book, which had an open coffin on the front cover and my father's lifelike picture on the back. In the photo, he was wearing a white New York Mets tank top and a full-fledged grin as he peered out from behind his laptop. Like him, it was original.

"Can't wait to read this." Brian winked at me.

My father patted him on the shoulder. "You're a good kid. Hey, Sal, did you happen to see who stopped by a few minutes ago?"

"No, I've been in the kitchen making cookies. Who was it? A literary agent on the prowl for *you* this time?"

He shook his head. "Nope. It was Jerry Maroon, in the flesh. He was hoping to do a live interview during the signing and get all the details on that whack job who held you and Mike at gunpoint last night."

I stared at my father in disbelief. "Dad, I told you what a jerk he was to me and Mike during our interview. He's nothing more than a dog sniffing for a bone. I can't believe you'd tell him yes. The man is a user."

"Hey," my father protested. "Give your old man some credit here. I told him to get lost and not come back. No one treats my baby girl like that—or my son-in-law for that matter.

Mike might not be Italian, but he's still all right in my book."

Brian stared down at the floor, but I spotted a small smile creeping across his face. Ally glanced from my father to Brian, obviously not understanding the joke. She didn't know my family like Brian did.

My father gave me a peck on the cheek. "I've got to talk to my publicist, and then your mom and I are taking off. The rental company will be here soon to collect the extra chairs and tables." He gave us all a wave and then crossed the room to my mother, who was chatting by the staircase with a woman about her age. She pirouetted around in a sequined, black halter minidress while clutching my father's book in her hand.

Brian watched them with amusement. "They're quite the pair, aren't they?"

"That's one way of putting it." I smiled at Ally. "It was nice of you guys to stop by and support my father's—ah, new venture."

"We wouldn't have missed it," Brian said. "Everyone in town is talking about his book. I saw a photographer from the *Colwestern Journal* snapping pictures of him. Looks like he'll be in the paper tomorrow."

More embarrassment for the family. Oh well, I should be used to it by now. Either my father or I always seemed to be the talk of the town. I addressed Ally. "Gianna had her baby late last night. A beautiful boy. He weighed nine pounds, three ounces."

Ally's gray eyes went wide. "That's wonderful! I didn't work yesterday, and my shift doesn't start until seven tonight. I'll stop by her room. Oh, I can't wait to see him."

"That's terrific, Sally," Brian said. "Please congratulate her and Johnny for me."

Ally glanced sideways at him slyly then swung her right hand that was entwined with his left. "Maybe it won't be too long before we're telling people the same type of news." She stretched her left hand forward for me to examine. "Look what Brian gave me last night when he got home."

On the third finger of her left hand was a lovely one-carat marquise diamond surrounded by a circle of tinier ones. Given everything that had recently happened, this was something I hadn't expected. "Wow, congratulations. Have you set a date yet?"

Brian's face reddened slightly. "We're thinking about June."

"Not very far away," I said. "Will it be here or in Boston?"

Brian looked at Ally and smiled. "I'm not going to Boston. I've decided to stay here in Colwestern. One of the detectives is retiring from the force next year, and I've been assured that I'm next in line for the job. Besides, Ally loves it here and working at the hospital. She doesn't want to leave. It's a great little town."

"I'm so happy for you both." Secretly, I wondered what had happened to make him propose to her. He'd been so insistent about leaving town the other day. Maybe he'd realized he was "in love" with Ally after all and didn't want to lose her. At least I hoped so. I wanted Brian to be happy and not think about me anymore.

"Thanks, Sally." Ally stepped forward and, to my surprise, gave me a quick hug. Then she glanced over at the display case. "Are those snickerdoodles I see?"

"Made fresh this afternoon," I said. "Better hurry before we run out."

Brian called after her. "Get me some chocolate chips, babe. Half a dozen. Wait, better make it an entire dozen."

Ally grinned over her shoulder at him, her perfect white teeth gleaming from the light above.

I leaned against the doorway. "Well, Officer Jenkins, you're certainly full of surprises. I'm so glad everything worked out."

"Yeah, me too." He fell silent and continued to stare at me. There was a sudden look in his eyes that startled me—an empty, sad-like quality that made me feel sorry for him, but I wasn't sure why.

"It was the right thing to do," he said quietly. "Ally deserves to be happy."

Brian started toward the display case, as if intending to join her.

Maybe I should have let him walk away and minded my own business, but that wasn't my style. "What about you?" I blurted out suddenly. "You'll be happy too, right?"

Brian had his back to me and froze at my question. His shoulders slumped forward slightly, as if someone had placed a heavy burden upon them. He turned around and pinned me with a somber gaze. "Sure, Sally," he said without conviction. "I'll be happy too."

My phone buzzed as I watched him join Ally. I'd said more than enough. Brian was a grown man, and if he and Ally wanted to get married, that was their business. But I sincerely hoped he *would* be happy. He deserved that much. With a sigh, I drew my phone out of my pocket and glanced down at the screen. "Hi, sweetheart."

Mike sounded excited. "Princess, you have Brian's number handy, right? I need a cop out here as soon as possible."

His words made me anxious. "What's wrong? Did you find a dead body?"

He laughed out loud. "No, that's your department. Can you call him and ask him to come to the house?"

"I can do better than that. He just showed up at my father's signing with Ally, but I don't think he's on duty. What's going on?"

"Well, I think Brian's going to want to see this, whether he's on duty or not," Mike replied smoothly. "I discovered a fake bottom in my toolbox."

"You mean a secret compartment?" I still didn't understand what he was trying to tell me. "Did it come from the manufacturer like that?" For what it had cost, it should have come with a gold lining.

"No," he said. "Apparently Trevor had it installed without telling me. I was so busy with the renovation that I let him use my truck and the toolbox for different jobs, remember?"

It finally dawned on me what he was trying to say, and my face broke into a wide grin. "Aha. Did you happen to find something green inside?"

"Oh, yeah. Lots of dough, baby. More than you've ever seen in that bakery of yours."

# CHAPTER TWENTY-TWO

"I think Alex looks like me," my mother said as she held the sleeping baby in her arms.

My father sat next to her on my couch, one arm casually slung around her shoulders. With his other hand, he tapped a copy of his book in his lap, in case someone here might happen to ask him for an autographed copy.

Dad stared down into Alex's face and grunted. "Sorry, hot stuff. You're gorgeous and all, but that kid looks like my father. One hundred percent Muccio."

"What you talk about?" Nicoletta bawled from her seat across from them. "Little Alessandro—he be a Gavelli. Just look at that nose. It the image of Johnny's. That is all."

Gianna frowned, but she said nothing. She was sitting at the kitchen table next to Mike and my grandmother while I served everyone coffee and Josie sliced up Nicoletta's chocolate cheesecake. Gianna and Johnny had decided to call the baby Alex. They both liked the name, and since it was a nickname for Alessandro, they hoped it might appease the new great-grandmother. However, Nicoletta still insisted on calling him Alessandro.

Johnny was sitting on the arm of his grandmother's chair. He leaned over and gave her a peck on the cheek. "For the last time, Gram, we're calling him Alex. Please stop making a fuss about it."

"Huh." Nicoletta grunted and folded her arms over her chest.

"Wow, he got brave all of a sudden, didn't he?" Josie said to Gianna, clearly impressed as she placed a piece of cake in front of her.

Gianna smiled. "Fatherhood agrees with him." She took a bite of the cake and then shook her head at me. "No coffee for me. We're going to have to leave soon, Sal. The baby needs to eat, and I'm exhausted."

"I understand, whenever you're ready. I'm so happy you were able to come for a little while. It wouldn't have been a family dinner without you and my new nephew. Now open your fortune cookie before you go."

Josie barked out a laugh as I held up the container with the cookies I'd made last week. "You saved them? They've got to be stale by now."

"There's personal messages inside for everyone. I thought it would be fun to still open them, even if they are a bit hard." I glanced at my husband, who was sitting next to Gianna and eating one of the sprinkle cookies I'd made earlier today. It was also my attempt to try to erase what had happened the night of the robbery, although the memories would never go away completely for us.

Mike's midnight blue eyes twinkled at me. "That's a great idea, princess. Things are looking up already."

He was referring to the cash he'd found in the toolbox yesterday. Brian had come to the house to remove the money and later told us there was almost a hundred grand inside.

Gianna broke into my thoughts. "It was so honest of you guys to turn the money over to the police. I'm proud of you both."

"Bah," Nicoletta snorted. "That your money Trevor take from you. Why give it to police?"

Mike glared across the room at her. "Because it was the right thing to do. Brian said that after the investigation is finished, there's a very good chance we'll get back the portion Trevor stole from us."

Grandma Rosa nodded her approval. "I too am proud of Mike and Sally. You have both been through so much, but I have a feeling that the tides are burning now."

Josie gave her a puzzled look. "I think you mean turning, Rosa."

"That is good too." To my surprise, Grandma Rosa winked at me, something she never did. "Let us all open these fabulous cookies and see what they have to say."

My mother cleared her throat noisily. "Gianna has an announcement to make as well. Tell everyone, darling."

Gianna watched Johnny take the baby in his arms and then grinned sheepishly at me. "Sal, I'm sorry I didn't get a chance to tell you, but Johnny and I have finally set a date."

"That's wonderful! What are you thinking? A summer wedding?"

She shook her head. "December. I love the idea of getting married at Christmas."

"We'll have a big affair." My mother beamed. "At least two hundred people. A red and white theme."

My father snapped his fingers. "That's a great idea. I'll give away a book to everyone at the reception. You know, they can be party favors."

My grandmother cocked her head at him. "No, *pazza*. This is their day, not yours."

"Why so far away?" Nicoletta wanted to know. "You should be married tomorrow now that little Alessandro is here."

"Hush, fool," my grandmother told her. "It does not matter when they get married. This baby will be greatly loved, and that is the important thing."

Gianna touched my arm. "You'll be my matron of honor, won't you, Sal?"

"Oh," My breath caught in my throat. "Yes, you know I will."

She looked at me strangely. "Something wrong?"

"Of course not." I gave her a warm hug but was aware of my grandmother's keen eyes focused on me. "I'm so happy for you." I crossed the room to hug Johnny. "For both of you." I leaned down to gently touch the little white cap on Alex's head. "Such a little sweetheart."

Grandma Rosa cleared her throat. "Everyone has not finished opening their fortune cookies yet, *cara mia*. Let them do this, and then Gianna must go home. We will talk about wedding plans later this week. I will make dinner, and everyone will come."

"I think that's a great idea." With a smile, I held out a fortune cookie to Gianna. "It seems that my message was spot on. Open it and see."

Gianna broke the cookie open between her two graceful hands and read the strip of paper aloud. "'Your new baby will look like its father.'"

"Did you know that Gianna was having a boy?" my mother squeaked at me.

"Huh," Mrs. Gavelli sniffed. "I could have told you that. Gavelli genes—they dominate over Muccio ones. That no mystery."

"Watch it, old lady," my father growled, then waved his message in the air. "Mine says, 'Your book will be a deadly success.' Ha-ha!" He placed the paper into his pants pocket. "That's a keeper, Sal. I'll have to mention it on the blog."

"What this?" Nicoletta said in apparent disbelief as she read her message aloud. "'Your bark is worse than your bite.' What, I a dog now?"

Johnny stared down at the floor, his mouth turned upwards at the corners.

Josie patted me on the shoulder. "Well done, girlfriend. Now, I've got to run too. Rob leaves for work soon, and someone has to supervise the little monsters."

I held up a finger. "Hang on. There's only one left." I handed the final cookie to my husband.

My father talked around the piece of cheesecake he had shoveled in his mouth. "Hey, Mike, I bet it says that you're going to get a big contract tomorrow."

Mike sighed as he drew me onto his lap. "Even if I did, Domenic, it's going to be at least six weeks before I can work again. Maybe Sal can start putting foundations in for me. There's nothing she can't do." He kissed me tenderly on the lips.

Grandma Rosa eyed me shrewdly. She smiled as she placed a piece of cake in front of Mike. "I think that Sally has other plans."

With his uninjured arm around my waist, Mike managed to break the cookie in half. "Hey, I'm getting better at this one-handed stuff," he joked. He unfolded the strip of paper and read the message to himself, then sucked in a sharp breath.

"Sal. Is it true?" His voice was barely above a whisper as he pinned me with his dark blue gaze.

Tears swam into my eyes as I lovingly stroked his cheek. "Definitely true."

"What's it say?" Gianna asked curiously and leaned over Mike's shoulder for a peek at the paper.

Mike waited a few seconds before he answered. He pulled me tightly against him, and there were tears in his eyes as well. "It says that I'm going to be a father."

## Sprinkled with Fun Cookies

Ingredients
For Cookies:
1 box Funfetti cake mix (15.25 oz.)
1 egg
⅓ cup unsalted butter, melted and slightly cooled
¼ cup sour cream
1 teaspoon vanilla extract
Preheat oven to 350°F. Line two baking sheets with parchment paper or silicone baking mats. Add all the ingredients into a bowl and mix until completely combined. Scoop cookie dough into tablespoon-sized portions and roll into balls. Place on prepared baking sheets about two inches apart and lightly flatten the dough balls with your hand or a spatula. Bake, one pan at a time, for 9–11 minutes. The tops of the cookies should start to crack a bit, but the centers should remain soft. Cool cookies on the baking sheet for 5 minutes, then remove to a wire cooling rack. Cool completely before frosting. Makes approximately 30 cookies.
For Frosting:
½ cup unsalted butter, room temperature
2 tablespoons vegetable shortening (optional, but helps develop crust on frosting)
Pinch of salt
3 cups confectioners' sugar
1 teaspoon vanilla extract
2–3 tablespoons half-and-half or milk
Garnish:
¼–½ cup sprinkles
In the bowl of a stand mixer, whip the butter, vegetable shortening (if using), and a pinch of salt until creamy—about 2 minutes on medium speed. Reduce the speed of the mixer to low and slowly add in approximately half of the confectioners' sugar and beat until incorporated. Add the vanilla extract and 2 tablespoons half-and-half (or milk) and beat until smooth. Beat in the remaining confectioners' sugar.

Increase the mixer speed to medium-high and beat for 2 minutes. If frosting is too stiff, slowly add additional half-and-half until desired consistency is reached. Frost the completely cooled cookies and garnish with sprinkles. Allow the frosting to set before storing in an airtight container.

Tips

For seasonal-themed Sprinkled with Fun cookies, substitute 15.25 ounces white or yellow cake mix for the Funfetti mix. Gently stir in ½ cup seasonal-colored sprinkles to the batter after all the other cookie ingredients have been mixed together. Bake according to directions above. Feel free to use your favorite pre-made canned frosting.

**Raspberry Cheesecake Cookies**

Ingredients
2 - 7-ounce boxes of raspberry muffin mix (You can also feel free to substitute blueberry or strawberry, whatever your preference might be. The Jiffy brand can be used. I used a brand called Martha White.)
½ teaspoon baking soda
4 ounces cream cheese, room temperature
4 ounces unsalted butter, room temperature
¼ cup brown sugar, firmly packed
2 eggs
1½ cups white chocolate chips
1½ cups chopped macadamia nuts (optional)
Combine butter and cream cheese until blended. Add eggs, baking soda, and brown sugar—then mix until blended. Add muffin mix, chips, and nuts (optional). Mix until blended. Place in the refrigerator for 1–2 hours. Scoop onto parchment paper-lined baking sheet, placing 2 inches apart. A two-tablespoon scooper will make cookies about 6 inches wide. Bake at 350°F for 12 minutes. Cookies will be puffy, almost a cake-like texture. If you want them thinner, flatten immediately with a spatula as soon as they come out of the oven. Cool completely. Makes about 18 cookies.

## Chocolate Brownie Cookies

Ingredients
5 oz. semi-sweet chocolate
3 oz. unsweetened chocolate
6 tablespoon (¾ stick) unsalted margarine, room temperature
⅓ cup all-purpose flour
1 teaspoon baking powder
¼ teaspoon salt
2 large eggs, room temperature
2 teaspoon vanilla extract
1 tablespoon Dutch cocoa powder
¾ cup sugar
¾ cup semisweet chocolate chips
⅓ cup chopped pecans (optional)
⅓ cup chopped walnuts (optional)

Preheat oven to 325°F. Line several cookie sheets with parchment paper. Melt the 8 ounces of semisweet and unsweetened chocolates and the butter in the top of a double boiler placed over simmering water. They can also be melted together in a microwave at 50% power, stirring at one-minute intervals until mostly melted. Remove from the microwave and stir until fully melted. Allow chocolate mixture to cool slightly.

Sift the flour, baking powder, and salt together into a small bowl and set aside. Using an electric mixer on medium speed, beat the eggs, vanilla, and cocoa in a medium-size mixing bowl until they are combined together—about 10 seconds. Add the sugar to the egg mixture and blend it all until thick—about 1 minute. Scrape down the sides of the bowl. Add the melted chocolate and blend 1 minute more. Scrape down the sides of the bowl again. Add the flour mixture on low speed and mix until blended—10 seconds. Fold in the chocolate chips and nuts by hand or with the mixer on low speed. Refrigerate dough for 30 minutes to 1 hour. Drop the dough by generous rounded tablespoons about 2 inches apart onto the prepared cookie sheets. Bake the cookies for 11–13 minutes or until golden brown. Remove from oven and let cool for 2 minutes before removing to wire racks to cool completely. This is most easily done by sliding the whole piece of parchment paper onto the cooling racks with the cookies still on it.

Makes approximately two dozen cookies.

## ABOUT THE AUTHOR

*USA Today* bestselling author Catherine Bruns lives in Upstate New York with a male dominated household that consists of her very patient husband, three sons, and assorted cats and dogs. She has wanted to be a writer since the age of eight when she wrote her own version of Cinderella (fortunately Disney never sued). Catherine holds a B.A. in English and is a member of Mystery Writers of America and Sisters in Crime.

To learn more about Catherine Bruns, visit her online at:
www.catherinebruns.net

Enjoyed this book? Check out these other fun reads available in print now from Gemma Halliday Publishing:

www.GemmaHallidayPublishing.com

www.ingramcontent.com/pod-product-compliance
Lightning Source LLC
LaVergne TN
LVHW041622290325
807232LV00026B/348